To Save Us All From Ruin

A Muldoon Adventure

By James Schroeder

ISBN-13: 978-0692564387 (Muldoon Publishing)
ISBN-10: 0692564381
CreateSpace Title Number 5822624

This edition published by arrangement with Create Space, 2015

Dedicated to my loving wife Kae

TABLE OF CONTENTS

FOREWORD

My father died in 2003 at the age of 84. His name was Earl Duane Schroeder. Like many of his generation he served in the military during World War II. I was the youngest of his seven sons and as the youngest I never really talked much with Dad about his experiences in WWII. I knew that he carried the moniker 'Easy Dog' based on his initials and the phonetic alphabet of the U.S. Army. This was eventually shortened to EZ Dog. I knew that he had been at some place called Anzio. I knew that he had an official military publication that he kept in the back of a bottom desk drawer in his home office. When I was a kid I sneaked peeks at that booklet with the word DACHAU on the cover. I wondered about the pictures of emaciated corpses stacked several high behind wire fences. I knew it was something bad but I could not fathom the depths of just how bad. I never thought much about the 1940s.

When I was a kid we occasionally went out to the artillery range at Fort Sill for public events. My brothers and I would cover our ears as the howitzers roared. I never considered that those guns could rain death down at the point of the far off explosion on the hillside. I couldn't connect the dots. Death was not real to me then. Now it is.

After my father died my brother Randy put together a labor of love. He took my father's WWII handwritten journal and did a painstaking page-by-page, word-by-word transcription and published it as the *EZ Dog Journals*, with the transcription side-by-side with scans of the actual handwritten pages. That diary covered Dad's experiences from Camp Hale in Texas to North Africa, through the Italian campaign, the shift to Anzio and on into France and southern Germany.

In the years since my father died I have learned more about the Anzio invasion. I have read through the diary several times and each time learned more about my father through his words on the pages of his journal. And I have learned something about myself and what motivates me in my own life. In spite of the darkness and death that my father saw in his early 20's he always maintained a lively sense of humor and a love of the English language. He taught me the simple elegance of words. He taught me how to stand up straight and be honest with myself although he may have despaired that those lessons would ever take hold. He tried to teach me how to fish and failed miserably in that endeavor. And he liked pie.

Now his journal serves as the inspiration for a fictional tale of three brothers. Raised on a farm in Colorado these ordinary boys went on to do extraordinary things—along with hundreds of thousands of their countrymen.

I worried at first that the whimsical elements of this story might make light of the more somber underlying story but in the end as I read my father's words I see the beauty that he was able to see in the midst of world war. I see that the threat of death adds to the value of life. I think he would have liked this story. In fact I can imagine him telling this story himself as we sit around a campfire after a nice day of fishing, together once again.

I have included excerpts from my dad's journal throughout the book to help provide the framework for the story. The tale is fictional but the broad picture and time line are true to the actual events of the time. The geography is mostly true to the area. I did have to relocate one town several miles, and have left that town nameless. The names have been modified, and any real persons mentioned in the diary have been anonymized. I have made only two minor tweaks to Dad's words in order to fit the fictionalized account in a couple of instances. One date from the journal was changed in order to make the time line fit a little better. All of Dad's words are italicized in a different font and labeled as coming from the EZ Dog Diaries.

The title of the story and the prominently featured Randall knife originated in the words of the song "The Randall Knife" by singer-songwriter Guy Clark. That song is worth a listen if you have a loved one who served during World War II.

I hope that in some small way this story entertains the reader and I hope the spirit of the Muldoon brothers has meaning for future generations.

With a wink and a nod this one is for you, Dad!

-Jim Schroeder—October 25, 2015

MAP 1- OPERATION "SHINGLE" THE ANZIO INVASION

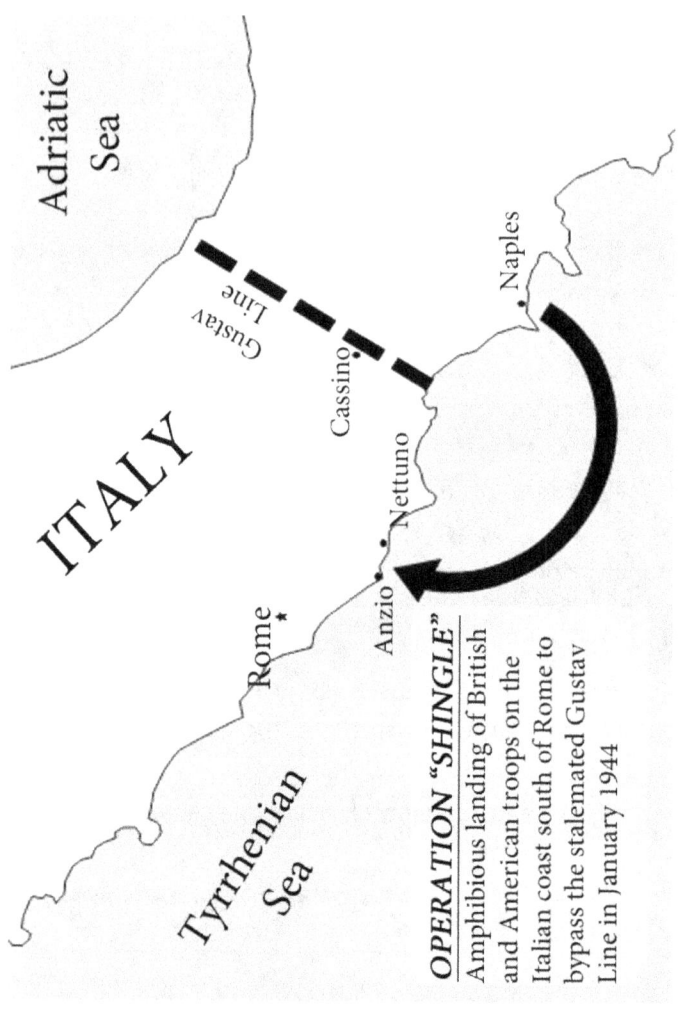

Adriatic Sea

Gustav Line

ITALY

Cassino

Nettuno

Naples

Rome ★

Anzio

Tyrrhenian Sea

OPERATION "SHINGLE"
Amphibious landing of British and American troops on the Italian coast south of Rome to bypass the stalemated Gustav Line in January 1944

MAP 2- ANZIO BEACHHEAD AND SURROUNDING AREA

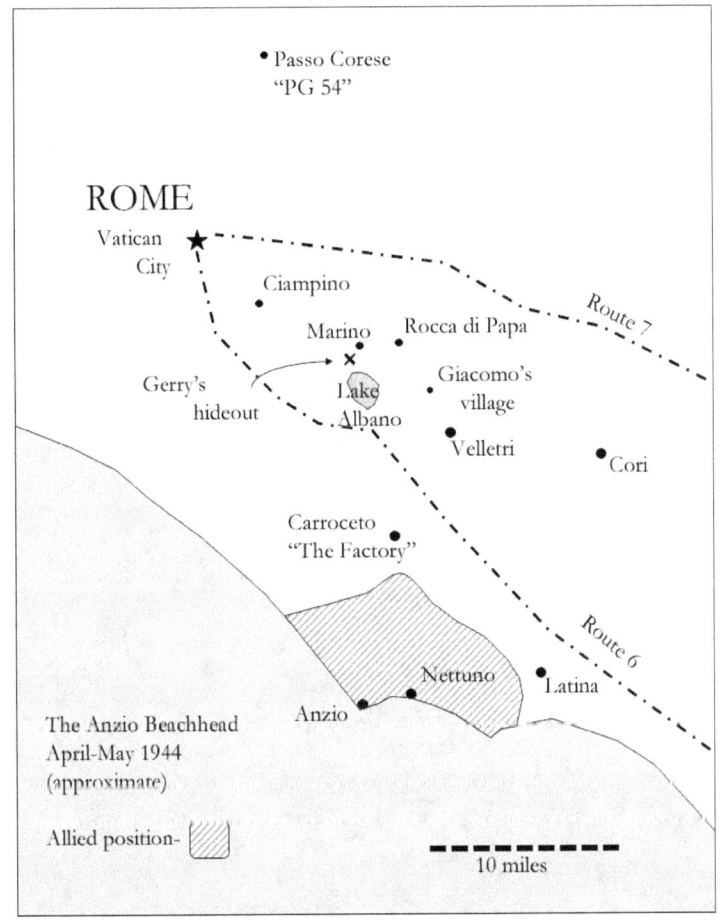

Passo Corese
"PG 54"

ROME

Vatican City

Ciampino

Marino   Rocca di Papa

Route 7

Gerry's hideout   Lake Albano   Giacomo's village

Velletri

Cori

Carroceto "The Factory"

Nettuno   Latina

Route 6

Anzio

The Anzio Beachhead
April-May 1944
(approximate)

Allied position-

10 miles

CHAPTER 1- TO SAVE US ALL FROM RUIN

"My father had a Randall knife, my mother gave it to him.
When he went off to World War II to save us all from ruin."
-songwriter Guy Clark, The Randall Knife.

January 1942- The Muldoon family farm, NE Colorado

The sun rose on a clear and crisp eastern Colorado day in mid-January 1942. As Seamus Muldoon leaned his tired head against the flank of yet another milk cow, his mind began to wander. He stripped the teats rhythmically making the frothy white milk sing a tinny tune as it sprayed against the inside of the shiny milk pail. Bessy (or was this one Flossy? Or Bossy? Seamus could never keep their names straight) munched placidly on the hay in front of her. It occurred to Seamus that for the last month the cows had been setting up their early morning ruckus earlier and earlier each day. The shortened days of winter seemed even shorter when the cows dragged you out of bed at "oh-dark-thirty". His father's words echoed in his memory, every winter morning milking session since Seamus was knee high to a Guernsey his father had cracked the same tired joke. "Hoo boy, it's colder than a well digger's ass, and twice as dark!"

1

Seamus usually thought to himself at those times, "Yeah, how would you know?" Seamus knew better than to give voice to those irreverent thoughts however.

Of course, the old man had not been joking much this past month. His jawline had been set in an attitude of grim determination ever since early December when the news of the Japanese attack on Pearl Harbor had come. The entire family had huddled around the radio in the living room waiting for "a momentous address from the President" as the surprisingly chipper-sounding announcer had put it. The president's sonorous baritone voice intoned over the usual faint crackle of static. "Yesterday, December 7th, 1941—a date which will live in infamy—the United States of America was suddenly and deliberately attacked by naval and air forces of the Empire of Japan." The President went on to lay out the full scale of Japan's widespread de facto declaration of war in the Pacific. "Last night, Japanese forces attacked Hong Kong. Last night, Japanese forces attacked Guam. Last night, Japanese forces attacked the Philippine Islands. Last night, the Japanese attacked Wake Island. And this morning, the Japanese attacked Midway Island."

President Roosevelt had closed his speech that night by saying, "I ask that the Congress declare that since the unprovoked and dastardly attack by Japan on Sunday, December 7th, 1941, a state of war has existed between the United States and the Japanese empire." The living room remained silent as the boys' father reached over and turned off the radio. The three boys knew what this meant. For most of the last two years the newspapers had been filled with stories of the war in Europe. The reports came in one by one as the Sudetenland, then Poland, then the Low

Countries and France fell under Nazi control, the inevitability of what was to come began to loom on the horizon. How much longer could the Brits hold out against the seemingly endless airstrikes from across the Channel?

During these past two years Seamus and his older brother Gerry had talked with the old man about their desire to join the Army, but he had always tried to downplay those ideas, hoping it would never be necessary. It was only with great reluctance that the old man had let his middle boy Eddie join the Army ROTC program during his second year of college at Colorado A&M University in Fort Collins. The old man's few mementos of The Great War were buried deep in a trunk in the back reaches of the attic of the old farmhouse and he had never spoken to the boys about the war. Boys being boys, however, they had found the rusty old bayonet, the campaign hat and the grey-green uniform tunic years ago. They had sometimes reenacted unimaginable feats of imaginary heroism as they played in the nearby fields. They aimed their fingers with care and boyish "pow-pow-pows" echoed through the trees.

Now as the radio fell silent, the three boys exchanged glances but dared not speak a word. This was the moment of truth and they all had a sense of what they had to do. The old man's shoulders seemed a little more stooped and his step seemed heavier with care as he mounted the steps up to the bedroom that night. Long into the night the three boys whispered excitedly about their plans.

Gerry was 23 years old. Long and rangy with muscles that had been hardened by years of farm chores Gerry was known around town as a tough customer. Serious to the point of being somber he wore the mantle of oldest brother with a burning intensity. Eddie at 22 was in his junior year at Colorado A & M University. He was home this week while preparing for his final exams. Eddie had a rugged muscular build that aptly fit his three years as starting fullback on the local high school football team. This body type combined with rugged good looks had characterized his mother's side of the family for generations. He was a solid young man with an easy good nature that made him well liked pretty much anywhere he went. Seamus, the youngest of the three was a 17-year-old high school senior and still had the slender body build of an adolescent. Seamus was the "hey-let-me-come-with-you-serious-you-guys-I-can-keep-up" brother.

Monday December 15, 1941 was a grey day. The clouds hung low over the chilly Northeastern Colorado countryside as the three brothers loaded the milk jugs onto the flatbed truck for the run into town. Seamus and Eddie jumped on the back while Gerry urged the engine to life. The truck lurched forward as they started down the quarter-mile long driveway. Eddie playfully punched Seamus in the arm and their laughter rang through the clear morning air. It was a long straight drive of about six miles to the milk processing plant in Nunn, a small town on the road north out of Greeley. After off-loading the milk at the plant and securing the empty replacement jugs to the rails of the truck the three boys headed downtown. Outside the Nunn General Store there was a cluster of young men. Seamus jumped down from the truck and elbowed his way to the front of the group. The men were clustered around an older man wearing an Army uniform with three sergeant's stripes on his arm. He was sitting at a small folding table on the front porch of the store, with a stack of forms. He was flanked on his left by a small stone-faced man with two corporal's stripes.

To the sergeant's right was a folding easel with a colorful red, white and blue poster. Out stared the familiar visage of Old Uncle Sam, tall top hat with a broad hatband of white stars on a blue background, big white stars on the wide lapels of his frock coat. The brows were lowered in an attitude of intensity that was only partially countered by the disheveled appearance of the long white hair, the shaggy sideburns and the long scraggly goatee. The large block text at the bottom of the poster read "VOLUNTEER" and the smaller text below elaborated, "AND CHOOSE YOUR OWN BRANCH OF THE SERVICE." Uncle Sam's signature was scrawled across the bottom. The artist's name was stenciled into the lower left corner of the poster—Arthur N. Edrop.

"One at a time, boys, one at a time," the corporal hollered. You'll each get your chance." Eddie and Gerry held back, watching from the periphery of the small crowd.

"What's going on?" Seamus asked one of the boys that he knew from school.

"War! Those dirty Japs killed a bunch of our boys out in Hawaii!" the boy said excitedly. "This fellow is here taking enlistments for the Army."

As the excited group made their way one by one to the table, the stack of blank forms to the sergeant's right began to dwindle while the stack of hastily filled-out forms to his left grew. As Seamus waited in line Eddie read the recruitment poster. Along the right side of the poster was an alphabetical list of military branches- "Army, Artillery, Cavalry, Engineers,

Hospital Corps, Infantry, Marine Corp, Nat'l Guard, Naval Militia, Navy, Quartermaster Corp. Which for YOU?"

Seamus solemnly and painstakingly filled out an enlistment form. Name, date of birth, branch preference, a brief health questionnaire and a signature block comprised the simple form. Seamus excitedly wrote "Infantry."

"All right, listen up you country bumpkins," the sergeant yelled. "Any of you who are younger than 18 years old are going to need signed permission from your parents before we can accept your enlistment. Raise your hand if you are not yet 18 years old." Three or four of the boys sheepishly raised their hands. So did Seamus. The older boys snickered and someone at the back of the group muttered sardonically, "Yeah, leave the hard work to us real men, junior!" Seamus felt his face redden with angry heat. Catching Eddie's disapproving look from the back of the crowd he bit his tongue and choked back his anger.

"All of you who have signed a form, go home and say your farewells to you family, kiss your girlfriends and report back here on Saturday, January 3rd at oh-eight-hundred hours. That's eight o'clock in the morning for all you civilians! From here we will transport you to the Recruitment Center in Fort Collins for induction. Take one of these lists that Corporal Jackson has in his hand. Pack one, I repeat one, small suitcase with only those items that are on the list and bring it with you that morning. Welcome to the United States Army gentlemen."

As the excited group of boys broke up into smaller groups of two or three and wandered off, Seamus ran over to Gerry and asked, "Aren't you going to join up?" Gerry shrugged noncommittally.

"Hey Seamus, let's go get a Coke," Eddie yelled. Seamus and Eddie ran up the steps and into the store, leaving Gerry alone on the porch with the two Army men.

"Well son, I've got one form left," the sergeant said, almost mockingly. Gerry hesitated a few beats, then reached out silently, took the form and slowly filled out his information. His hand paused almost imperceptibly and then he scrawled his signature.

All three boys sat up front on the drive back to the farm. Seamus and Eddie joshed back and forth while Gerry sat silently, gripping the steering wheel intently. Just before the turnoff to the home place Gerry brought the truck to a stop by the side of the road. "Knock it off, you two. Mom and Dad are not going to be happy about this, you know. And there's no way in hell Dad is going to give you permission, Seamus. You do know that don't you?"

Seamus downplayed it, "Aw shucks, Gerry. I know I can talk Mom into it. She always lets me get my way. Besides, I've been thinking about leaving home anyway as soon as I graduate at the end of this semester. They can't stop me."

Eddie muttered wryly, "Hoo boy you better not underestimate Mom when she sets her mind to something."

That evening, as the family gathered around the dinner table, the boys were uncharacteristically quiet. The boys bowed their heads as Dad intoned his usual simple but heartfelt prayer. "Heavenly Father, we ask that you watch over this house in thy mercy. Bless the fruits of our labors. Bless this food to the nourishment of our bodies. Guide us in thy paths of righteousness." This concluded Dad's usual

7

dinner grace but before the boys could utter their "Amens" and dig in Dad added one more sentence, "...and we humbly ask you to guide the leaders of this nation in this time of impending war. In Jesus' name we pray. Amen."

The three boys filled their plates with crispy country fried chicken, mounds of steaming mashed potatoes with brown gravy and fresh corn from the family garden. They washed it all down with heavy fresh cream-laden milk. One of the biggest benefits of living on a dairy farm was that they always had plenty of heavy whole milk and fresh butter. Mom was not a fancy cook but she could make the massive dining table groan with the weight of the good country fare. There was rarely much conversation around the table but this night everybody was more reticent than usual as if the weight of a great secret hovered over the place.

The sweet smell of apples, cinnamon and buttery crust filled the room as Mom pulled a fresh-baked apple pie from the oven. She placed the pie pan in front of Eddie and said, "Ed would you please cut the pie?" Eddie took a table knife, lined it up carefully with the far edge of the crust and boldly made one firm cut across the middle of the pie. With a practiced hand he twirled the pie ninety degrees, deftly stopping it on the perpendicular. The second cut neatly bisected the first, dividing the pie into four precise quarters. Each of the boys and their father in turn lifted their quarter of the pie onto their dinner plate. Dad took his knife and cut a thin wedge from his piece of pie and silently slid it onto Mom's plate. "Just a tiny piece for me," she always said. For as long as the boys could remember, every pie Mom had ever baked was cut into four equal pieces, with just a tiny piece for

Mom. Eddie often joked that he didn't realize a pie could be cut into more than four pieces.

Mother produced a small pitcher of cream from the cool box and each poured a serving of the rich foamy cream onto their pie. The room remained silent except for the contented munching sound of three young men eagerly enjoying their apple pie. As Dad used his finger to pick up the last few crumbs of crust from his plate he pushed his chair back from the table and cleared his throat.

"So boys! I noticed you were in town a little longer than usual this morning. Anything happening that I should know about?"

Seamus looked down at his plate, feigning interest in a small piece of cinnamon-covered apple. Eddie inclined his head imperceptibly for Gerry to field this one. Gerry slowly chewed his last bite of pie, swallowed deliberately, drained the last mouthful of milk from his glass and looked back and forth between his mother and father.

"Welp, I joined the Army!"

CHAPTER 2- THE DRY LAND WHEAT

"Granddad grew the dry land wheat, stood on his own two feet. 'Til his mind got incomplete and they put him in the home."
- James McMurtry, American singer-songwriter

Mom and Dad Muldoon were solid. They had scraped together enough money back in Nebraska to move to Northeastern Colorado in 1925 with their three sons. Gerry was seven years old, Eddie was six and the baby Seamus was still in diapers at the time. They bought a quarter section of prairie, sank some roots and tried to hang on. As farms go in that part of the state the Muldoon farm was not big. Most of the serious farmers had multiple sections. A section is the equivalent of one square mile or 640 acres. The main farm compound on the Muldoon farm sat among a hardscrabble cluster of trees that served as a meager windbreak against the howling northwesterly Colorado winds. The main farmhouse and a barn with metal corrugated siding along with three or four small outbuildings sat on about three acres at the northeastern corner of the quarter-section. A rickety windmill adjacent to the house pulled water from the deep water table for the family's use. A bountiful vegetable garden at the east side of the house produced every kind of vegetable you could imagine, from succulent sweet corn to the bitter yet sweet stalks of rhubarb. A dozen or so chickens reliably provided eggs. If one of the chickens ended up on Mom Muldoon's bad side there was the occasional chicken dinner. Mom ran the house and the garden while Dad was in charge of everything else. The barn housed the small dairy herd of about fifteen head. The remaining acreage was devoted to raising dry land wheat. This was one small corner of a section that was one small part of a township that was one small part of the Colorado plains that was just the western fringe of the vastly larger portion of North America known as the Great Plains. This was the world's Bread Basket. This is where the Star Spangled Banner's 'amber waves of grain' poked up above the surface of the mostly flat prairie lands. Old Man Muldoon sometimes looked like a grizzled sea captain as he drove the combine across the rolling waves at harvest time.

Hard red winter wheat was the main crop on the Muldoon farm. Ideal for breads the winter wheat was well suited to the weather and soil of northeastern Colorado. Winter wheat farming involved two main phases. The planting of the seeds took place in the early fall around September or early October. If soil conditions, moisture and temperature were good the young plants would germinate and take root. The establishment of a good strong root system was critical to the later production of the grains of wheat. As the winter months arrived the plants would then go dormant for several months only to resume active growth in the spring. By early summer if things were going well the stalks of wheat were mid-thigh high and the spikes or head of the plant that contained the actual grain were about 4 inches. The wheat harvest in northeastern Colorado usually began in June and peaked in July.

The art of knowing when to plant was probably the hardest part of wheat farming in this region. Old Man Muldoon used a combination of intuition and observation. He kept a daily diary of weather conditions such as precipitation and high/low temperatures for year by year and month by month comparisons. He watched and recorded the barometric pressure. He frequently picked up clumps of dirt in his fields. He felt the texture, squeezed tightly to form a clod and sniffed the aroma of the soil. He sometimes even tasted the soil as if he could divine the moisture and nutrient content of the soil. Sometimes he would sit on the tractor with the seeder mounted behind and just wait. Finally when the day of planting arrived he would employ what his sons took to calling "The Old Man's Fudge Factor". He would lick his finger and hold it up in the air. Gauging the wind speed and direction to be suitable he would push the starter button on the old tractor and head out into the field to plant the wheat seed. As he started down the furrows he would silently mouth a prayer for a good harvest.

The Muldoon farm with its wide open fields was a wonderful place to raise a family. The Muldoons had been blessed with three healthy boys in fairly rapid succession before leaving Nebraska for Colorado. Gerry was born in 1918, Eddie in 1919 and Seamus joined the family in 1924. The boys hit adolescence as the Great Depression held its grip on the nation. Living as far from town as they did, and with the self-sufficiency that the vegetable garden and the dairy cattle provided the family did not really feel the effects of the Depression as much as some. The three boys were always busy with something. In the small periods of free time that weren't taken up by schoolwork and farm chores Gerry and Eddie would wander the dry creek beds and ridges of theirs and neighboring farms. They often found remnants of the transient passing of the American Plains Indians. There were several old tepee rings in the vicinity formed by stones placed where a tepee had stood once upon a time; sort of a miniature Stonehenge. Eddie in particular developed a keen eye for spotting stone chips and even intact arrowheads along the creek beds. He learned to look along the edge of the creek bed where the soil had been freshly eroded by rain and to let his eye spot the piece of rock that looked out of place, looked like it didn't belong. Brushing the loose dirt away from an innocuous piece of flint would reveal the small inch-long arrowhead.

Seamus on the other hand, being several years younger tended to stay back at the farm while the two older brothers were out on their adventures. He developed a strange affinity for small animals and when he was twelve years old his parents allowed him to get his first pair of hamsters. Seamus built an elaborate cage system in one of the farm's outbuildings, with a series of tunnels, rope ladders, traverses and obstacles for the hamsters' enjoyment. He would spend most of his spare time with the hamsters and he usually had a hamster sticking its head up out of his shirt pocket as he went about his chores. Mom always smiled knowingly when she saw him with his little pets and would furtively hand him a little piece of cheese as a treat while she was in the kitchen preparing supper. Dad on the other hand could never quite see what Seamus saw in the little rats (as he liked to call them). "Dirty filthy russin' sussin' flappin' rats," he would mutter under his breath whenever Seamus was out of earshot or even when he was not. The three boys went to school five days a week at a little one room schoolhouse in the town of Carr, several miles north by northwest of Greeley.

During the inter-war years, land grant colleges around the country began expanding the 4-H Club program. Often confused with the Future Farmers of America the 4-H Clubs were social development organizations based in local communities under the aegis of Land Grant Colleges such as Colorado A&M. Head, Heart, Hands and Health is the foundational motto of the 4-H Club. Participating youngsters gained valuable life skills during their participation in the 4-H Club. Leadership, teamwork, industriousness and innovation were fostered. Local 4-H groups each began to develop their own specialized interests under an offshoot of the 4-H program known as the 4-H+H clubs. The fifth "H" stood for the local club's particular interest. For instance a city group interested in blues music might form a 4-H (Harmonica) group and learn about music history, learn songs and perform in local concerts. Similarly a group interested in flowers might call themselves 4-H (Horticulture) and practice the delicate arts of the hot house gardener. Around the country there were 4-H Clubs for horsemanship, hairstyling, hand puppetry, hog calling and even haberdashery.

When Seamus reached the seventh grade he joined the local 4-H+H Club. Head, Heart, Hands, Health & Hamsters meetings were held every other Tuesday in the school multipurpose room after classes had let out for the day. In the Rocky Mountain region during the 1930s under the broad umbrella of the American Hamster Club there was quite an active program of hamster training with particular interest in an activity known as Homing Hamsters. Here's how it worked.

Under supervision of an AHC official, a competitor would release his competing hamster into the wild at a distance of up to 5 miles from the school buildings. The youth would start a timer and would return to the school. An official would then turn on a powerful sonic transmitter that emitted an extremely high pitched sound, well beyond the range of human hearing. In fact the sonic homing beacon was even beyond the range of dogs' sensitive hearing. Hamsters though not only could hear the sound but loved it. Apparently it triggered a region of the hamster hypothalamus that evoked the high-pitched squeaks of a mother hamster. Upon hearing this sound even from a distance of several miles a well-trained homing hamster would set out to find the source of the sound. During a competition the hamsters would return to their home base as quickly as they could and upon entering their cage at the school multipurpose room would be assigned their completion time. Fastest time won. It was as simple as that. Some of the biggest and fastest hamsters could make a three-mile trip in less than four days. In 1934 a boy from Idaho had a seven ounce hamster (massive by hamster standards) make a nearly five-mile trip in under four days, a national record that stands to this day. Understandably many hamsters never found their way home. The ones that did were prized as accomplished athletes and celebrated like...well...like celebrities. Fortunately hamsters are also quite prolific, so despite the high hamster mortality rates there never seemed to be a shortage.

As the 1930's went by and the Muldoon boys grew through adolescence into early adulthood the winds of war were brewing in the Pacific and in Europe. On Saturday mornings while Dad read the comics pages of the Greeley Tribune the boys would kneel in front of him and read the front page articles. In 1931 Japan invaded the Manchurian region of China. In 1933 Hitler was elected Chancellor of Germany. In 1934 the saber rattling intensified as Hitler assumed full dictatorial command of the country's government and began threatening his neighbors. In 1935 Mussolini's army entered Ethiopia. In 1937 Japan declared war on China. In 1938 Germany annexed the Sudetenland region of Czechoslovakia and in 1939 they invaded Poland virtually unopposed. Certainly by the time Eddie graduated high school in 1937 it was becoming evident that war was coming. About the only big question was whether the United States would help against the Axis powers or not. There was a strong sentiment of hemispheric isolationism. American lives lost in the First World War had led to fairly strong public opinion against willingly joining another European fray.

Although the Muldoons lived on a rural farm they were not bumpkins. Dad and the boys often discussed world affairs around the dinner table. The boys' father possessed a wisdom that came from his connection to the earth. As a farmer he relied on his ability to read subtle changes in the weather and nuances in the texture of the soil. He could gauge the strength of a coming storm by licking his finger and checking the wind. Knowing the optimal time to start the harvest of the wheat did not depend on how he felt. It relied on keen observation and prompt analysis. This same keen eye and analytic capability suffused his reading of the news. He would pick a news report and read it aloud at the dinner table between the meal and the dessert. He would then pick one of the boys and quiz him first of all on the facts of the report and then on a critical analysis of the report. Did the facts as reported fit with facts previously known? Did the details ring true in context? Did the main characters in the report act consistently with their known history? Their father taught the boys how to reach a reasoned conclusion, how to defend that conclusion with factual data and how to present a synopsis of their conclusion concisely and dispassionately.

It was on this backdrop that Eddie Muldoon graduated high school in 1937 and went off to college at Colorado A&M, more formally known as the Colorado College of Agriculture and Mechanical Arts (now Colorado State University) in Fort Collins. Although he was there to study Agriculture with the intent of returning to the family farm Eddie signed up for the Army ROTC program. His father was not pleased to hear this news nor was he surprised. Eddie had a keen eye and incisive analytical skills. It was no wonder that he was selected as Cadet Commander for the ROTC Corps of Cadets at the end of his junior year.

With the growing unrest in Europe Eddie knew that his destiny would lay not on the family farm. Ironically, although Eddie did not know it yet his future lay in farm country of a different sort, the farm country of southern Europe where he and much of his generation were bound in order to save the world for Democracy. While Gerry returned to the farm after two years at college and Seamus spent more and more time with his pet hamsters, Eddie was learning his trades. Eddie was learning how to be both a farmer and a soldier.

This is the setting in which Gerry had dropped his bombshell announcement at the dinner table that early December day in 1941.

"Welp, I joined the Army!"

The room fell silent when these words left Gerry's lips. The boys' mother quietly set down her fork, took the napkin from her lap and laid it meticulously on the table. Beneath the edge of the table she placed her hand on top of her husband's, feeling the muscle tension building. After a slow ten count Dad slowly and loudly exhaled, resignation settling over his face.

"Son, I suppose that deep down I knew this day would come. We all know there's work to be done in Europe and now in the Orient as well. You are a solid man and I know I can trust you to do your duty."

Gerry finally allowed himself to breathe. He had expected his dad to explode in anger. He snuck a glance at Eddie and gave him a wink and a lopsided grin.

"When will you be leaving?" his father asked. Eddie piped up and said, "I'm heading back into Fort Collins after Christmas. I can drop them off at the assembly area on my way." Eddie quickly caught himself and rephrased, "Yeah, I'll drop **him** off on my way."

Dad glanced up sharply and saw the red creeping up onto Eddie's face and then quickly shifted his intense gaze to Seamus. Seamus gulped a bite of pie, swallowed noisily, sat up straight and puffed his chest out. "That's right Dad, I signed up too."

"I forbid it!" the old man exclaimed. "You are staying here and you will pick up the slack on your brother's chores. There's going to be plenty of work just keeping this old place running, I can't do it without you. Eddie in the ROTC and now Gerry enlisting, two is enough. You're staying here."

"But Dad, you yourself said those dirty Japs…" "NO!"

"I'm almost 18, in just a few months, I'm a man…" "NO!"

"But there's work to do Over There…" "NO! I FORBID IT!"

The old man's tone suggested that he had heard enough. Seamus pushed his chair back from the table, leaped to his feet and shouted, "Well I'd like to see you try and stop me!" His father began to stand and raise the back of his hand toward Seamus but Mom reached out calmly and firmly laid her hand on his forearm. She said nothing but shook her head almost imperceptibly. The old man sat back down in his chair and his shoulders slumped as he fixed his gaze firmly on the middle of the table.

"Seamus, run along now, tend to your evening chores," Mom said quietly. Seamus and the other two boys quietly left the room, leaving their father sitting at the table. Eddie and Gerry went out to the tenant farmer's shack next to the barn where the three boys had their sleeping quarters. They began to talk quietly but excitedly about the coming trip to the Army Induction Center. "They are going to whip your skinny farmer's ass into shape, Gerry! We do a two mile run every morning at school. Have you ever heard of burpees? Some folks call it a squat thrust and some call it an eight count push up. You start in a standing position and go (1) squat, (2) shoot your legs back so you're in a push up position, (3)

19

down, (4) up, (5) down, (6) up, (7) back to squatting and (8) back to standing. We do twenty-five of those.”

Gerry scoffed, “No big deal little brother. I've been running almost every day, out to the tepee rings and back, that's about a mile and a half. And I can do 20 pull-ups! I'll show them what kind of shape a real man is in!”

While the two older brothers continued to talk, Seamus was out in the equipment shed next to his hamster cage. He idly pushed snack pellets through the mesh for his best hamster, Houdini. As he did that he talked mostly to himself, although if you watched carefully you might have seen Houdini tilting his head first one way then the other. It was as if the little rodent was actually pondering what Seamus had to say which was, “It's just not fair. He doesn't understand how important this is to me. It's always been ‘Gerry this’ and ‘Eddie that’. Those two get to do whatever ‘the gosh’ they want. Nobody lets me do anything. They just don't understand me like you do, Houdini.”

Seamus didn't hear the door open behind him as he continued his whining. He startled abruptly when his mother laid her hand on his shoulder. “Son, I talked with your father and got him to change his mind. He's going to sign the permission form. He just, well he is just scared of losing you. Did you know you have always been his favorite? I think it's because he was the youngest in his family also. That and the fact that you two just look so darn much alike. Anyway, don't you ever tell him I told you this but he's afraid of losing you boys. Deep down though, he and I both know that you need to do what you need to do. We know you will make us proud. We know that you know right from wrong and that you will do the right thing in the end. We just want you to stay safe and come back home when this horrible business is finished."

Seamus didn't say anything for a long minute. He surreptitiously dabbed at the corner of his eye with his shirt sleeve. He sniffled once, then swallowed big and said, "Okay Mom. Thanks!"

"We were going to wait until your graduation day to give you this, but what with the big things happening you father wanted me to go ahead and give you this," she said as she pulled a long narrow box from her apron pocket. The box, wrapped in brown paper and twine felt heavy in his hand as she gave it to him.

"What is it?" he asked.

"Go ahead, open it," his mother urged.

Seamus carefully untied the twine then peeled the paper back. The box had the single word "Randall" printed in block letters on the front. Seamus removed the top and his eyes gleamed as he saw the blade glinting in the fading evening sunset through the window. "Wow" was all he could manage to say. The six-inch blade of polished steel curved gently toward the tip. The polished maple handle just looked right as if it would fit his hand perfectly. Seamus lifted the knife from the box and read the small paper label hanging by a string, "The Outdoorsman- by Randall".

"Mom? Thanks. Thanks for the knife. Thanks for talking to Dad. Thanks for well, everything!"

As Seamus rushed off to show off his new hunting knife to his brothers his mother stood by the dingy window and watched the sun sink below the horizon. She silently uttered a simple prayer, "Dear Lord, watch over my boys. And help them to save us all from ruin."

CHAPTER 3- YOU'RE IN THE ARMY NOW

"You're in the Army now. You're not behind a plow.
You'll never get rich, by digging a ditch, you're in the Army now"
- WWII Army song

January 1942- Northeastern Colorado

Saturday dawned clear and cool. The small crowd of farm boys shuffled their worn brown work boots restlessly in the dry prairie dust. A few family members and girlfriends stood by to bid the boys farewell. Seamus and Gerry stood apart from the main group, talking quietly. Eddie had returned to the campus at Fort Collins earlier in the week leaving his brothers to endure the uncomfortable silence of their father during these last several days. Mealtime had been strained ever since the boys had announced their intention to join the Army. The old man had been spending more time in the barn, avoiding the boys. When they had left the farm early this morning before sunup he had avoided coming outside to say "goodbye". Mom had given each of them a quick, brusque hug. She held Gerry's gaze for a few moments and implored, "Keep an eye on Seamus for me."

The bus pulled up at the General Store in Nunn right at 8:00. A handful of young men from other towns were already on board. The nice man in the Army uniform herded Gerry, Seamus and the others onto the bus, calling out their names as he checked them off the list on his clipboard. As the bus pulled away, the gaggle of folks left behind waved and a brief cheer went up. During the 45 minute trip to the induction center in Fort Collins the eager chatter slowly faded away as a nervous anticipation settled over the young men. This was it. They may not have been quite sure what "it" was, but they knew this was it.

The bus stopped outside a simple two-story brick building a block or two from the Colorado A&M campus. The plank sign over the door read simply "Induction Center". The boys bantered with each other as they filed off the bus onto the sidewalk. An air of cocky assuredness seemed to be the attitude of most although the quick darting of eyes revealed an underlying uncertainty. They were greeted by a short but formidable man in a crisp khaki uniform.

"All right ladies, quit your gawking! You're in the Army now! Form a line right along here," he indicated with a sweep of his arm.

A wise guy in the back of the group muttered, "Who died and left this little runt boss?"

"Knock it off, sister," the sergeant yelled. "Lefffft…FACE!" Most of the group looked around while five or six turned slowly to their left. One red-headed kid from Ault turned toward his right in utter confusion, causing a loud snicker to sweep over the group. "THAT WAY!" the sergeant thundered, his face growing redder with each passing second. "All right, if you're taller than the man in front of you move forward," he instructed the group. After a few seconds of shuffling around the group was arrayed generally from tall to short. "When's lunch?" the wise guy muttered when the sergeant was turned the other way.

"Listen up you yahoos! My name is Sergeant Wilkins. I am going to be your baby sitter for the day. The first order of business today is a medical examination. Follow me and stay in line." Wilkins led the group down the sidewalk and up the steps to the side door of the building. The men were herded into two straight lines facing each other along the sides of a sparsely furnished room. Along each wall was a row of clothes hooks. A young attractive brunette nurse with her starched white cap and rustling white nurse's uniform marched into the center of the room. "Gentlemen, kindly remove your coats, shoes, socks, pants, shirts and undershirts and hang them neatly on the hooks behind you." A couple soft wolf whistles rang out as the boys hurried to comply. As the boys turned their backs the brunette quietly left the room and was replaced by a group of dour old men in white lab coats. Each of the doctors took up a station arrayed around the center of the room. The boys were now clad only in a variety of thin cotton boxer shorts or tattered briefs. There were just three exceptions. Two brothers from a wheat farm up on the Colorado-Wyoming border were wearing what looked like homemade burlap undershorts and the wise guy was standing stark naked with his hands crossed over his private parts demurely. "Nobody told me to bring underpants," he griped.

Gerry's voice carried across the whole room, "Looks like somebody wants to join the Commandos!" Wise Guy's face blushed red while the others all laughed at his expense.

He grabbed a towel and wrapped it around his waist, still muttering under his breath.

As the recruits turned to face the team of doctors a strange game of medical musical chairs began. Each of the doctors was responsible for one body part. "Read the letters on the third row." "Open wide and say 'ahhhhh'." "Turn your head and cough." Seamus winced as the rubber-gloved hand jammed into his groin. "Next," the hernia doctor intoned. "Bend over and grab your ankles." "Do a deep knee bend." "Touch the tip of your nose with your index finger." On and on the examination went like a stylized minuet. Step, twirl, bend, swoop, repeat.

Seamus cruised through all the stations with flying colors. The last doctor had him turn to face the wall. "Walk forward, one foot in front of the other heel to toe," he instructed. "Sit here," he said brusquely, indicating a small hard stool. He raised each of Seamus' feet one at a time, pushing, wiggling, prodding and manipulating them. The doctor scribbled a few notations on his clipboard as Seamus got dressed again. Sergeant Wilkins marched the group back outside to the sidewalk. "Listen up ladies, we're going to get you all a bite to eat and then we're going to have a little welcoming ceremony. If I call your name sound off with "Yes, Sergeant".

"Muldoon!" the sergeant barked.

Gerry and Seamus simultaneously echoed "Yes, Sergeant."

"Which one of you is Muldoon?" Wilkins asked.

"Both of us," they replied.

Wilkins consulted his clipboard. "Seamus?" Seamus replied, "Yes, Sergeant."

"You step aside here. The rest of you men go with Corporal Hopkins." The corporal marched the group of men down the street to the mess hall for lunch. Seamus figured that he had been singled out for specialized training because of his obviously superior physical condition. "Come with me Muldoon." Seamus followed the sergeant into a small windowless office at the corner of the induction center. A pale thin clerk with tortoiseshell glasses sat behind a small desk. "Tough luck, kid." Sergeant Wilkins muttered. He turned on his heel and left the room while Seamus turned to the clerk. A puzzled look came over his face.

"Sign this form. Initial here and here. Write your home address here," the clerk intoned.

"What's going on?" Seamus asked.

"Here's a voucher for a one-way bus ticket back home, Muldoon."

"What?" Seamus sputtered.

"Looks like you failed your medical examination. You're one lucky S.O.B. Muldoon. Flat feet. Go figure!"

Corporal Hopkins led the group of recruits down the street in a rough semblance of a four-wide formation. Learning to march would come later. For now the corporal was happy that the boys were walking in approximately the same direction. "Listen up ladies! We've got one quick stop on our way to the Mess Hall."

Gerry found himself next to the wise guy. "What the heck is a Mess Hall?" he asked Gerry.

"That's Army talk for where we eat."

"They sure talk funny in the Army." Wise Guy replied.

"Pipe down back there," Hopkins growled. "Squad! Halt!" The group came to a ragged halt outside another nondescript building. The plank sign on this building said only "Barber". A collective groan went up from the recruits. Following Hopkins instructions, the boys formed a single line and filed up the four concrete steps and through the door. Through a thick haze of cigar smoke, the boys could barely make out four barber chairs, two on each side facing each other. Behind each of the chairs was a swarthy, balding man with a cigar chomped between his teeth. Three of the four were of average height, the fourth was no more than four feet tall. Each chair was surrounded by a pile of hair clippings close to eight inches deep; black, blonde, brown and an occasional splash of red gave the piles of hair the appearance of autumn leaves piled in the yard. Two by two the recruits took a seat on the barber chairs and another bizarre but finely choreographed minuet began. The three normal-sized barbers stepped up behind their intended victims and draped a barber's cape over their victim's chest and shoulders. The thin cloth smelled faintly of lilac water and garlic. The undersized barber (who rather un-ironically was called "Shorty" by the other barbers) mounted a little wooden platform three steps high like a Mayan high priest climbing the pyramids to perform a virgin sacrifice and assumed the same stance as the other three. Each of the four barbers took a set of electric shears in their right hand while their left hand firmly grasped the top of the hapless victim's head.

"Just trim the back and sides, don't take much off the top," Wise Guy cracked.

As if on cue, the four electric clippers clicked on with a loud snap and a buzzing sound. In unison the four barbers pushed each head sharply toward its owner's left shoulder. Right arm extended, clippers engaged the side of the head just in front of the right ear and in one long smooth sweeping motion to the rear cleared off a swath of hair like a miniature Zamboni ice machine smoothing a rink before a hockey game. A deft flick of the wrist tossed the accumulated hair onto the ever growing pile and the arm repeated that long buzzing arc from front to rear. Two sweeps for the right side of each head, three sweeps for the top. Like a baton twirling troupe the four barbers tossed the clippers from their right hand to their left in unison and hesitated just long enough to take a deep puff on their cigars. They then violently tilted the nearly bald head of their victim back toward the right shoulder and took two quick sweeps clearing the final remnants of civilian life from the recruit's head. From start to finish the entire process took about 30 seconds per man.

The group of recruits at the Induction Center in Fort Collins grew as busloads of young men arrived from all around northeastern Colorado. By the end of the week the group numbered well over 150. The Mess Hall was so crowded that some of the new arrivals had to eat standing up along the wall, tray held in one hand, fork in the other. Bright and early Monday morning the entire group was loaded into buses and a convoy of 5 buses led by a jeep headed down the highway to the south. Their destination was Camp Carson, Colorado.

Just to the southeast of Colorado Springs Camp Carson had been quickly erected on a 137,000 acre expanse of pinon pine and arroyos as an Army Mobilization Training camp following the Japanese attack on Pearl Harbor and America's entry into the war just a few short weeks ago. At the time of Gerry Muldoon's arrival at Camp Carson there were several dozen mobilization style wooden barracks buildings and the smell of new paint still hung in the air. Construction was still ongoing on many of the camp buildings. Among the hundred-plus military camps that were beginning to churn out raw soldiers by way of a 6-week-long regimen of training, Camp Carson had arguably the most beautiful setting of all. To the west the looming grandeur of Pikes Peak looked down on the western edge of the American Great Plains. Even on cloudless days the higher reaches of Pike's Peak seemed to be wrapped in a fine blanket of haze as if floating lightly off the surface of the earth. Of course the new Army recruits did not have any spare time to enjoy the scenic beauties of the Rocky Mountains. From the instant the buses groaned to a halt outside the barracks building and the boys were herded inside it was go, go, go. There was a mad scramble for bunks as the training platoon entered the barracks. Gerry was not the quickest but he had an uncanny knack for seeing an opportunity. He managed to elude the tangled mass of recruits in the center of the room and stake out a claim on a top bunk in the far back corner of the barracks.

They only had enough time to toss their suitcases on the thin threadbare mattresses before the drill sergeant and his ever present corporal entered the room. "Ten-HUT" the sergeant bellowed while the corporal steered the boys to their expected post at the foot of their respective bunks. "Listen up gentlemen! When I give the command 'Fall Out' you will exit this building on the double time to the front the building where you will form up in platoon formation on a

10-man front, 5 deep. We will size you by height and the position you are in at the end of that process will be your own individual position for all platoon formations for the remainder of your time here at Camp Carson. Do I make myself clear?"

A few of the men responded weakly, "Yes Sir!"

The drill sergeant bellowed, "I'm not a 'Sir' you ninnies! I *work* for a living! Now I want to hear you sound off! Do I make myself clear?"

A few more men joined in, but still weakly, "Yes Sergeant!"

The corporal put in his two cents worth, "I CAN'T **_HEAR_** YOU!"

The whole platoon in unison chorused, "YES SERGEANT!"

"Fall out!" the sergeant snapped.

There was a mad scramble as the platoon rushed for the door. After a couple dozen seconds of scrambling around on the small apron in front of the barracks the boys were arranged in a 10-across 5-deep formation arranged by height from right to left and front to back. Gerry's lean and lanky build put him in the front row third from the left. The rest of the first day at Camp Carson involved basic equipment and clothing issue. The recruits joined long lines of other platoons stretching as far as the eye could see. Entering the Clothing Disbursement Center a hamster-like man with a tape measure deftly measured chest, waist and inseam in exactly 2.7 seconds. Yelling the numbers out loud the man pushed the recruit down the counter and reached for the next in line. Moving down the long counter each recruit's stack of clothing began to grow. Two pairs of pants, three shirts, five undershorts, five T-shirts, five pairs of green socks, one floppy fatigue hat, one belt. The stack soon became perilously tall, like the leaning tower of Pisa. But the government issuing did not stop there. One class "A" khaki uniform with garrison cap and black tie, one field jacket with flannel-lined hood one pair of government-approved pajamas and finally a toiletry kit containing a double-edged razor, toothbrush, soap, shaving mug, hairbrush and comb. Gerry chuckled softly at the irony of these last two items as he ruefully ran his hand across his bald noggin. The final item of attire in the assembly line was a pair of brown leather service shoes with lace-up canvas leggings that covered the ankles and strapped under the mid-portion of the shoe. The shoes were sized quickly by having each recruit stand with his heel against a wooden block nailed to the floor with shoe sizes marked on the floor in white paint. There were no half-sizes and your best possible outcome was to have a shoe that was half an inch too big rather than one that was half an inch too small. The last item plunked on top of the stack was a large canvas duffel bag with shoulder strap. The final stop in the clothing disbursement shed was a large changing room. The recruits shucked their civilian clothing and donned their new fatigue uniforms. The civilian clothes were dropped into mesh cloth bags, labeled with the recruit's name, serial number and platoon number for long-term storage. They wouldn't be needing them for quite a while as it turned out. The boys emerged from the clothing building like newly minted candies popping from a gumball machine.

After a late supper in the Mess Hall the several new platoons of recruits were herded into a large assembly hall, basically a stripped out barracks building with no furniture and a small raised platform at one end. A microphone stood in the center of the platform. "Ten-Hut" rang out as the Camp Commander entered the building with his staff. A bespectacled Captain in a khaki trench coat took to the microphone. "At ease, men! On behalf of the United States Army, the training cadre of Camp Carson and a grateful American people I welcome you to the United States Army."

Gerry's mind began to wander as the Camp Commander stepped up and made a few comments. He wondered how his brother Eddie was doing back at college in Fort Collins. He wondered how Seamus was coping with the sudden rejection from the Army. He wondered whether his father was still angry. And mostly he wondered about whether his mother had made an apple pie lately and if so whether it was cut into more than four pieces.

Gerry's reverie ended when the captain called the room to attention. "Raise your right hand and repeat after me. I, (state your name) do solemnly swear or affirm that I will support and defend the Constitution of the United States against all enemies, foreign or domestic; that I will bear true faith and allegiance to the same; that I take this obligation freely, without any mental reservation or purpose of evasion; and that I will well and faithfully discharge the duties of the office on which I am about to enter. So help me God."

Gerry solemnly recited the oath along with his fellow new soldiers and added a soft, "Amen" at the end. "You're in the Army now," he thought to himself.

The next morning began with a pre-dawn two mile run and 20 minutes of calisthenics. Gerry was accustomed to running and exercise from his football playing days in school.

His long loping stride allowed him to cover the two miles with only a light sweat. The high dry air of Camp Carson allowed the sweat to evaporate quickly and kept his body cool. Although he was used to basic calisthenics like jumping jacks and push-ups some of these Army exercises were new and puzzling at first. Thanks to Eddie's coaching Gerry was familiar with the "squat-thrust" exercise but it still took a while to get accustomed to the rhythm of squatting, putting hands on the ground, kicking the feet back to a forward leaning rest (push-up) position and then returning back to squat position and return standing. "One-two-three-four, Two-two-three-four, Three-two-three four," and on it went. This was the four-count burpee. They also got a taste of the more elaborate eight-count burpee which included two push-ups with every squat-thrust repetition. The remainder of the first week of basic training was a blur.

Rousted out of bed at 0530 every morning the boys learned to square off the corners of the blankets and tuck the blankets so tightly under the mattresses that a fifty-cent piece would bounce twice when dropped from about 18 inches above the bed. Each trainee was allotted two sheets. Some of the boys adopted the expedient of fake-making the bed by using one sheet as the bottom sheet at the head of the bed, then doubling it back on itself to form the top sheet as well. Essentially this looks the same as the old prank of short sheeting somebody's bed. The blanket would then be tucked in using the standard technique of hospital corner with the edge of the top sheet folded back over the top edge of the blanket. The second sheet would then be hidden inside the pillowcase. When "Lights Out" rolled around at 2200 hours the second sheet was produced and served as a light covering.

Sleeping on top of the blanket meant that when they rolled out of bed it was already made. A quick tuck of the blankets to tighten them up and you were off and running.

Literally off and running. The morning runs and calisthenics were followed by a quick but calorie-dense breakfast. The boys filed quickly through the chow line, trays piled high with good hot food. Scrambled eggs, slabs of ham, crusty dry toast, oatmeal and mugs of hot coffee disappeared as if part of a third rate magician's stage act. After breakfast the trainees were packed into classrooms for a couple of hours of book learning. Military traditions, history, recognition of military rank and insignia, flag etiquette and military decorum were covered in the first week. Subsequent weeks would bring classes on weapons, recognition of enemy vehicles and weapons, squad tactics and awareness of operational security along with dozens of other topics.

Following their morning classroom session the troops would return to barracks where they gained invaluable experience in polishing shoes and brass belt buckles. Late morning brought a return to the great outdoors for an hour on the parade grounds learning close order drill. On the first full day of drill the boys were a ragtag collection of feet, knees and elbows going all different directions. Each boy got a one-on-one session with a drill instructor to learn the basics.

"To assume the position of attention, you will stand erect but relaxed. Your heels should touch together. Your feet should form a 45 degree angle. Your knees should not be locked straight unless you want to pass out in the middle of formation like a girl! Your hips should be thrust forward as if you are slow dancing with your best girl back in high school. The small of your back should be flattened, not arched. Your chest should be out and your gut should be sucked in. Imagine a string attached to the top of your chest pulling it straight up toward the ceiling! I said suck that gut in, soldier! Your arms must be down at your sides, elbows slightly bent, hands clenched but not tightly, as if holding a roll of quarters in your fingers. Your thumbs should be in line with and just behind the seam of your government issued gabardine trousers. Your wrists should be rotated backwards so that the tips of your fingers lightly touch the fabric of your government issued gabardine trousers. Your head should be straight ahead, eyes focused on the horizon. Do not gaze to the left. Do not gaze to the right." This mantra was repeated so often in the first week of basic training that Gerry began to hear it in his sleep.

Once the majority of the new troops had mastered the military art of standing still the drill team began to put them into motion. "Forward march!" The litany of marching commands came ever faster and ever more furious as the first week of training progressed. "At short intervals dress right, dress!" "Left face, right face, about face!" "Forward march!" "Quick time march!" "Column left march, column right march, to the rear march!" "Eyes, right!" "Present arms!" "Eyes, front!" "Squad, halt!"

Most of the boys quickly figured out that marching was simply walking in unison and once they adjusted the length of their arm swing to the cadence of the march ("Nine inches to the front, six to the rear!") were able to fall into a synchronous marching style. It was just walking after all. One ungainly farm boy though simply could not grasp the concept. In spite of intensive one-on-one sessions with the Drill Sergeants he persisted in marching with a style that drew snickers from the group. This boy was one of the two farm boys that had been wearing the burlap underwear during their medical examination back at the Induction Center in Fort Collins and the rigors of basic training were beginning to overwhelm him. He marched with knees locked stiff as if freshly returned from a tour with the Nutcracker Ballet. His arms also swung stiffly without any natural bend of the elbows. The oddest part of his marching style though was the fact that he insisted on swinging his right arm forward when his right leg stepped forward and his left arm forward when his left leg stepped forward. This awkward movement required him to rotate his hips from side to side and threatened to result in him tipping over entirely once he got up to speed. On the third day of drill training he was removed from the group and taken aside for an individual session. The following morning his bunk in the barracks was empty, his footlocker was gone and his mattress was folded up double, indicating that he had washed out.

At the beginning of the second week of Basic Training the boys were introduced to the obstacle course. Initially conceived at Ft. Belvoir, VA in 1940, the obstacle course was implemented at Army training camps throughout the system in 1941. The purpose of the obstacle course was to build physical stamina, balance, improvisation and performance under duress capabilities. The now-familiar elements of the Army obstacle course included horizontal logs for balance, rope swings over mud-filled ditches, low crawl under barbed wire, low vaults, a 10 foot tall scaling wall and a rope climb among other nefarious devices.

A spirited competition broke out during Obstacle Course week. The first three days involved familiarization with the various obstacles, instruction in proper technique and practice sessions. Some of the taller men did well on the scaling wall but struggled with the low crawl. Some of the stockier men did well with the strength elements of the course but had a hard time with the balancing portions. Gerry's lean lanky build with farm hardened strength suited all of the various parts of the obstacle course quite well. During the week the platoon was graded according to their preliminary performances during the week. On the final day the trainees were paired according to their rankings for a final head-to-head competition. Gerry at #1 for the week was paired up against a boy from Denver who had been a star high school athlete. Throughout the early days of Basic Training this boy had managed to irritate every single member of the platoon with his bragging. Runner-up in the Metro Conference wrestling tournament, back-up quarterback on the football team that lost the state championship game in '39, dated the homecoming queen's less attractive younger sister, National Merit semifinalist (alternate) his senior year, this boy had almost done it all and wasted no opportunity to regale the boys with tales of his near greatness. The platoon had taken to calling him The Contender, as in "I coulda been…"

The rest of the platoon gathered around as Gerry and the boy from Denver toed the starting line. "Take your marks, get set…" "Tweeeeeeet!" The race was on. Gerry's shoes lost traction coming out of the start and he almost fell to his knees. The stumbling start gave The Contender a slight edge as they reached the first obstacle. Quickly navigating the horizontal zigzag log he left a trail of mud from his shoes. This slime resulted in Gerry slipping again as he started across the logs. Falling hard to the ground Gerry narrowly avoided emasculating himself. He jumped up again, re-entered the obstacle from the beginning and took off after the other boy who was already halfway through the barbed wire crawl. Lungs bursting with effort Gerry put everything he had into the race. He gained steadily until the rope swing. Upon reaching the pit Gerry found that his rival had cleared the pit but then wrapped the rope around one of the stanchions on the far side of the pit so that Gerry could not reach it for the big swing across. Gerry gritted his teeth, backed off several paces and took off at a full sprint. Gaining precious footing on the near side of the trench he launched himself headlong into the air. It seemed as if the entire platoon collectively held their breath and Gerry sailed as if in slow motion across the gap. His feet landed a few inches short of the lip of the trench but he was able to stick just enough that his forward momentum carried him face first into the dirt on the other side of the pit. Back to his feet he was off and running again.

Two obstacles to go. Gerry was once again gaining ground. As he reached the climbing wall, Gerry saw that The Contender was already at the top, about to drop down to the other side. Gerry fought to catch his breath and was almost resigned to losing this race when in a gesture that surprised all the observers the braggart reached down to Gerry offering his hand. "Come on, farmer! Take it!" Gerry smiled gratefully and reached up with his right hand. The Contender clenched his hand to Gerry's and pulled steadily while Gerry leaned back and put the soles of his shoes against the wall and began walking up. At about the six foot mark Denver laughed, muttered "Sucker!" and turned Gerry's hand loose.

Gerry fell back onto the ground landing squarely on his back on the packed earth. His air was knocked out of his lungs with a resounding "Oof." The Contender dropped down onto the far side of the climbing wall and raised his arms triumphantly as he trotted toward the final obstacle, the rope climb. Behind him, Gerry struggled to the top of the climbing wall and saw the insurmountable lead. As Gerry dropped back onto the course he saw the braggart pitch forward awkwardly. Celebrating too soon he had managed to twist his ankle and had fallen to the ground. He struggled to get back up as Gerry pulled even with him. His eyes pleaded with Gerry for a little help. Gerry quickly flashed back to his upbringing on the farm. He thought of his hard-working father, a man of principle. He thought of his gentle but strong mother. He thought of his brother Eddie about to head off to Fort Sill with the Field Artillery. He knew what each of them would have done. Finally though he channeled his youngest brother Seamus. He reached his hand out toward the man on the ground. As The Contender reached up to take Gerry's hand Gerry quickly altered the course of his hand and patted the boy on the top of his head as if petting a stray dog. "You coulda been a contendah!" Leaving the startled boy on the ground Gerry leaped to the rope climb, dug into his last reserves of energy and quickly pulled himself to the platform at the top. He sat down heavily, draped his feet over the edge, took a deep breath and smiled to himself.

April 1942- Muldoon family farm, northeastern Colorado

In the weeks following Seamus' return to the farm he and his parents settled into a new routine. Picking up the slack for the absence of Gerry and Eddie, Seamus and the old man each increased their workloads. They seldom spoke as they labored side by side keeping the farm running. Once the daily chores were done however Seamus was able to carve out some free time. For a couple of hours each day he began working intensively with his hamsters. For the last several months he had been toying with a novel idea. He had one particular hamster who seemed very adept at manipulating things with his front paws. Seamus had been forced to create a hamster proof latch for this one's cage, because this particular hamster had the annoying habit of opening his own cage and diving into the hamster chow bag. He had become such an accomplished escape artist that Seamus had dubbed him Houdini.

The new idea Seamus had been working on involved a model airplane kit he had received for his 16th birthday. Seamus had quickly assembled the scale replica of a World War I Sopwith Camel biplane in a matter of days. Not content with merely having the plane on display Seamus and Eddie had then Gerry-rigged an actual functioning control system including up and down ailerons and left-right tail rudder. They had launched the plane on test flights from the second story hay loft in the barn and it demonstrated incredibly functional aerodynamic stability, able to glide smoothly for almost a hundred feet. When Seamus and Gerry had left to join the Army he had put the plane on top of the dresser in his bedroom. Now that he was back on the farm with no role to play in the war effort other than growing the dry land wheat Seamus dusted off the Camel and got to work. He fashioned a compartment for Houdini in the rear seat of the Camel. He installed a simple single stick control that connected to the steering mechanism. The basic function was simple, push forward for down, pull back for up, tilt left or right to turn. The stick was identical to a standard airplane pilot's control stick.

Seamus started Houdini's airplane training by suspending the model from the ceiling in the chicken coop. He pinned a simple bullseye target to the wall and put Houdini in the cockpit. The final element of this flight simulator was a tube that was attached to the front of the cockpit. Down this tube Seamus could roll a hamster alfalfa treat. They were ready for flight simulation training.

"All right, Houdini. Here goes nothing!" Seamus exclaimed. Standing behind the suspended plane, Seamus gently moved the tail to the right so that it was not pointing straight at the target and gave the command "On Target, Houdini!" After a few random tries Houdini accidentally pushed the stick toward the target. When Seamus sensed this he brought the nose back into alignment with the target and dropped a pellet down the treat tube. "Way to go fella!" Seamus said. You can almost imagine Houdini's eyes lighting up as the association was made. It took several days but Houdini soon became very skilled at operating the pilot's stick and had mastered the basics of left, right, up and down. Seamus bean to introduce some pitch and yaw and more complex rotational motions into the training regimen and Houdini proved quite skilled at handling these maneuvers.

At the same time Seamus had been constructing a launch ramp in the hay loft. The launch ramp was about eight feet high and very much resembled a ski jump. Pitched at about a 50 degree angle the ramp extended for about six feet horizontally. The last 18 inches curved back upward to achieve about a 30 degree angle of launch. He included a guide rail to keep the plane heading straight down the ramp.

The morning of April 19, 1942 was bright and cloudless. There was a light northerly breeze but Seamus decided that this was to be the day. He took one of his mother's old unused bed sheets and painted a bullseye target on it. He placed it on the ground about 30 yards from the hay loft door. Mounting to the hay loft with the Camel in one hand and Houdini in his left breast pocket Seamus prepared for launch. He positioned the plane at the top of the launch ramp. He gave Houdini a pellet and a pat on the head before placing him delicately in the cockpit. He playfully stood to attention, gave a brisk salute and a thumbs up. Pulling the release lever on the launch ramp Seamus commanded, "On Target, Houdini!" The plane gathered speed rapidly down the ramp. There was a clattering of wheels on wood as the plane entered the transition zone. The plane cleared the end of the ramp. The nose tilted up for a brief second. The plane then tilted forward into a steep nose down dive. It dropped quickly out of sight.

Seamus lunged forward to the edge of the hay loft door. He looked down just in time to see the plane pull out of its dive. Houdini had managed to pull back on the control stick at the last moment. Unfortunately, the sudden adjustment resulted in an overcorrection. Barely missing the ground the plane tilted back to an almost vertical position. This caused the plane to lose all forward momentum and it stalled out about 6 feet above the ground before dropping like a brick. It landed roughly with the brunt of the fall absorbed by the tail section. Seamus scrambled down the ladder to the ground and ran over to the plane. He scooped Houdini out and cupped him gently in his hand. Houdini opened his eyes, blinked twice, shook his head, looked around, scrambled up Seamus' sleeve and dove headlong into the relative safety of his shirt pocket.

Over the next two weeks Seamus and the hamster kept at it. Every evening after supper Seamus would patch up a busted tail section or a wingtip and make minor adjustments in the ailerons or the steering system or the paw-holds. Every morning after morning chores he would work with the hamster on conditioning and strength training. Early afternoons before evening chores when the wind conditions were just right Seamus and Houdini were out at the barn doing actual flight training. Seamus had extended the launch ramp by adding ten additional feet at the back end and had adjusted the angle of the ramp several times by trial and error. On the last Friday in April all of the minor adjustments finally bore fruit. For seemingly the hundredth time Houdini rumbled down the launch ramp with the wheels clattering like an empty boxcar. The ungainly looking biplane left the end of the jump and time seemed to stand still. The plane dipped down and Houdini banked it gently to the left. They caught a little lift from a steady breeze that was coming around the side of the barn and gained altitude steadily for about five seconds. Houdini then put the plane into a steep rightward bank and tilted the nose down. The plane picked up speed steadily and the slipstream began to pull the loose skin of Houdini's cheeks fluttering backward. The flapping of the hamster's cheeks became audible and Seamus was able to hear it from his vantage point in the barn loft. "Wocka-flappa- wocka-flappa-wocka" went Houdini's cheeks as the plane approached the target laying on the ground. Seamus let out a long slow breath and then started yelling, "No! No! You're going too fast, you're going to overshoot the landing!"

Houdini paid him no heed. The Sopwith Camel hurtled toward the target at a steep angle. Just when it seemed another crash landing was inevitable Houdini pulled steadily back on the control stick and held it firmly to his belly. The plane pulled out of the dive and began to climb as it rapidly dumped airspeed. Arcing gracefully up and backward Houdini held the plane in a steady loop. As the plane completed the loop Seamus was astonished to see that it was directly on line with the target. Easing toward the ground, Houdini pulled back on the stick once again. The plane stalled out a few inches above the sheet, plopped back to earth smack in the middle of the target, bounced lightly a couple of times and rolled to a stop.

"That was awesome!" Seamus shouted. In the cockpit Houdini reached up, smoothed his cheek flaps back to their normal position and crawled out on the wing of the biplane to await his hamster treat.

At the front window of the house where he had been watching the proceedings Old Man Muldoon dropped the window curtain back into place. He sat back in his armchair, tapped the cold ashes from his pipe, scratched his head, chuckled softly to himself and muttered, "Well I'll be. Ain't that something?" Ma rested her hand on her husband's shoulder and smiled knowingly.

"I always told you that boy was going to do something amazing! But Lordy Pa I never dreamed it would be a flying hamster!"

The first week of May brought the three Muldoon brothers together once again. Gerry had a short week's vacation before he had to report to his new infantry unit mobilizing down in Texas. Eddie was on break awaiting college graduation, following which he was off to Fort Sill, Oklahoma to begin his Field Artillery career in earnest. The three boys talked as they sat on the edge of the dry creek bed west of the house watching the sun set.

"Man, I wish I was going." Seamus muttered. "You guys get all the breaks."

Eddie elbowed him in the ribs. "Aw quit your whining. You know what they say, an army marches on its stomach. Somebody has to grow that wheat to make into flour and it might as well be you! I'll be damn proud to eat a biscuit made with flour from the Muldoon farm."

"You know what I mean," Seamus sulked.

Gerry began to regale his brothers with stories of infantry training. In particular Gerry had excelled at hand-to-hand combat training. He went on and on about how to immobilize a sentry or how to break a man's neck by giving him a sudden twist of the helmet. He described in great detail the knife fighting techniques he had learned at his Advanced Infantry Training course. Jumping to his feet he grabbed a stick from the ground and brandished it toward Seamus while crouching and circling warily. He lunged with the stick toward Seamus' midsection. Seamus reacted instinctively by deflecting Gerry's hand to the side while grasping the wrist. He stepped across with his right leg and turned away from Gerry. Simultaneously bending at the waist, throwing his hip into Gerry and pulling down on

Gerry's wrist he managed to flip Gerry up and over, putting him flat on his back in the sandy soil of the creek bed.

"You'd better work on that knife fighting technique, Zorro!" Eddie laughed.   Gerry's face broke into his trademark lopsided grin and the three brothers shared a hearty laugh. Tomorrow they would go their separate ways.

Back at the house, while Gerry and Eddie went in to say their goodbyes to Mom and Dad, Seamus held back. He went to his dresser and opened the bottom drawer. There, still in its box sat the Randall knife. He picked it up and opened the box one last time.

"You're going to need this a lot more than I will," he thought to himself. Seamus knew that Gerry would not accept the knife as a gift, so he had to make sure Gerry didn't know. Reaching deep into Gerry's duffel bag he pushed the knife in its box all the way to the bottom and hid it in a rolled up pair of pants. "That ought to do the trick," he muttered under his breath.

Not a single member of the Muldoon family slept soundly that night.

CHAPTER 4- ABLE BAKER CHARLIE

"I do not have to tell you who won the war. You know the artillery did."
- Gen George S. Patton

June 1942- Fort Sill, Oklahoma

During his Reserve Officer Training Corps training at Colorado A&M College in Fort Collins Eddie Dean Muldoon had spent two summers in basic training courses learning the basics of soldiering. He achieved basic competence with the M1903 .30-06 rifle which had been the standard U.S. Army rifle since the early 1900's as well as the newer M1 Garand semiautomatic rifle that was slowly replacing the M1903. He qualified on the M1911A1 .45 caliber semiautomatic pistol; standard sidearm for Army officers. He learned how to salute, right face, left face and about face. He learned that as a lowly ROTC cadet he had four answers for any question asked by one of his instructors. The four answers were "Yes Sir", "No Sir", "No Excuse Sir" and "Sir I do not understand." He also learned basic map reading and orienteering skills, how to shoot an azimuth and a back azimuth, how to estimate distance travelled by counting his steps with a measured stride of 2.5 feet per stride and complex triangulation. He learned the meaning of the phrase "double the angle on the bow". He learned basic radio technique, including the phonetic alphabet. Here is the phonetic alphabet used by the U.S. Army in 1942.

A – Able
B – Baker
C – Charlie
D - Dog
E – Easy
F – Fox
G – George
H – How
I – Item
J – Jig
K – King
L – Love
M – Mike
N – Nan
O – Oboe
P – Peter
Q – Queen
R – Roger
S – Sugar
T – Tare
U – Uncle
V – Victor
W – William
X – X-ray
Y – Yoke

Z – Zebra

Nobody remembers exactly when it happened but by the time Eddie Muldoon had finished his second summer of basic training one of the instructors had tagged him with the nickname that would stay with him for the rest of his life. Edward Dean became E.D. which morphed into "Easy Dog" which was soon shortened to "EZ Dog". This moniker would stick for the duration of the war and for decades beyond.

Eddie's agile mind grasped the phonetic ABC's so quickly that he would amuse his classmates on slow Thursday nights around the barracks by using the phonetic replacements to turn newspaper headlines into doggerel.

For example, when Eddie and his pals read the news from the Battle of Midway the first week of June, 1942 the headline "Jap Fleet Smashed" was rendered by Eddie Muldoon as "The Jig enAbled Peter's Fox to Love the Easy Easy Tare Sugar. Mike enAbled Sugar, How Easy for a Dog." Delivered in Eddie's Midwest twang these nonsense verses sounded like some quirky poetry and served as a great source of amusement for his mates. Before dismissing this notion out of hand the reader must keep in mind that this was the same culture that by 1943 had given us such gems as the popular hit song "Mairzy doats and dozy doats and little lambsie divy".

Following his graduation from Colorado A&M in May 1942 EZ Dog Muldoon was ordered to report to Fort Sill, Oklahoma for Basic Officers Leadership Training in the Field Artillery. He arrived at Fort Sill on June 15 and was soon swept up in a growing sense of impending significance. Big things were afoot and there was a buzz in the air. At least that was the case until the boredom and drudgery set in a few days later.

On yet another late June morning EZ Dog Muldoon gazed out the window at the rolling hills of southwestern Oklahoma. The morning air held the promise of a hot afternoon to come but for now he allowed himself to enjoy the crystal blue skies and gentle morning breeze. The voice of the instructor droned on with a recitation of Field Artillery History. During his ROTC days EZ Dog had read extensively about military history. He was particularly interested in discussions of lessons learned during the Great War. There were two different schools of thought in the U.S. Military during the interwar years.

One group held that the Field Artillery was still the "King of Battle" and that no large scale military operation could be fought and won without massive application of artillery. Bigger, more powerful and intimidating guns were expected to play a major role in any future conflict, heaven forbid they should be needed.

The other school of thought held that the mobility provided by the tracked vehicles known as tanks that had emerged near the end of World War One would quickly supplant the usefulness of field artillery. Artillery was derided as a dinosaur, a thing of the past, a mode of war that had seen its day but now should be mothballed.

As it would later turn out, both philosophies were simultaneously right and yet wrong. The rapid strike and movement capabilities of a mobile tank army could quickly overcome a less mobile enemy force. Fixed emplacements of large artillery weapons quickly became useless if they were pointed the wrong direction as the French had learned along the Maginot line in the early summer of 1940. The mobile German blitzkrieg was able to do an end run through the Low Countries and render the French big guns worthless.

The flip side of this coin is that as the terrain became rougher and more mountainous or swamp-like the advantage shifted to the field artillery. A tank that has been immobilized by terrain is much less effective as an offensive weapon and relatively more vulnerable to attack. The range and trajectory capabilities of the Field Artillery enables concentration of fire from batteries that are widely separated on the battlefield onto a single target. When guided by a forward observer, artillery fire can be incredibly accurate and devastating. In addition, not only can a single object be targeted by multiple batteries it is possible to adjust the timing of the incoming rounds from different locations. By application of a little trigonometry, physics and knowledge of local wind and weather conditions the time in flight of shells from multiple guns can be calculated and the time of firing adjusted for each battery so that a huge amount of firepower can be focused on the target with all arriving at the same time. This technique is known as 'time on target'.

EZ Dog continued to daydream as the instructor droned on. He came out of his reverie just in time to hear the instructor tell the class, "Your assignment for tomorrow is to calculate a program of fire for a single gun, multiple round time on target exercise. You are to calculate charge, range, azimuth and time of fire requirements for a single 105 mm howitzer crew to rapidly fire two rounds from the same weapon, one on a high trajectory and one on a low trajectory at a target 6,000 yards down range at an elevation 800 feet above your firing location. This single gun, multiple round time on target technique is more commonly referred to as a High-Low shot. Next week on the range we will put your calculations into practical application. Class dismissed!"

As he sat in the day room at the barracks that evening EZ Dog mulled the problem in his mind. The basic calculation was actually pretty straightforward. Using a higher powder charge, the first round would be fired at a steep trajectory which would carry the round high into the air and taking a little under 25 seconds to reach the target. A second round fired at a flat trajectory with a smaller explosive powder charge would take just over 10 seconds to travel from the gun to the same impact point. This give the gun crew about 12 or 13 seconds to manually crank the angle of elevation (range) of the weapon down to the lower trajectory and load the second shell into the breech in order to fire at the exact instant that would allow the two rounds to reach the target simultaneously. These mathematical calculations had been incorporated into extensive tables of data that artillery fire control centers used in the real world and were readily available. The more Eddie thought about the problem however the more variables he realized had to be considered. Wind speed and direction could be known with some accuracy at the location of the gun battery but wind speed and direction do not remain constant during the flight of an artillery round. The elevation of the target relative to the firing battery had to be considered. Believe it or not, at longer distances even the curvature of the earth and the small but real Coriolis effect (deviation in the course of an object relative to the rotation of the earth) had to be taken into consideration. Shell rotation, tumbling, air temperature, relative humidity; the list went on and on. In a small room, lit only by a dim table lamp, with a couple of sharpened pencils, a slide rule and a stack of ruled paper EZ Dog Muldoon was in his element. He worked until the small hours of the morning, finally wrapping up at about 0300.

Satisfied that he had prepared a complete and accurate program of fire he took a few minutes to write a brief one page letter to his parents.

> *"Dear Mom and Dad- Working hard here, late nights and long days. It is already nearly the end of June and still no word on when and where we'll be heading overseas. All the boys are eager to "get to it". I guess you will have heard the news from the Pacific. It sounds like the fellas really gave the Japs a walloping at Midway! Hooray for the Navy boys! I heard from Gerry that he will be in Texas for another couple of months before his unit heads out for Europe. Rumors abound but it looks like the first place we can get into the war will be in North Africa. I haven't heard a peep out of Seamus since he headed back east. Have you gotten any word from him? How is the wheat shaping up this year? Hopefully it will be a banner year. Were you able to find any field hands to help out? I think I will be able to come home on leave briefly at the end of August. Save me a piece of pie. You know apple is my favorite but I'll settle for rhubarb if that's all you can manage. Love to all. Eddie."*

He stuffed the letter into an envelope, addressed it and dropped it in the outgoing mail box outside the day room before shuffling off to bed.

The young officers filed into the classroom the next morning promptly at 0800. The senior instructor collected the varied worksheets from the officers and retired to his office while the junior cadre launched into a presentation on timing fuses. As the class filed out after nearly 3 hours of lecture, the senior instructor was waiting at the door. He pulled Eddie aside brusquely, "Muldoon, step into my office."

Eddie stood stiffly at attention in front of the instructor's desk with his eyes locked onto the map of Europe that hung on the wall. "Well Lieutenant Muldoon. I've been reading through everybody's firing solution for this high-low shot." Eddie remained silent, a bead of sweat beginning to form on the tip of his nose. He wanted to reach up and wipe it away but remained at attention. "The average length of the solutions submitted by the class runs about half a page. The average number of variables considered in the solutions is three. Barrel elevation, powder charge and time of firing."

He continued, "Your solution on the other hand takes up seven pages and considers 13 different variables. Would you care to elaborate?" Eddie started to formulate his reply but before he could utter a word the instructor interrupted, "Never mind! I think you elaborated quite enough in your two paragraph dissertation on wind speed variation in the American Plains states on page 5."

Eddie swallowed a big dry lump with difficulty and felt the drop of sweat wobbling as it threatened to fall from the tip of his nose. His eyes focused on the center of the map of Europe, picking out the "W" in Switzerland. Could he have already washed out of the Field Artillery? Why had he over analyzed this problem? Why couldn't he remember the acronym K-I-S-S they had learned during the first semester of ROTC back in Fort Collins? Keep. It. Simple. Stupid!

"Here's the thing though, Muldoon," the instructor interrupted Eddie's self-reflection. "I can't find a single wrong element in this entire analysis. You have included a mathematical adjustment for every known variable that we can give a measured value. You have made a reasonable assumption and adjustment for the variables we can't put a value on. This is the most comprehensive firing solution for a high-low shot that I've ever seen. Fine work, son! Now let's get out to the range and see if we can translate this formula into practical action."

Eddie allowed himself a quick grin and a surreptitious wipe of the tip of his nose as he snapped a salute. "Yes Sir!" he barked.

The instructor hesitated briefly then said, "One final question, Muldoon. I saw the parenthetical footnote at the bottom of page seven and couldn't quite decipher its meaning. What is 'LYFACTW-OMM'?"

Eddie's face lit up and he said, "Oh that's my old man's advice, Sir. OMM is for Old Man Muldoon. Whenever he took us out shooting jackrabbits back on the farm he would tell me and my brothers to Lick Your Finger And Check The Wind. L-Y-F-A-C-T-W. That's my ultimate fudge factor."

The bus full of young artillery officers pulled up at the main howitzer range in the barren hills of Fort Sill. The young men filed into the wooden bleachers overlooking the three gun 105-mm howitzer emplacement. The gun crews lounged over by the sand-bagged bunker off to one side. The enlisted men eyeballed the peach-fuzzed young officers and a couple muttered something about "damn butter bars!" One-by-one the junior instructor called the students to the front where a simulated fire control center had been set up. In turn each student was given ten minutes to relay their fire solution to the gun crew. Powder charge, range and azimuth for both rounds. The exact time of firing was called out by the student officer.

The first student nervously took his place. The gun crew loaded the first round and aimed the weapon. On the command "Fire!" the cannoneer sharply pulled the lanyard triggering the firing mechanism and sending the first round hurtling high into the air. The young lieutenant eyed his wristwatch as the gun crew leaped into action. Furiously cranking the elevating handwheel they rapidly lowered the barrel to the designated elevation while the loaders opened the breech, extracted the spent cartridge, inserted the second round and locked the breechblock back into "ready" position. The lieutenant watched as the final two seconds ticked off and then yelled "Fire!" once again sending a round downrange. The watching students waited breathlessly while the next 10 seconds ticked off. Looking downrange they saw first one and then the second far off explosion marked by a cloud of Oklahoma dust on the side of the hill. Half a minute ticked off while the scorers made their calculations. The junior instructor stepped in front of the bleachers and hollered, "Distance separation 12 yards! Time separation 3.5 seconds!"

Over the next two hours this process was repeated over and over with similar results. One hapless student endured the catcalls from the audience when his results were shouted out, "Distance separation 160 yards! Time separation 15 seconds!"

The instructors had saved Eddie Muldoon for last. As his ten-minute preparation time began Eddie dashed around the gun crew. He pulled a tape measure from his pocket and measured the length of the cannoneer's right arm. Pulling out his slide rule he ran through some last minute calculations and scribbled furiously on his notepad. Throughout the morning he had been using a stopwatch to time the arm swing of the cannoneer and made a slight time adjustment for the soldier's reaction time. Finally, after giving his final load and range instructions he stepped to the firing line. Licking his finger he stuck it up in the air and felt the coolness on the left side. "Ready, Fire!" Eddie barked. The gun barked and sent the first round high into the late morning air. The gun crew leaped into the now-familiar furious routine of adjusting the barrel's elevation and loading the second round. Eddie watched the sweep second hand on his stop watch. At the last possible instant Eddie jumped to the side of the gun and gave the traversing handwheel a counterclockwise half turn changing the final direction of fire slightly. Leaping back away from the gun he yelled "Fire!" It seemed like slow motion as Eddie watched the arc of the cannoneer's arm and the brief delay as the pull took up the slack in the lanyard. The release of the trigger mechanism looked even slower as Eddie watched with all sense of time suspended. Finally the blast and recoil of the howitzer brought time back into alignment and the second round left the muzzle.

Eleven seconds later the onlookers saw a single puff of dust and smoke on the distant hillside. They waited in anticipation for the second round to hit. And they waited. And they waited some more. The men began to look around and a murmur ran through the crowd. "What happened?" "Did he miss the hillside completely?" "Was there a dud?"

"At ease! Listen up!" the senior instructor brought the group to silence. "We have results. Distance separation one-half yard! Time separation zero seconds! We have a simultaneous impact gentlemen!"

The men broke into a cheer, spilled out of the bleachers and mobbed Eddie with congratulations! They mussed his hair, rumpled his clothes, punched his shoulder and slapped his back until he was sore. As the instructors loaded the men back on the bus the senior instructor pulled Eddie to one side and said, "Congratulations Lieutenant! I think you are going to do well in the Field Artillery. Tell me though, what was that last second traverse adjustment?"

"Well sir that was just Old Man Muldoon's fudge factor!" Eddie grinned.

"Easy Dog Muldoon indeed!" the instructor grinned back.

CHAPTER 5- SEAMUS JOINS THE WAR

"It has long been known for sure that the sight of tasty food makes a hungry man's mouth water."
- Ivan Pavlov, Russian scientist

December 1942—Special Warfare Animal Group, War Department, Chicago, Illinois

The jeep pulled up outside a nondescript warehouse in the industrial district of Chicago. The bitter winter wind blowing off Lake Michigan cut right through Seamus' light jacket, chilling him to the bone. Seamus watched as the driver pulled away, leaving him outside a rusted metal door. The sign over the door read "Harkinson Dry Goods". Huddled against the side of the building, sheltered only slightly from the wind, Seamus waited, not sure what he was waiting for. After what seemed like an hour but in fact had only been five minutes, the door creaked open. A tall, hawk-faced man with thinning light brown hair stepped out. He was dressed in a plain khaki uniform with no insignia. The only adornment was a simple black nametag over the right breast pocket with one word, 'Smith'. A half-smoked cigarette hung languidly from his lips as he approached Seamus. "Muldoon? Come this way." As they entered the large, mostly empty storeroom, Seamus' eyes struggled to adjust to the dim light. The thin man walked quickly across the room, Seamus following hesitantly along. A single bare light bulb over an interior door struggled in vain to push back the darkness of the windowless room. The unlikely pair passed through the door into a long, narrow, featureless hallway. Interspersed at irregular intervals were several doorways, unmarked. The two sets of footfalls echoed blankly in the otherwise empty hallway. Seamus began methodically counting his steps. When he reached "one hundred and eighty three" the thin man stopped.

They stood outside a blank wooden door. Smith reached for the knob and pushed the door open. A bare metal table stood in the center of the room. A single three-legged stool sat empty on the near side of the table. On the far side of the table were three folding chairs facing toward the door. A short round man sitting in the middle chair gestured toward the well-formed stool. "Have a seat Mr. Muldoon." Seamus nervously sat down. The room reminded him of the principal's office at his high school back home. The round man was dressed the same as the thin man, right down to the name tag with the name "Smith". A third man occupied the second facing chair, looking intently down at a stack of paperwork in front of him. A black leather coat covered this man's shirt leaving Seamus in the dark about his name. Seamus assumed the obvious; another "Smith". Thin

Smith walked around the table and took the empty chair facing Seamus.

Round Smith cleared his throat noisily and said, "Welcome to the Department of the Army, Special Weapons Animal Group, Mr. Muldoon. May I call you Seamus?"

"Sure, I guess," Seamus replied vaguely. "That's my name. Why am I here?"

Round Smith shrugged and replied cryptically, "Why do you think you are here?"

"You've got the advantage on me there Mr. Smith. May I call you Smith?" Seamus shot back. "All I know is I was enjoying a cold beer in a comfortable tavern when your driver shanghaied me and drove me way out here to the middle of nowhere. Maybe you can fill me in."

Round Smith glanced at Thin Smith and both glanced at the man in the black jacket who nodded almost imperceptibly. "We have been watching you for quite some time, Seamus. We…well not we…rather the American people…need your help. You possess certain, shall we say, talents that are unique in this country. I am speaking of course about your expertise in the area of hamster training."

Round Smith interjected, "We understand that you were president of your hometown Homing Hamster Club, is that correct?"

Seamus nodded. Thin Smith piped in, "And we know that you were three time State Champion at the Colorado State Homing Hamster competition in 1939, 1940 and 1941 with your number one competitor, Hammie, correct?" Seamus nodded again.

Black Leather Jacket looked up from his paperwork and grunted, "Clever name for a hamster," before burying his nose back in his paperwork.

Round Smith once again took the initiative. "We also know that you were champion at the Mountain Regional Interstate Hamster Trials in 1941." Seamus nodded yet again.

"So what does this have to do with why I'm here?" Seamus queried.

Black Leather Jacket pushed his chair back from the table and lurched to his feet. As he did so his jacket fell open briefly and Seamus was able to read the name tag. 'Smythe'. Seamus muttered to himself, "It figures."

Smythe pulled a thumb-thick cigar from his inner jacket pocket, bit off the tip, spat it into the corner of the room and lit up with a series of short quick puffs. The flaming end of the cigar flashed briefly, then settled into a faint red glow as Smythe took in a deep pull. Tilting his head back, he sent seven or eight quick smoke rings chasing each other toward the ceiling.

"Allow me to explain. We represent a Top Secret wing of the United States Army known simply as the Special Warfare Animals Group, more commonly known as S.W.A.G. This is our headquarters building. We are largely staffed with a group of elite scientists led by the renowned behavioral scientist B. F. Skinner. You may be familiar with his work with both humans and animals. Our mission is to develop novel ways for our animal friends to assist in the war effort. We have dolphins working with the Navy, pigeons working with the Army Air Corps and working dogs in the Military Police. Until recently we have not had any use for rodents."

Seamus waited silently until Smythe continued, "One of our most troublesome military problems is that the German artillery exceeds ours in terms of range and accuracy. We are working on ways to improve the accuracy of our counter artillery units in order to neutralize some of that German advantage. One of our scientists has developed a program that could potentially use small rodents as little furry pilots, if you will, to help guide artillery shells with a degree of precision that conventional weapons cannot achieve. We have developed a prototype artillery shell but have run into some obstacles that have kept us from achieving a practical deliverable weapon system. That is where you come in. We think that your unique skills can help us overcome these obstacles."

The room fell silent as Smythe ended his sales pitch. Seamus could almost hear his own heart beat as he looked from Black Leather Jacket Smythe to Thin Smith to Round Smith and back to Smythe again. A faint grin began to creep onto his face and then he burst into laughter. The three Smiths watched impassively as he snickered, tittered, guffawed and then giggled a little. As Seamus regained his breath he shook his head and said, "You're kidding, right? Hamster guided bombs? Little suicide missions by patriotic hamsters?" He chuckled some more then continued, "Who put you up to this? It's a prank, right? Did one of my brothers put you up to this?"

The three Smiths relaxed slightly and began to chuckle right back at Seamus. Thin Smith turned to Round Smith and said, "Pay up!" Round Smith pulled a crumpled five dollar bill from his pocket and handed it to Thin Smith. "I told you he would react like that," Thin Smith gloated.

Smythe strode over to the door and snapped, "Come with me, Muldoon!" Seamus pushed himself to his feet and followed Smythe down the hallway to the first door on the left. Smythe opened the door and gestured for Seamus to enter. As they entered the room, Seamus blinked in amazement. Spread out on a massive raised counter in the middle of the large room was a miniature landscape with paths, hills, buildings and three small athletic fields. Around the table were several somber looking men with white lab coats and clipboards. They consulted stopwatches and made notations on their clipboards as they observed the table. A muscular man in an undersized T-shirt stood at the far end of the table flexing his considerable biceps self-consciously while holding a stop watch and a whistle. "Tweeeeeet!" On the middle athletic mini-field three hamsters wearing form-fitting one-piece exercise garments came to a halt as the trainer clicked the stop watch and barked, "All right fellas! Good work today. You improved your time by two seconds Number Three! Take a break." The three hamsters scurried off into a little building in the corner of the table with a small sign that read "Locker Room". As they entered the miniature doorway each of the hamsters received a hamster treat from one of the scientists.

Seamus stood with his mouth hanging open. Smythe grabbed him by the collar and pulled him back out of the training room, then steered him back into the conference room. "No, Mr. Muldoon, we are not kidding, this is not a prank and your brothers are not involved in this. We are deadly serious."

Seamus sat back down with a stunned look on his face. He looked silently from one Smith to the next, unable to form any words. The seconds ticked by. After a delay of what seemed like half an hour but was probably more like sixty seconds Seamus uttered the only words that came to mind.

"Wow! That was COOL!!"

Seamus quickly agreed to sign on for the hamster project. The next two days were a whirlwind of activity as he received a rapid fire series of briefings bringing him up to speed. His mind had trouble absorbing it all but the picture was made clear for him during a briefing given by Black Leather Smythe on Seamus' second day on the job. Seamus sat in a darkened conference room while a slide projector flashed a series of images on a white bed sheet hung from the wall. Smythe began.

"Listen up Muldoon. Americans have always had a creative and inventive spirit. The current hostilities have brought out some of the most creative and imaginative thinkers in history. Radio is well established as a means of communication but we are finding that radio waves can be used in other ways. We think that by the end of this war we will be using radio waves to see into the skies and across the seas and to steer our bombs on target. This new technology has been dubbed RADAR which is short for Radio Detection and Ranging. Unfortunately, using RADAR as a means of improving the accuracy of weapons systems is only in the theoretical stages. As you may know in World War I trench warfare bogged down into a pattern of infrequent full frontal infantry assaults that gained only a couple hundred yards of hard-fought territory separated by long tedious days of artillery duels. The weaponry that emerged from WWI has a terrible destructive capacity. Unfortunately the accuracy still leaves something to be desired. During the 1930's a large number of both civilian and military groups were working on different ideas to improve the accuracy of delivering an attack with maximal effect. Our mission here at the Special Warfare Animal Group Laboratory falls into the category of nonconventional weapons systems development. There are three innovative programs in particular that we are working on.

"Most people have at least passing familiarity with Pavlov's dog. A Russian physiologist named Ivan Pavlov worked with classical conditioning of animals. He was most well-known for his work with dogs. As you undoubtedly know Pavlov was able to condition dogs to salivate at the sound of a bell by making a strong association between being fed and hearing the bell. With time the dogs would salivate before the food was placed in front of them. The sound of the bell became the trigger for the salivation response."

Smythe gave Seamus a few seconds to digest this and then continued, "You may have heard of a scientist named B. F. Skinner. He got some play in the national news last year. He is a Harvard-trained psychologist. Professor Skinner has worked extensively with animal behavior modification along the lines of Pavlov's conditioning experiments. Skinner's contribution to the war effort has been focused on a Top Secret project named "Project Pigeon". I have been authorized to discuss this program with you, Seamus.

"Skinner knew that it was fairly easy to condition pigeons to peck at an image on a screen in order to trigger the release of a food pellet. Pigeons who had been conditioned this way would peck repeatedly at a picture on a screen. With Skinner's input Army Air Corps weapons engineers have developed a nosecone that can be fitted on a high-explosive bomb. Within the nose cone are three separate compartments each with enough room for one pigeon. Small harnesses hold the three pigeons in position. In front of each of the three pigeons is a small viewfinder that shows whatever the bomb is heading toward. In theory, as the bombardier releases the bomb toward a target such as a naval vessel the pigeons will see the target on their view screen and begin pecking at the center of the image just as they have been conditioned to do. Each of the image screens is connected to a guidance system in the tail section of the bomb. The guidance system is actuated by an array of wires and pulleys that manipulate three guidance fins at the back of the bomb. As the bomb comes closer to the target the image grows larger and the average position of the three pigeons pecking creates a crude form of triangulation. This allows small adjustments in the bomb's final glide path and results in a more precise strike on the target. This system has been hampered by the fact that pigeons are in fact rather stupid and have short attention spans. They are not quick learners."

"Maybe the bombs should be pigeon-towed," Seamus quipped in an attempt to lighten the mood.

Smythe went on without missing a beat, "Our folks are also working on a second little-known weapons program dubbed Project Bat Bomb. This weapon is in its early stages. If we can develop a working prototype it will consist of a bomb casing with multiple small compartments. Each compartment will hold a Mexican fruit bat to which a small fire bomb is attached by a harness. This bomb would be deployed from an airplane shortly before dawn with its descent toward the ground slowed by a small parachute. The outer casing would open up before impact with the ground. The bats would then do what bats naturally do. They would fly off and find places to go to sleep for the daylight hours. The hope was that the bats (by the thousands) would seek out remote crevices within buildings in time for the delayed-trigger incendiary bombs to detonate, thus setting widespread fires that would cause panic and property destruction as well as require enemy resources to be used fighting the fires. This could be particularly effective in the Pacific Theater given the widespread utilization of bamboo, wood and paper for construction in that part of the world.

The third unique weapons system utilizing animals is the one that we recruited you to work on. We think this system has potential to be deployed in real war action within the next two years. We call this program "Operation Hamster".

The next morning Smythe took Seamus into the lower floors of the building. They ended up in a small laboratory behind a door marked "Top Secret". In the middle of the room lit by a single spotlight was a rather ordinary looking artillery shell. "Do you know much about artillery, Muldoon?" Smythe asked.

Seamus wished he had listened last summer when his brother Eddie had come back from ROTC summer training at Fort Sill, site of the U.S. Army's artillery headquarters. Eddie had been droning on and on about calibers and elevations and trajectories and fire control centers with an excitement Seamus had never seen in his older brother. Eddie had regaled Seamus and their older brother Gerry with stories of the 105 mm howitzer versus the new 155mm

M1A1 guns. He had expounded at the dinner table about the differences between guns, howitzers and mortars. Seamus had found the conversation pretty tedious and had tuned Eddie out pretty quickly. Now in this small room in the basement of a nondescript warehouse building on the lakefront in Chicago Seamus struggled to remember his brother's words.

"Umm. A little bit," he fudged.

"We know your brother is in the Field Artillery. Quite an up-and-coming young officer judging by the reports coming out of Fort Sill. He may be able to help us down the road but for now we are going to give you just the basics about field artillery," Smythe continued. "The shell that you see in front of you is a modified 155 mm artillery shell. That's a hair over six inches across. The new M1A1 155's are affectionately referred to by our artillery friends as the "Long Tom. These guns are highly accurate and have an effective range of 23,000 meters. That's a hair over 14 miles."

As the briefing went on Seamus learned about other prevalent weapons in the current Field Artillery arsenal including the 105 mm howitzer. He learned that 105 mm is a hair over 4 inches. The 105 mm howitzer was much more mobile and had a more rapid set-up procedure than the "Long Toms" but had a much shorter effective range. The Army envisioned the 105 mm howitzer as being useful in direct combat support at the Infantry Division level while the 155 mm guns with their longer range and larger payload capacity would be used at Corps and Army level. By being able to reach well beyond the front lines in a combat situation the Long Tom was well suited for taking out or neutralizing enemy artillery. This function is known in Field Artillery circles as counterbattery operations. Seamus learned that the German Army had several huge artillery pieces that were so large that they had to be mounted on railroad cars. These behemoths were not very accurate and could not sustain a high rate of fire but they were able to deliver a 280 mm caliber projectile weighing 255 kg a distance of almost 65,000 meters. He learned that that was a hair over 11 inches, a hair over 500 pounds and a hair over 40 miles.

The specific mission of Project Hamster was the modification of an artillery shell so that it could function effectively as a counterbattery threat against long range German artillery pieces.

Seamus plunged headlong into his new role. Over the next few weeks Seamus, Smythe and the team reviewed the obstacles facing them in their mission. The biggest problems to overcome were the physical effects on the pilot hamster. They focused on the 105-mm howitzer as their preferred weapon due to much better on-target accuracy. They calculated rate of acceleration, muzzle velocity and spin rates of typical shell configurations. The concussive shock of the firing of the gun, the sudden acceleration and the high velocity spinning of the shell were obviously not conducive to hamster well-being. Overcoming the physical effects on the hamster was their first hurdle. If that could be surmounted the training of the hamsters to steer the shell to its target would become the next obstacle. Finally they had to figure out a way to recover the hamster at the end of the projectile's flight. "We shall leave no hamster behind!" became the mantra of the S.W.A.G. hamster team.

The scientific team performed a series of biometric measurements on the test hamsters. Seamus learned that an average adult hamster weighs 220 grams or a hair over 7 ounces. Hamsters are remarkably strong. An adult hamster can lift a weight equal to five times his body weight. The skeleton of a hamster is largely made of cartilage so is remarkably flexible. A typical adult hamster can compress his body and deform his skull in such a way that he can fit through a hole the size of a dime. That's a hair under three quarters of an inch.

The technical problems involved with loading a hamster into the nose section of an artillery shell proved to be anything but straightforward. The S.W.A.G. technicians had built a simulator room. A dummy artillery shell was mounted on a tripod in the center of the room, attached to a high-powered electrical motor that could rotate the shell at speeds ranging from 10 up to 10,000 rpm. A projector screen was mounted on the far wall where footage of various potential targets could be shown. A small light mounted parallel to the side of the shell shone on the screen, indicating the hamsters aiming point. This room became the main focus of Seamus' life during early 1943.

In order to overcome the dual problems of explosive acceleration and high-speed rotation the team had brainstormed a number of ideas. Thin Smith suggested a timed short acting sedative that would put the hamster to sleep during the firing of the round but allow him to wake up during flight in time to take the controls and guide the shell to its destination. When they tried this in the mock-up lab the timing could not be controlled with any regularity. Hamsters either slept through the entire mission or woke up too soon and panicked during firing. Those hamsters that did wake up in time were too groggy and disoriented to do a very satisfactory job of steering an artillery shell.

Round Smith came up with an idea for protecting the hamsters from the massive G-forces they experienced upon launch. A relatively new product known as foam rubber had been developed by the Dunlop tire company about a decade before. This product was lighter than standard rubber for the same size due to incorporation of thousands of tiny air bubbles within the structure. It was well suited for shaping by way of a mold into a large variety of configurations. Smith spent close to six weeks in the early spring of 1943 designing and building prototype hamster shock absorber suits, vests, trousers and helmets. There was even a jaunty scarf to complete the ensemble. Ultimately this experiment failed because the hamsters quickly developed a taste for the foam rubber garments and would quickly nibble them to pieces. Any protective benefit was quickly lost as the suits were filled with holes; not to mention the effect of a stomach full of foam rubber on a hamster's mobility and mental sharpness. The bloated lethargic rodents just couldn't muster the wherewithal to operate the steering mechanism.

Tensions began to run high at team meetings. The phrase, "That's the stupidest idea I've ever heard!" became at least a daily occurrence. Finally, one day near the end of April Smythe pulled Seamus aside saying, "Come on Muldoon! Let's get outta here for a few hours." The two men jumped into one of the S.W.A.G. jeeps and headed toward Lake Michigan. They soon found themselves sitting in the outdoor section of a bar/restaurant on the lake front near the Navy Pier. The cold beer went down easily as the two men sat and watched the activities along the waterfront.

They could see a group of Navy sailors in a spirited game of touch football on the beach. Off in the distance they could see a couple Navy planes taking off and landing on a flattop boat that had been fashioned from an old steamer for pilot aircraft carrier practice. To the east a pair of speedboats were pulling water skiers around in a sweeping circle. Closer in they could see a banner strung above one of the small piers that dotted the waterfront. The banner read "1943 Midwest Lumberjack Championships. They could see a group of rather burly bearded men on the pier with a small crowd of onlookers. Seamus caught the flash of the sun reflecting off an axe blade swinging high before coming down with a resounding "ka-chunk" as the lumberjack hewed through a 12 inch log in about 20 strokes. Out on the water to the left of the pier a pair of lumberjacks were balancing precariously on a log in the water. The two burly men ran swiftly in place with a nimbleness that belied their bulk. The log spun first this way then the other as the two men tried to throw each other into the drink. A smile began to spread across Seamus' face and he slapped his hand down sharply on the table. "Finish your beer, Smythe. I've got it!"

"What? What have you got?" Smythe countered.

"The answer to all of our problems." Seamus replied cryptically. "Come on, I'll fill you in on the trip back!"

When the two men arrived back at S.W.A.G. Seamus rushed into the storeroom. Rummaging among the cages, water bottles, and other spare hamster parts he quickly found what he was looking for. "How big is this hamster wheel?" he blurted. Not waiting for an answer he pulled a ruler from the desk drawer and measured. The diameter was exactly 5 inches. All of his training came suddenly into focus as he quickly calculated 155 mm artillery shell was just over 6 inches. Smythe looked on bemusedly as Seamus rushed to the blackboard. He scribbled out a series of mathematical conversions, divided by six, carried the two and multiplied by the square root of something or other. When he was done he plopped down in a chair and ran his hand through his prematurely thinning hair. "Call a team meeting for first thing in the morning, Smythe. I'm about to knock your socks off."

The team gathered around the battered metal table in the sparsely furnished conference room right at 0800 the next morning.

"Gentlemen, I maintain that we have been going about this all wrong. From the beginning we have been working under the presumption that our best platform for this project was the 105 mm howitzer because they are deployed so close to the front that they could reach any reasonable target with high degree of accuracy. But the 105 mm shell is barely four inches in diameter. This has placed size constraints on all of our prototypes and those size constraints in turn have limited our ability to overcome the problems of rapid acceleration and high-speed rotation. But, if we allow ourselves to accept a change in premise, perhaps we can see our way clear to completing an effective system. Forget about optimizing throughputs or aligning your synergies. Consider for a moment the 155 mm "Long Tom" guns. The difference between the 105 mm and the 155 mm is a full two inches. That should give us the room we need to overcome the technical problems. We will have a lot more room in the nosecone for apparatus, as well as room for more explosives in the payload. Any decrease in accuracy will be more than made up for by the hamster guidance mechanism." Seamus looked around the room at the expectant faces of the various Smiths.

Round Smith piped up first, "That's not exactly the stupidest thing I've ever heard. But let me ask this question. We still have the problem of explosive instantaneous acceleration and a substantial amount of spin to overcome."

"That's where this comes in," Seamus almost crowed, holding up the hamster wheel defiantly. "All we have to do is mount this inside the nosecone and let the hamster pilot do what hamsters do naturally. If we can set up a counter rotation inside the nosecone at anything close to the rotation rate of the shell, the spin will cancel out and once the shell is in stable flight the outer casing will be rotating around the inner element with the hamster in his wheel riding without any rotation at all. The shell will be spinning along merrily outside the hamster wheel. And as far as the sudden acceleration goes, I think if we position the hamster on a flat surface, facing forward, that the natural flexibility of his cartilage skeleton will deform to a flattened position and then recoil so that he can begin running almost immediately. Keep in mind that these animals can deform their skeletons enough to fit through a hole the size of a dime. Why can't they flatten out to be as thin as a dime?"

Tall Smith stroked his chin thoughtfully before muttering, "It just might work. Dammit, I think it just might work. Only now we have to find the world's fastest hamster."

The team began to talk excitedly among themselves. The tension that had been building for the last 8 weeks was released from the room like air from a balloon. Team leader

Smythe quickly made up a new assignment roster and the team jumped back into the testing rooms with renewed enthusiasm.

CHAPTER 6- THE ITALIAN JOB

Sept 8, 1943 - heard report Italy surrendered.
Sept 14, 1943 - was going swimming in the Mediterranean
Sea but developed a toothache - pulled.
-The EZ Dog Diaries

September 1943- North Africa

Eddie "EZ Dog" Muldoon's war started with a whimper, not with a bang. Leaving the hot, dry summer of Camp Bowie, Texas in mid-August Eddie's unit had crossed the Atlantic Ocean and landed near Casablanca. They were now moving quickly across northern Africa towards their embarkation point in Tunisia. From there they would cross the Mediterranean to join the U.S. 5th Army attempting to advance up the Italian mainland against stiff German resistance along the Gustav Line near Monte Cassino. Eddie's toothache had started during the Atlantic crossing and grown steadily worse over the past week. As he sat in the waiting area at the dental clinic of the Divisional mobile hospital his mind wandered back over the recent world events that he was about to join personally.

Back on the family farm the Muldoons had followed the events in Europe as they unfolded in the late 1930's and early 1940's. The sense of a looming catastrophe built with each step along the way. British Prime Minister Neville Chamberlain fed the Sudetenland portion of Czechoslovakia to the Nazi alligator in 1938, hoping that the beast's appetite would be curbed. In 1939 the German army marched almost unopposed into Poland. Seizing the opportunity provided by momentum and encouraged by the conciliatory stance of England and France, the Germans looked to push their expansion by invading the Low Countries (Belgium, The Netherlands) and France in May of 1940. Within a month, scrambling in retreat, the British Army narrowly escaped annihilation by means of the massive deployment of thousands of watercraft, retrieving the remnants of the British forces from the shores of collapsing France at Dunkirk.

Pausing to regroup and consolidate the tremendous territorial gains, the Germans launched the Luftwaffe in waves of bombing raids against the British homeland, gamely opposed by the outnumbered but valiant RAF fighters during the summer and autumn of 1940. By the end of 1940 Britain was reeling, stubbornly clinging to survival by their fingertips. Southern Europe was fairly secure, consisting of ostensibly neutral Spain, Axis controlled Italy under Mussolini and the Balkans countries, with pockets of partisan resistance but no major battle sites. In North Africa, at the beginning of 1941 Erwin Rommel took command of the Afrika Korps which soon held sway across the majority of the Mediterranean coast extending all the way from Morocco in the west and into Egypt to the east.

On the eastern front, a tenuous standoff had remained in place since the Hitler-Stalin Non-Aggression Pact of 1939. By the beginning of 1941 the Axis powers of Germany and Italy controlled the bulk of the European mainland and there did not seem to be much the Allies were going to be able to do about it. The United States steadfastly refused to engage in combat against the Axis. Although supportive of Britain and Russia through the Lend-Lease program, the U.S.A. remained essentially isolationist. Early reports of atrocities being committed at German internment camps were unsettling to many in the States and a sense of inevitability began to emerge. Fighting the Nazis began to be seen as a moral imperative.

In 1941 Hitler shifted his attention from Britain in the west to the Russian bear in the east. In June of that year the Germans launched Operation Barbarossa, the invasion aimed at the heart of the Russian nation. This gave Britain a small space to catch its collective breath and begin to organize for a push-back. Meanwhile, as we know, December 1941 brought the Japanese attack on Pearl Harbor which heralded the U.S. entry into World War II at long last.

Sheer inertia meant that it would take some time for America to gear up to a war footing, but as 1941 turned into 1942, it appeared that the German expansion was running out of steam. Mid-1942 marked the high-water mark of Nazi territorial expansion. Britain held solid in the west, and in Egypt was able to gain a much-needed military victory at the first Battle of El Alamein in July 1942. The German invasion in the east stalled out and began to be pushed back as the Battle of Stalingrad turned in favor of the Russians in the waning months of 1942.

U.S. ground forces first substantive entry into the war in Europe took place as a joint British-American flotilla launched simultaneously from ports in the U.S. and the U.K. against French North Africa in Morocco and Algeria. Stepping off in November 1942 Operation Torch, at the western extreme of Northern Africa, roughly coincided with Rommel's defeat by Field Marshall Montgomery at the second battle of El Alamein in the east. The landings met with only spotty resistance but provided a first taste of combat for the unseasoned U.S. forces and a toehold that could be quickly expanded to provide a base for launching an amphibious assault against Fortress Europe on the Southern Front. Within a matter of a few short months the Germans were forced out of North Africa. As the Nazi forces regrouped in Italy, the Allies began a buildup of troops and landing craft that would allow an amphibious invasion of Europe.

Operation Husky kicked off on July 9, 1943 with American and British troops landing on the southern coast of Sicily. Some heated battles ensued and the Allied troops began to get their first real taste of the rigors of armed combat. The Germans made a strategic decision to minimize their losses in Sicily and withdrew to the Italian mainland about six weeks after the initial assault. As the Germans withdrew to the mountainous areas of south central Italy in the narrowest portion of the Italian "boot", the Allies were hot on their heels, making another amphibious landing at Salerno on September 3, 1943 (Operation Avalanche). By September 8 the Italian government had capitulated and the Italian military was out of the fight. The optimism that sprang from reaching the European mainland coupled with the surrender of the Italians and the sense of having the Germans on the run was quickly snuffed out as the Allies were stymied by stiff German resistance at well-prepared hardened defensive positions in the vicinity of Monte Cassino along the so-called Gustav Line. Rousting the battle-seasoned German divisions from this line of defense was going to be a tough nut to crack.

This is the situation young EZ Dog Muldoon found himself heading into on that mid-September day in 1943.

"OWWWWW!" he wailed as the dentist simultaneously snapped Eddie out of his reverie and extracted the offending molar from his jaw. As I said, Eddie's war started with a whimper not with a bang. The bangs were soon to come however.

Nov 25, 1943—EZ Dog Diaries

Thanksgiving. Rainy, cold. Battery moved up to its first position vicinity of Piccilli, approx. 4500 meters behind front lines. 937 [FA Bn] moved up at night. Our baptism under fire was purely Baptist, i.e. Full Immersion.

Sound sleep was an elusive goal for many of the men in the unit once they entered the combat zone. EZ Dog Muldoon however never really had that problem. Whether it was laying on bare ground under open stars, crammed in a pup tent with a sleeping bag, huddled under an earthen embankment or in the fluffy embrace of a feather bed at a rear area hotel he was able to sleep restfully. Growing up on the farm he and his brothers had often camped out under the stars on the open prairie of northeastern Colorado. Whether it was purely a physical trait or whether it arose from a deeper sense of knowing that he was doing the right thing, Eddie always rested well.

Early in the morning of November 25 however, he was roused from sleep by the loud explosions of a rolling German artillery barrage. Ducking under his cot he sought cover behind the shallow barrier of sand bags he had built up along the outside edge of the tent. The ground shook violently as another wave of the barrage washed over the bivouac site. Following each shell burst he could hear the pit-a-pat of dirt and shrapnel raining down on the tent. As the German artillery adjusted their target to a more likely spot the rumbling explosions receded gradually into the distance like the thunder of a sudden summer thunderstorm moving on across the grasslands of home.

Eddie emerged from his tent in time to see his buddy Ace trotting up the road from the HQ building. Ace was yelling something but all Eddie could make out was "…message from Gerry."

"Yeah, they sure sent us a message, eh? Nobody hurt I gather. All in all, a little too early for my tastes," Eddie quipped.

"No, no, I said you got a message from Gerry." Ace repeated. "Your brother, Gerry. His unit has been pulled from the line for a rest and refit and he's going to be in Naples next week."

The first week of December was cold and grey as Ace and EZ Dog climbed aboard the single engine Stinson L5 observation plane. EZ Dog always marveled that the ungainly little plane that was not much more than plywood and fabric could gain enough groundspeed to make it into the air. Ace was particularly skilled as a pilot and could maneuver the little plane over a short grassy airstrip and into the air as well as anybody. As the plane gained altitude EZ Dog looked out to the north and could make out small columns of smoke rising from the battle lines below Monte Cassino. Ace banked the plane to the south and set a course for Naples. They landed just outside of Naples and the pair were met by a staff officer from Division who took them on a 45-minute ride along winding Italian country roads to the small farmhouse that was serving as headquarters for the Division Artillery. After a quick meeting to brief several of the 5th Army bigwigs Ace and EZ Dog borrowed a staff car and headed into Naples.

Reaching the Army rest area at Sorrento, just outside of Naples the pair pulled up to the main camp building. After asking several times for directions EZ Dog was able to find out where Gerry's unit was staying. As they neared the barracks building EZ Dog spied Gerry's tall lean frame among a group of soldiers engaged in an impromptu game of softball.

"Gerry!" he yelled. Gerry's face broke into a crooked grin and he ran over to EZ Dog. The two brothers embraced warmly as Ace looked on. After introductions were made, the trio made their way to the nearby canteen. Over glasses of frothy Italian beer the brothers brought each other up to date.

"Man, I haven't seen you since just before you shipped out back in May," EZ Dog exulted. "Mom always asks about you in her letters. Are you eating enough, all of that sort of thing? You do look thinner than last time. So, how's the war treating you?"

Gerry took a long drink from his beer and hesitated before answering, "It's been rough. We made good progress the first two weeks but we've been hung up since then. Every week seems like a re-run of the same old movie. The German lines are tough enough as it is, but the rain has been just horrendous. Each week we launch an advance and seems like we gain a thousand yards before the trucks bog down in the mud. I don't think I've been dried out below the knees since late September. Knee deep mud everywhere you turn. We spend more time pulling trucks out of the mud than we do shooting at the Krauts. Once we bog down the German artillery starts zeroing in on us. Just last week we were humping some equipment around a mud hole when the shells started falling. I dove into the ditch on the left side of the road and my buddy Santini dove into the ditch on the right side of the road. Once the barrage let up I pulled my face out of the mud and went around to the other side of the truck. Santini was dead as a doornail. Took a big chunk of shrapnel right through the neck. Could have been me just as well as him. Just so god damned random, you know?"

EZ Dog sat quietly for a minute or two. "This new fire plan we're developing over at Division HQ will hopefully help with that. We are stepping up our counter battery operations in a big way. The new battery of Long Toms should help as well. Part of our problem is that the Kraut howitzers are hunkered down on the north side of the mountains and from our firing positions the rounds we fire don't have the right trajectory to touch 'em. The shallow trajectory clears the ridgeline but the shells then carry on right over their heads. We think we've found the right angle though. I'll tell you what, though, I'm going to do everything in my power to bring some counter fire in on 'em enough to at least keep them hunkered down and give you guys some breathing room. Ace and the other two pilots have been doing some fine work spotting for us from up in the air in this little Stinson observation plane. Fortunately our boys control the air so there haven't been any Messerschmitts chasing them down."

After finishing their beers the three men hopped into the car and drove into Naples where they found a small local restaurant that was serving mostly Allied servicemen with a few locals scattered among the crowd. The Italians were exuberant and seemed generally happy that the Germans were gone. The conversation continued as they enjoyed a simple meal of cutlets that purported to be lamb but may very well have been goat. Compared to weeks of Army chow and with the assistance of a couple more glasses of beer the meal went down quite nicely. After dinner the locals mounted a floor show with a dancer doing a traditional Tarantella dance accompanied by an attractive local singer named Giannina Marie. The bandleader made a point of stopping by the men's table and introducing himself and Miss Marie. For a couple short hours the three forgot about the war.

As the evening wore on, Gerry opened up a little more. "Here's a strange little tale," he said. "Have you heard of these Moroccan fellows called 'Ghoums'?" he asked.

"What's that, gooms? What's a goom?" EZ Dog responded.

"That's Ghoum. G-H-O-U-M." Gerry elaborated, "The Ghoums are a group of Moroccan mercenary soldiers, like Ay-hab the Ay-rab. There are probably four or five hundred of them, attached to the French Expeditionary

Corps up near our sector. They dress in these colorful native costumes, big billowy pants, turban type headgear, scimitars at their sides. Most of them carry old Enfield rifles although I've seen a few with actual blunderbusses or muskets of some sort. Big long curved stocks with a barrel that seems to be about 10 feet long." Gerry took another swig of beer before continuing, "Anyway, these guys have a big group of women and goats and mules that follow them around to wherever they are bivouacking, like whatchacallits, camp followers. The women cook the meals and generally help keep the equipment up and running. These guys are some real maniacs. They aren't really very cohesive as a military unit, but they move like ghosts in the night.

"Anyway, one night about a month ago I'm asleep in my tent. A puff of wind seems to move the tent flap a little bit, and I sort of wake up. Next thing I know I feel a hand at the base of my neck, moving down toward my chest. I can't quite reach my pistol, so I just lay there as still as a church mouse. In the faint moonlight I catch a glimpse of a curved blade held in the air above me. The man's hand reaches my dog tags, lifts them up off my chest and then lays them gently down again. I close my eyes, expecting the worst, and another puff of wind blows through, rustling the tent flap again. When I open my eyes he's gone. When I told the platoon sergeant about it the next morning he explained that the Ghoums always check for dog tags before slitting the throat of their victims. Apparently these guys go up behind German lines in the night and inflict a good deal of terror on the Krauts. Creepiest thing that ever happened to me in my entire life. I'm glad they are on our side. I think."

"Oh, and hey speaking of knives, did I ever tell you what your kid brother Seamus did last year?" Gerry added.

"You mean YOUR kid brother don't you?" Eddie retorted.

Gerry ignored him and continued, "You remember that beautiful hunting knife Mom and Dad gave him for graduation? The Randall knife? Well that little turd hid the knife in my duffel bag. Must have been that last night we were all together at the farm back when you graduated. Stuffed it into a rolled up pair of pants. I didn't find it until two months later. I guess he thought I needed it more than he did."

"Yeah, every time I think that boy isn't quite all there he does something thoughtful like that. Mom always told Dad he would accomplish something in his life." Eddie said somberly.

"Well, that knife fits my hand like it was custom made. It never leaves my side." Gerry lifted up his shirt tail and Eddie saw the maple handle of the Randall knife gleaming in the reflected light.

Gerry and EZ Dog shared another brotherly hug when they dropped Gerry off back at the rest camp. "You be sure to write Mom and Dad a letter Gerry. I'm tired of making excuses for you," EZ Dog chided. He knew as Gerry disappeared into the darkness of the night that it might be the last time he ever saw his brother.

Ace and EZ Dog made their way back to the airfield and caught a couple hours of sleep before dawn, which found them in the air again headed back to the front.

Dec 10, 1943—EZ Dog Diaries

Air attack on forward installations. Three planes, at least, shot down. Tanks moved toward San Piedro at noon. Heavily smoked and shelled. Temporarily stopped. Infantry started on Lungo at 1700. Moving forward. 936 & 937 [FA Bn's] shelled again. V**** had both legs blown off about 2200 1730. [Margin note: Correction: Only one leg lost at the knee. Other one mangled but saved.] Clear.

The day after seeing EZ Dog in Naples Gerry's unit was ordered back into the line. Scuttlebutt had it that this was going to be the big push to try to dislodge the Germans from the Gustav Line. Gerry and his squad were part of a larger infantry column that was advancing toward the Rapido River. Establishing a bridgehead on the north side of the river would enable the Allies the leverage they needed to wheel on Monte Cassino and bring overwhelming force to bear on the German positions.

Huddled by the side of a nondescript dirt road in the drizzly early morning hours of December 15 Gerry struggled to keep his cigarette lit. Ever since returning to the front he had been unable to shake a feeling, almost a premonition. His fitful sleep had been interrupted night after night with images of raging water. In these dreams Gerry found himself swept along by a massive current of water while his brothers Eddie and Seamus ran along the bank trying to reach out to him. Their flailing hands were always just out of his grasp and Gerry found himself washed further downstream while his brothers' faces faded into nothingness. Slipping beneath the surface of the water Gerry found himself closing his eyes and relaxing. Every time he awoke sputtering from these dreams, chest heaving as he gulped for air. He had become accustomed to the cold clammy sweats that these dreams brought on.

As the squad waited for the "Go" signal Gerry and the boys heard the beginning rumblings of the artillery batteries beginning their pre-assault barrage. He knew it would be just a matter of minutes before they moved out. Their job today was to act as an advance unit for perimeter defense during the initial stages of crossing the Rapido River. A battalion of engineers was positioned to make the initial crossing via flatboats. Once a few troops were landed on the far bank they would push out a couple hundred yards or so to establish an initial beachhead while the engineers deployed the floating bridge that would allow the tanks and other vehicles of the Brigade to cross the river.

Just as the platoon sergeant called, "All right you guys, move out!" the rain clouds opened up once again and the drizzle turned into a downpour. "Crap! Here we go again." the squad muttered in unison.

The dirt road quickly turned into a mud road. Footing was treacherous and the brown oxford Army-issue shoes provided little added traction for the men. Moving down the slope toward the river Gerry's feet went out from under him and he slid down the hill taking the legs out from under four or five of his mates like a game of ten pins. They finally reached the riverbank and loaded into the three flatboats that were waiting for them. The river was running higher than usual on this morning but the crossing was uneventful. Reaching the north bank Gerry and his buddies reassembled and started moving forward. In the aftermath of the Allied artillery barrage it was eerily quiet in the woods. Taking up their forward positions the men started to dig shallow defensive foxholes in anticipation of probing German counterattacks.

In the grey rainy dim light of morning Gerry could not see or hear what was happening on the south side of the river. It was probably a good thing that he couldn't. The advance of the main body of troops had been halted cold in its tracks, not by German resistance but by Mother Nature. Once again the heavy military vehicles had become mired in the mud of the Italian country roads. Engines roared, diesel smoke billowed and creative curse words flew through the air as men and machines struggled vainly to make forward progress.

The pontoon bridge sat empty waiting for the armored column to extricate itself from the mud. The morning wore on. The clouds began to lift. As the mountain slopes to the northeast began to emerge from the mist everybody knew what was about to happen. Positioned on the south-facing slopes of the mountains German artillery observers began to mark targets. Radio traffic relayed this targeting information to the German artillery batteries and the howitzers began to limber up.

The artillery rounds began to fall. Initially the Germans targeted the south end of the bridge. They soon walked their barrage further up the road toward the stalled tanks. The intensity of the shelling picked up as the batteries found their range.

Oddly enough, from Gerry's position on the north side of the river he was able to watch this barrage like a spectator. None of the rounds were falling on his side of the river. Looking up in the air toward the east Gerry spotted a small single engine airplane flying in and out of the edge of cloud cover. In the plane, Ace was tacking back and forth while his passenger quickly made annotations on a map. This observer's job was to spot the muzzle flash of German artillery pieces and locate their position on the map. He would then relay this sight ranging information to the Fire Control Center where Eddie Muldoon's boys would make the calculations of range and azimuth to the German positions and relay the firing program to the gun batteries.

Although Gerry and the rest of the squad could not see or hear any of this, the flurry of activity back at Division counterbattery section soon brought a wave of counter fire down on the targets that Ace and his spotter had identified. What Gerry could tell was that the incoming German fire was slowing down. Looking back across the river valley Gerry could see the armored column beginning to move once again. To his dismay however he discerned that they were heading south, back toward the rear. Just then the half-whispered, half-yelled word was passed up the line, "Pull back boys, we're pulling back across the river!"

"What a SNAFU!" Gerry yelled. Situation Normal All F(ouled) Up! Yet another Allied advance had been stymied by the odd coalition of Mother Nature, geography and the Wehrmacht.

Gerry's group was among the last to reach the pontoon bridge. They had still not encountered any German forces or taken any direct fire. The artillery activity had all but stopped as they approached the bridge. When they were within about 25 yards of the bridge a single German shell came whistling in. The force of the explosion blew Gerry back several feet momentarily stunning him. When the dust, water spray and debris had settled and he had gathered himself he saw that the final section of the bridge had been obliterated by a direct hit.

The damaged bridge was now separated from the north bank by a gap of about 15 feet. "Let's go for it fellas!" somebody shouted. The men scrambled down the bank and into the water. Hand in hand they formed a human chain that was able to reach the edge of the tattered section of bridge. The first in line scrambled up onto the platform and then reaching back began to pull the other men up onto the bridge. One-by-one the men were pulled out of the water. Gerry was the last in line and the others yelled encouragement as he made his way through the waist deep water. Just as he reached his hand up toward the men on the bridge another stray artillery round hit the water a mere 15 feet from the side of the bridge. The men on the bridge were knocked off their feet. Gerry on the other hand was knocked unconscious by a large piece of shrapnel that struck his helmet a glancing blow. His body fell back into the water. Before his mates had picked themselves up from the blast the strong river currents had carried Gerry so far downstream that they could no longer reach him by hand. They watched helplessly as Gerry bobbed along with the current, face bloodied and eyes closed. Gerry lapsed in and out of consciousness and began to see the faces of his brothers Seamus and Eddie. Eddie reached out for him in vain while Seamus called out, "Gerry!!" He vaguely felt himself slipping beneath the surface of the water.

Seamus Muldoon sat up in bed wide awake. The alarm clock read two minutes before six a.m. The alarm was set to ring at six o'clock. He clicked off the alarm, pulled on his gym shorts and a faded black sweatshirt and headed for the front door of his tiny apartment. Hitting the pavement he headed north toward the lakefront at a brisk jog. The cold December air cut straight to the bone but he ignored it as he got into the rhythm of his run. The old canvas sneakers made an odd smacking noise on the nearly deserted sidewalks of the city's business district and the clouds of vapor as he breathed made him look like a steam locomotive chugging along the horizon. Most of the businesses he passed were dark with the exception of the occasional bakery or deli with early morning food preparation beginning. A garbage truck pulled out of an alley in front of him and he had to swerve diagonally across the street to avoid it.   A boy in the back of a Chicago Tribune panel truck half a block ahead slung a stack of newspapers onto the sidewalk in front of a newsstand. Seamus looked down at the stack and jogged in place.   Chicago Tribune December 10, 1943.   "NAZIS LASH BACK IN ITALY, BUT 5TH ARMY PUSHES ON" he read.   He was able to scan the first couple of lines of the article above the fold.

> *"Driven from the crests of a chain of mountain ridges which formed the outer wall of their defenses before Rome, the Germans with their backs to the upper Garigliano River fought back savagely today against Lt. Gen. Mark W. Clark's 5th army."*

The only news that Seamus got these days regarding his brothers Gerry and Eddie came from letters his mother wrote. She wrote regularly about once a week but the missives were skimpy when it came to details and usually contained information that was at least a month out of date. He knew that Eddie was attached to Division Artillery somewhere near Naples and that Gerry's infantry unit was part of Lt. Gen. Mark W. Clark's 5th Army (as the newspaper put it). The most recent letter from his mother had informed him that Eddie thought Italian food was much spicier than the meat and potatoes they had grown up with. Reading between the lines of his mother's letters he gathered that both Eddie and Gerry were frustrated with the slow progress up the "boot". He often wondered if the news reports that were released for public consumption on the home front were tidied up a bit in order to maintain morale for the war effort.

The pressure was on down at the Special Warfare Animal Group where Seamus was still working on the hamster project. Twice in the last two weeks teams of Army big shots had toured the facility. Seamus and the Smith/Smythe team knew that results were expected in a big way and soon. Common sense told them that since the principal invasion of the European mainland was nowhere near imminent that the pressure for results had something to do with the Italian campaign. They had speculated that the ability to place artillery shells with pinpoint accuracy might have something to do with dislodging the Germans from the slopes of the Italian mountains, but somehow Seamus thought something else might be in the works. For now however the team remained in the dark.

Finishing his five-mile circuit in a little over 30 minutes Seamus started a pot of coffee while grabbing a quick shower. The little pot was percolating at full tilt as he toweled off and pulled on a pair of jeans and a pullover. Today was a big day for Seamus' team. Their first completed prototype shell was fully assembled and ready for testing. The hamsters had been winnowed down to the top five prospects, each of them an athlete in his own way. Today the team was scheduled to run a full speed simulation for the first time.

As he sipped his coffee and munched on a piece of dry wheat toast Seamus mentally reviewed the design for seemingly the five thousandth time. A specially modified 155 mm artillery shell was used. The two inches at the very tip of the shell was made of a special hardened non-refracting glass that acted as a transparent windscreen. Mounted just behind the nosecone on a floating spindle, with a nearly frictionless graphite coating was a modified hamster exercise wheel. The front end of the wheel was open, while the back end had a solid metal plate coated on the inside surface with a padded rubber lining. This gave the wheel the appearance of a snare drum. Suspended from the axle of the wheel were two handsets connected via a system of pulleys to a gyroscopic guidance system that rode just behind the hamster wheel. By exerting pressure on the two handgrips the pilot hamster could manipulate small fins on the back end of the shell to induce subtle changes in shell trajectory and alignment within a deviance of about 1 to 2 degrees of angle. This small range of adjustment would allow the accuracy of the shell to be reduced from a range of plus or minus 50 feet down to a pinpoint range of within 5 feet. The last little piece of technical innovation is something Seamus had insisted on against the objections of the rest of the team. Seamus had no desire to send a hamster on what would amount to a kamikaze suicide mission. He had insisted that the shell include an escape hatch for the last second bail out of the pilot hamster.   He was relying on his hamsters' homing instincts to enable eventual recovery of the pilot following the mission.   The rearward 2/3 of the shell was packed with standard military grade explosive. Seamus had crafted a small tunnel down the center of the explosives that led to the rear plate of the shell.   This was the location of the hamster escape hatch, complete with a small silk parachute.

As the shell was loaded into the gun for firing, the hamster would position himself lying flat on the back plate of the hamster wheel. As the round was fired, the G-forces of the sudden acceleration would force the hamster's supple skeleton completely flat.   The elastic nature of the cartilaginous skeleton would allow it to quickly rebound in time to jump down onto the wheel. As the round sped down the barrel of the gun, the rifling of the barrel would set the shell to spinning at almost 10,000 rpm.   Initially, the hamster wheel would not spin, due to inertia.   Even the special graphite coating was not entirely frictionless though, and the wheel would begin to spin in the same direction as the shell, accelerating quickly.

Now came the most critical part of the whole process. The hamster pilot would begin to run along the hamster wheel in the opposite direction, providing enough rotational energy and speed to keep the wheel relatively steady without net rotation while the shell continued to rotate around outside the wheel.   Once a steady state was achieved the hamster would position his front paws into the handgrips and direct his attention out the nosecone. As the shell arced up at the apex of its trajectory and began to descend toward the target the pilot hamster would acquire a visual lock on the target and using the conditioned responses would tweak the final trajectory of the shell onto the final destination. Seconds before impact the hamster was to jump to the back of the shell, grab the parachute and pop the escape hatch. If all went according to plan, the hamster would float gently to earth a couple of hundred yards from the point of final impact while the shell would impact within the five foot target radius.

Seamus had not quite worked out the details of the hamster recovery team's role, given that the impact zone would be well behind enemy lines but there was still time to figure that part out.

Seamus entered the prototype testing room with an intent look on his face. He checked, double checked and triple checked the rig. He cross-referenced some figures on a clipboard that he carried under his left arm. He popped open the transparent nosecone of the prototype shell that was mounted on the rotational simulator and pulled training hamster #7 from his cage, popping him into the shell and re-attaching the nosepiece. Once the technical team was in position and Seamus gave him a nod round Smith gave a perfunctory countdown. "10… 9… 8… 7… 6…"

"Here goes nothing!" Seamus muttered under his breath.

Gerry awoke in the dark with a splitting headache and a face full of mud. He could feel water lapping at the lower half of his body. He groaned and reached up to check his aching temple. His hand came away bloody. Propping himself up on his elbows he raised his head, ignoring the splitting pain. His eyes gradually came into focus in the pale moonlight. He could hear the faint sound of the river current. In front of him was the gentle slope of the riverbank. He could not hear any voices or machinery and there was no sound of battle. There were no lights to be seen. Pulling himself to his feet he half stumbled and half crawled up the slope and found a small grove of trees. He sat with his back propped against the gnarly trunk of one of the trees and began to take inventory of his situation.

The last thing Gerry could remember was reaching up toward the pontoon bridge and then falling backwards toward the surface of the water. That had been in the early afternoon but he had no way of knowing how long he had been unconscious or how far downstream he might have drifted. Aside from the wound on his right temple he felt an aching in his shoulder. He did not have much sensation at all in his legs or feet but was able to move his legs and wiggle his feet. His pants were soaking wet. His tunic was covered in partially dried mud. Feeling in his breast pocket he found a half pack of cigarettes and he still had his battered lighter in his trouser pocket. Placing a cig between his lips he flicked the lighter and on the third attempt a steady flame flared up. To his dismay he was unable to light the waterlogged cigarette. Tossing it aside with disgust he continued with his assessment.

His supply pack and rifle had been stripped off of him sometime in the scramble back toward the bridge or after he was in the water. His helmet was also missing. This struck him as probably a good thing because the combined weight of the equipment would have certainly dragged him down and drowned him. On his web belt he still had a canteen that was three-quarters filled with water and Seamus' Randall knife secure in its sheath. He had a K-ration tin labelled "Peanut Butter" in one of his pants pockets and a rain poncho secured to his web belt.

Gerry found himself beginning to shiver from the damp and cold of his clothing. He gathered some fallen branches from the copse of trees and cleared a space on the ground for a fire. He figured he must still be on the German side of the river and hoped the fire would be shielded from the eyes of any passing German patrols. As the shivering became more violent he knew he didn't have a choice. He pulled the knife out and made a generous pile of wood shavings on the ground. Using the smallest twigs for kindling he built a teepee of dry wood above the thin shavings. He then build a "log cabin" arrangement of medium sized sticks surrounding the teepee. He tapered this to keep it in close contact with the teepee. Flicking his lighter once again he placed the small flame at the bottom of the wood shavings and watched as the flame took hold and began to rise up the pile of shavings. Steadily and surely the fire rose within the teepee and the kindling caught fire as well. Within a minute he had a nicely burning campfire and he warmed his hands over the glowing flames. Keeping the fire small he fed larger branches in one by one. He huddled close to the fire and soon saw steam begin to rise from his sodden pants.

After he had dried out and the shivering had subsided Gerry began to look around. He could just barely make out the faint light of pre-dawn. Knowing that the sun was coming up in the east he was able to confirm that he was on the north side of the river. Tucking the knife back in his belt he sat back down to rest. He remembered the surprise he had gotten when he opened up his duffel bag during the

Atlantic crossing last summer and found the Randall knife. That little turd Seamus had managed to fake him out. At the time he had been angry, but now as he sat in the cold twilight of dawn on a riverbank in Italy behind German lines he was actually very grateful. The knife was the only weapon he had. It might be the key to his survival and evasion as he tried to figure a way to get back to Allied lines.

Using the small disposable can opener all the G.I.'s kept attached to their dog tags Gerry worked to open the can of peanut butter. Using his finger as a scoop he made a light breakfast of the gooey mess. Ordinarily the nasty tan glop was barely palatable but this morning it tasted like the sweetest stuff on earth. He closed his eyes and imagined he was eating a big slab of Mom's mincemeat pie back on the farm. Eating only half he replaced the lid and stuck the can back in his pocket knowing he would probably want lunch in a few hours.

As daylight broke Gerry moved on up the slope above the trees to where the land flattened out. At the top was a narrow dirt road. He was able to make out a rickety fence line and an olive orchard on the far side of the road. There was a thin wisp of smoke rising from a farmhouse chimney perhaps 300 yards away beyond the olive trees. Suddenly Gerry heard the sound of an approaching vehicle from the west. He scrambled back into the bushes and hid as well as he could. He watched as a German soldier on a motorcycle with sidecar preceded a troop transport truck with canvas sides and German insignia around a bend in the road. A small cloud of dust arose as the two vehicles motored past Gerry's hiding spot. As they passed he caught a glimpse of a squad of soldiers sitting in two facing rows in the back of the truck.

When the coast was clear Gerry returned to his spot in the trees by the riverbank. He started to formulate a plan of action. Somehow he had to get back across the rain swollen river. The waters were too deep and the current was too strong to allow him to cross here. He racked his brain trying to remember the area from his earlier study of the sector maps. He did not know how far to the west he had been carried by the water but figured it had to be less than five miles. He could not recall any of the villages in this area. It was possible if he could find a village near the river he could liberate a rowboat from the local pier and cross the river that way.

Gerry also knew that since the Italian army had surrendered and Mussolini had fled last September (had it really only been three short months?) that the civilian population of Italy was largely sympathetic toward the Allies and had no great love for the German soldiers who now occupied their country. Although there was not a well-organized system of underground resistance in the Italian countryside there was certainly a good chance that a sympathetic Italian civilian might be willing to help him. The dilemma he faced was not knowing how to tell which Italians he could trust and which might still be collaborating with the Germans. He figured that he might just have to roll the dice and take a chance.

For the rest of that day Gerry hunkered down and tried to stay out of sight. As he waited he tried to recall the little bit of Italian he had learned to speak since being in the country. He rehearsed in his mind what he might say. Two or three times during the day he heard vehicles traveling along the dirt road. By late afternoon he was ready to make his move. He crossed the road and made his way through the olive grove toward the farmhouse. As he rounded a small shed and approached the barnyard he saw an older man chopping firewood with a small axe. Gerry stepped out into the farm lane and softly called, "Ciao signore, mi scusi!" The old man was startled by the unexpected voice with the odd accent.

Brandishing the axe the farmer hissed, "No! Andare! You go!"

Gerry held his hands palms facing forward in a nonthreatening gesture. "Uh, per favore signore. Americano, er, Yankee! Er, can you uh help, er aiuto?"

At the word 'Yankee' the farmer's face lightened up as if a switch had been flipped. A big smile broke out on his face and he lowered the axe to his side. "Ah si bella, Yankee! Molto bene! Benvenuto signore Americano."

Through a series of gestures and poorly phrased attempts at speaking each other's language the two men tried to communicate. The old man looked down the lane to make sure there were no other strangers or more importantly no German patrols looking on. He gestured for Gerry to quickly come into the shed. A small donkey and two goats shared a simple stall with a bed of straw. The air was redolent with the smell of animal dung but it was warm in the shed. The old man indicated Gerry should sit down on a bale of straw while he pulled out a three-legged stool from a corner and sat down himself. Gerry was able to indicate that he was thirsty. The old man nodded, "Si, Si," and gestured for Gerry to wait.

After about five minutes the shed door opened and the old man entered carrying a tin cup filled with water. Right behind him was a scowling man of about thirty with a black bushy mustache and a pistol in his belt. The younger man walked with a noticeable limp, favoring his right leg.

Gerry stood up and said, "Buon sera, signore!" reaching out to shake the man's hand. The younger man kept his hands at his side and glared at Gerry who stammered, "Mi scusi, er…friend…er…Americano?"

"Relax, I speak English. I am Vittorio. My father told me he had an American soldier hiding in the shed looking for help. What is it you need?"

Gerry explained that he had been separated from his unit and found himself lost behind enemy lines and that he just needed a way to get back across the river so that he could rejoin the Allies. After several minutes of discussion Vittorio and his father stepped outside the shed. Gerry could hear them speaking in rapid fire Italian. He was unable to make out the gist of their talk but he did gather that the conversation was heated and that there was some disagreement between the two. When they returned, Vittorio said, "We have decided that we will help you. I know a man who has a small boat with a motor that can take you across the river. I will go into the village tonight and make the arrangements. We will take you across at first light tomorrow morning."

"Oh goodness, thank you, thank you so much!" Gerry enthused. "How can I ever repay you?"

"You can repay us by leaving and never coming back to this farm," Vittorio replied sternly. "The German army is brutal to anybody caught helping the Allied troops. Just last month a family in our village was executed in broad daylight at the front door of their house when the Germans learned that they had helped a British soldier. Both parents and two young girls. I cannot allow you to put my parents in such danger. For tonight you sleep here in the shed, first thing in the morning I want you gone from this property."

Vittorio slipped back out the door. Gerry tried to make himself comfortable by pushing a couple bales of straw together into a crude bed. At about nine o'clock the old man brought a bowl of soup and a large hunk of crusty peasant-style bread to the shed and sat watching quietly while Gerry filled his belly. Noticing the maple knife handle of the Randall knife the old man smiled and gestured. Gerry eased the knife from the sheath and handed it butt first to the farmer. The old man admired the craftsmanship of the blade, testing the edge with his thumb. He then smiled and made a motion of slicing across an imaginary throat. "Kill Nazis? Si?" Gerry raised one eyebrow, nodded glumly took the knife back. "That's the general idea," he muttered under his breath.

"Buona notte" the farmer said as he took the empty soup bowl and extinguished the lantern by the door.

Gerry's entire body ached as he dropped into a fitful sleep. As he slept he dreamed of camping out on the prairie with his brothers. In the dream both of his brothers were there but he could not see their faces. They were speaking a strange language that Gerry could not comprehend. Seamus was strutting around like a prairie chicken and Eddie was crowing like a rooster. Before long morning light was filtering through the gaps between the side wall of the shed and his dream faded away while merging with his waking reality. An anemic sounding rooster was half-heartedly crowing whatever it is that roosters say in Italy. He had never considered that an Italian rooster would speak a different language than an American rooster.

Gerry opened his eyes as three German soldiers burst in at the door of the shed brandishing rifles. "Hande hoch, hande hoch," they yelled. They quickly disarmed him. The one who seemed to be in charge looked at the Randall knife admiringly and slipped it into the pocket of his great coat as he said in heavily accented English, "Wilkommen Herr American. You are now a prisoner of the Wehrmacht."

CHAPTER 7- PEONIES IN THE LATRINE

Apr 10, 1944 — A beautiful day. The flowers are coming out by the hundreds. There is a large peony bush beside our outdoor latrine. One of the buds is about ready to open. Enemy fire is still quite heavy. -The EZ Dog Diaries

As 1943 drew to a close the front in south central Italy was largely a standoff. The Gustav Line continued to hold, assisted by geography and weather. The relatively narrow isthmus of the Italian "boot" essentially funneled the Allied troops into a few select corridors of advance and enabled the German defensive positions to straddle these limited avenues. In addition, the formidable mountains of central Italy presented terrain that neutralized the maneuverability the Allied troops needed for offensive operations. An exceptionally rainy fall and early winter had added to the treacherous situation as well.

Meanwhile, on the home front there was mounting political pressure. The much anticipated main invasion of the European mainland in France was still beyond the visible horizon. The civilian leadership of the U.S. and Britain wanted a victory to boost support for the overall war effort. Stalin, via emissaries was putting additional pressure on

Churchill and FDR.   Military leaders in the Italian theater favored a continued effort up the center of the country, believing that bringing focused pressure to bear would eventually crack the Gustav line.   Winston Churchill on the other hand was pushing for an "end around" amphibious landing.   After extensive discussions (some of which were no doubt very heated) a plan began to emerge.   Using whatever scant amphibious and naval resources they could scrounge up the British and Americans decided to launch an attack on the west coast of Italy.   The planners settled on an obscure resort area a mere 35 miles from the center of Rome.   The twin towns of Anzio and Nettuno provided a gently sloping shoreline that would enable an amphibious landing as well as a small deeper water port.   The area was lightly defended by a thin German force.   The strategy was to land a force of three or perhaps four divisions, establish a beachhead and push rapidly inland creating a break in German lines of supply to the Gustav Line and pull valuable German forces away from the stalemated situation on the southern front. The planners envisioned a campaign of one to two weeks to take control of the two main highways, Routes 6 and 7.   In theory, once the Germans felt the threat of being cut off from their supply chain they would withdraw from the Gustav Line back to northern Italy and their second line of defense.

Operation Shingle stepped off on January 22, 1944 with VI Corps, a combined force of British and American troops under the command of Major General John Lucas.   Due to limited availability of landing craft the size of the invasion had been reduced to two divisions, one British and one American.   The Brits were to cover the Anzio sector on the left side of the battlefield and the American 3rd Division of General Lucian Truscott had the right flank or the Nettuno sector. The initial phases of the invasion went better than anticipated. German resistance was indeed light and the landing forces were largely unopposed on the beaches. Advancing a few miles inland very quickly the Allies had established a beachhead at very low initial cost. The first few days of the operation brought encouraging news to Eddie Muldoon back at Division HQ along the Italian front, but by the 27th of January it started to become evident that the advance at Anzio had stalled.

Late January 1944- EZ Dog Diaries

Jan 22, 1944- …Word came of landing of VI Corps at Anzio. Sounds good. Hope it relieves our pressure.

Jan 23, 1944- … VI Corps at Anzio seems to be doing very well. All of 3d Div landed. Rest of 45th going to beach tonight…

Jan 24, 1944- …Bombers flew over all day - presumably to VI Corps. VI is pushing well in - ahead of schedule - meeting little resistance. Germans thought they would land at another point.

Jan 25, 1944- …VI Corps progressing with little opposition. About 10-12 miles inland…

Jan 26, 1944- … No word from VI Corps…

Jun 27, 1944- … Little news from VI Corps. Seem to be doing O.K.

Jan 28, 1944- … Troops are being constantly pulled from this sector and moved up to VI Corps. Very little word from there, but it is apparent that sector is to be the main effort.

.

I will leave it to the war historians to explain the specific details but suffice it to say that the initial success at

Anzio was not exploited. It seems a combination of factors came into alignment very quickly. The countryside inland from Anzio was essentially reclaimed marshland. Very swampy lowlands had been drained by a system of canals to the south and east. To the northeast the coastal lands were essentially impassable. Rail lines and major roads pretty much ran parallel to the long axis of the country, also parallel to the shoreline, from northwest to southeast.

Following the initial landings at Anzio and Nettuno General Lucas made a fateful decision to stop and regroup at the perimeter of the initial beachhead, perhaps seven miles deep on a front of about 20 miles rather than pushing further inland. Within days the Germans had redeployed battle hardened troops to the Anzio beachhead. The Allied troops were quickly bottled up within this shallow emplacement. The Germans once again used the terrain and weather to their advantage. The marshy ground and canals served as natural defensive barriers to Allied tank movement. Mud and canals prevented movement anywhere but along existing roads. The high ground of the Alban Heights outside of Rome gave the Germans a distinct edge in terms of artillery warfare. Before the Allies could bring in decisive reinforcements the Germans had mounted a counterattack and by early February were threatening to push the embattled Allied troops back into the Tyrrhenian Sea. German artillery bombardment had the Allies hunkered down in bunkers and cellars all along the beachhead. Movement of troops and supplies from ships in the temporary harbor and within the beachhead itself was almost constantly harassed by German artillery fire.

Feb 1, 1944- EZ Dog Diaries

Cool and cloudy. Off to rest camp at Sorrento. Left CP at 0800. Got in Naples in time for dinner at the 106th. On to Sorrento at 1530. Beautiful place. Tourist town in peace. Music for dinner - and no thoughts of war.

Feb 4, 1944

Btry has orders to move to Anzio. 77th [FA Brigade] taking over at Lungo. Went to assembly area at Caivano near Casserta - then on in to Naples with General and a night at the Parco. Miserable day - cold and rainy.

It always amazed Eddie how quickly his mind could shift between war zone and regular life. As the action at Anzio continued during the first two weeks after the landings the activity at the main front around Monte Cassino lagged. EZ Dog welcomed a two-day pass for rest and relaxation near Naples, but he was interrupted by unexpected orders to return to HQ. He barely had time to grab a quick dinner at the Parc Hotel. As he ate he listened to the beautiful songstress Giannina Marie that he and Gerry had met back in December as she performed a rendition of "Lili Marlene". Eddie had always considered that tune to be the theme song of the Desert Fox Erwin Rommel but enjoyed Miss Marie's version nonetheless.

Returning late that night to the command post at Lungo EZ Dog learned that the counterbattery group was being pulled from the front and sent to Anzio as the Allies scrambled to maintain their tenuous foothold on the Anzio beachhead. EZ Dog Muldoon had direct orders from the General to establish a Division level counterbattery presence on the Anzio beachhead to help provide the Allied forces with the breathing room they needed to reestablish the momentum.

The debarkation port was a hive of activity. Men, trucks and equipment were scattered seemingly helter-skelter across the docks. Creating order out of chaos was EZ Dog's goal for the day. One of the saving graces of the Anzio invasion was the highly efficient use of the limited landing craft that had been allocated. Rather than loading and unloading equipment by hand onto the landing craft trucks were preloaded with equipment and supplies at the docks and driven directly onto the waiting LST landing ships. The LST's chugged up the Tyrrhenian Sea to Anzio where the trucks drove straight off onto the docks and waiting empty trucks were driven immediately back aboard for the return trip to Naples. This enabled fairly rapid turnaround time for the crucial resupply that the stalled invasion force so badly needed and also limited the length of time the LST's were exposed to enemy fire at the docks in Anzio.

EZ Dog Muldoon accompanied the General aboard LST #403 at 1400 hours on February 5, 1943 along with forward elements of his unit. The straight line distance from the port outside of Naples to the beach at Anzio was roughly ninety miles. Leaving the docks in Nissida at about 1900 hours the convoy headed into a light headwind. It would take about 14 hours to cover the distance. EZ Dog once again showed his talent for being able to sleep pretty much anywhere by curling up on the back seat of one of the jeeps. The gentle rocking of the boat over the waves put him into a deep dreamless sleep.

Waking in the dark hours just before dawn EZ Dog stretched, worked the kinks out of his neck and strolled over to the side of the boat. Pulling a battered cigar out of his shirt pocket he lit up and took a long draw. The tip of the cigar glowed orange in the dark as the smoke swirled skyward in the light breeze. He could just barely make out the outline of the Italian coastline in the faint pre-dawn. As he smoked his cigar he heard a sound coming from the front of the boat. Walking forward EZ Dog spied the shape of a man hunched over the railing of the boat. One of the jeep drivers, a mere kid of 19 years was vomiting into the sea.

"There, there son. Breathe through your mouth. Stand up straight here. Try to keep your eyes on the horizon, it'll balance out the movement of the boat." The young soldier wiped his mouth on his shirt sleeve.

"Thank you, sir! I ain't ever been seasick before. Of course I'm from Kansas so I ain't been at sea all that much. I'm sorry to bother you," the boy tried to put a brave face on it. He continued, "Sir, is it true what I've been hearing, that the Krauts are kicking our butt up here at Anzio and that's why we're being moved?"

EZ Dog hesitated a few seconds before answering. "Well, Private, here's the thing. We got sent over here to do a job that needed doing. You're from Kansas, eh? A farm boy?" The soldier nodded. "Well, so am I. Dryland wheat farmer from Colorado. So just think of it like this. Each of us, each soldier, each squad, each battery, each platoon, well, we're just like all of the gears and cogs and what-not on the inside of a grain harvester. By ourselves separately we can't do a damn thing, but if each of us just pays attention to doing our own job, the whole thing will run like a John Deere. And our job is to go up here to the beachhead and help our boys push those Gerries back. So square your shoulders, face forward and do your job. Got it?"

The boy stood up a little straighter, set his jaw and replied firmly, "Yessir!"

"Good. Now go try to get an hour or two of sleep. We'll be landing a little after daylight." EZ Dog turned back to the rail and took another puff on his cigar. He wished that he was as wise and confident as he had just pretended to be. He ran his hand through his prematurely thinning scalp and thought wryly to himself, "Well, aren't you just the picture of wisdom and leadership?"   Eddie was 24 years old when he landed at Anzio.

Early February, 1944 Chicago, IL, USA

Young Seamus Muldoon sat in the small closet that served as his office at the Special Weapons Army Group building in Chicago thinking about the state of things. The winter of 1943-44 seemed like it would never end. Since the successful prototype test demonstration of the hamster-guided artillery shell back in December work in the Hamster Section had largely come to a standstill. The team still spent time on minor equipment and design tweaks. They continued to train and condition their small cadre of hamsters. But the overall attitude was one of expectation. Every morning Seamus would peek in at Mr. Smythe's office door with one eyebrow raised, "Any word?" Every morning Smythe would give him the same terse response along with a shake of his head, "Nope."

The team had been following in the news the progress, or more properly, lack of progress of the Italian campaign as well as the war in the Pacific. The island hopping campaigns of the Pacific did not really lend themselves to Field Artillery operations and were not likely to be the site of the first wartime deployment of their pet project. The smart money around the office was betting that Monte Cassino on the Gustav Line was going to be their target. Others were guessing that the main Allied invasion in France that was expected at any moment now would be their opportunity to shine. After signaling that the project was "good to go" back in December the team had been waiting for their deployment orders. The Anzio invasion had bogged down quickly and many of the newspapers in the U.S. were deriding the stalled invasion as failed and a waste of precious invasion resources.

Seamus scanned the newspaper each day looking for news of the campaigns in Italy that might help him know how his brothers Eddie and Gerry were faring. Articles in the Tribune such as "Great Peril Seen in Allies' Delay at Anzio Beachhead"- Feb 9, 1944 and "Anzio's Gloomy News Blamed on Allied Leaders"- Feb 17, 1944 did not reassure him. Actual news about Eddie and Gerry however was not to be had from newsreels or newspaper stories.

Mom's weekly letters were much more useful in that regard. In early January she had written Seamus that the Army had notified her and Dad that Gerry had been separated from his unit during operations along the Rapido River in December and that he was reported by the Red Cross as being held by the Germans as a POW. There was no word on whether he was injured or not and his folks had received no direct communication from Gerry although they had sent several letters of their own via the Red Cross. They had no way of knowing if Gerry had received the letters. They also had no way of knowing where he was being held.

It was on this backdrop of anticipation and uncertainty that Seamus waited out the month of February, 1944. He had started having real misgivings about Project Hamster when he noticed a dramatic decrease in overall activity at the S.W.A.G. building. He had made the acquaintance of a young man who worked somewhere in the upper reaches of the big S.W.A.G. warehouse building on a different Top Secret project. The young man was not allowed to discuss his project with outsiders and had adhered rigorously to this code of secrecy. Despite that veil of secrecy Seamus was able to surmise that the project had something to do with birds (probably pigeons). He based this guess on the simple observation of two stray feathers on the man's clothing and a distinct streak of bird droppings on his left sleeve helped Seamus in his deductions. Seamus had not seen the mysterious pigeon man since early-January. The amount of foot traffic in and around the building had also dropped off considerably. Rumors abounded that many of the S.W.A.G. programs (including the pigeon warfare group on the top floor whose existence was supposed to be a great secret) were being shut down. The men of the Hamster Team (or H-Section as they were officially designated) could not help but wonder if they would be next.

In the H-Section the men made note of reports that the new RADAR technology was progressing to field trials of radio guided bombs. Another technologically-driven weapon in development was the new field of rocket-propelled missiles. If the RADAR could be incorporated into missiles the range and accuracy would quickly surpass anything a hamster-guided artillery shell could muster.

As February wore on Seamus began to shift his expectations from the hope of a deployment order to a fear of a deactivation notice.

February 4, 1944- PG-54, Passo Corese Italy

Many British and other Allied military men who had been captured during the campaigns in North Africa during 1941 through 1943 had been moved to Prisoner of War camps on the Italian mainland. Most of these camps were run by the Italians. With the collapse of the Italian military in September 1943 many of the Italian camp guards walked away from their posts. This presented an opportunity for many of those prisoners to make their escape and try to work their way back to Allied lines. The window of opportunity was only open for a brief time though as German forces recaptured many of the escapees and reorganized the camps under German command. Many of the Italian camps were converted to transit camps or temporary holding sites for Allied prisoners. The Germans carried out a net relocation of POW's toward northern Italy and eventually into more permanent facilities within Germany. Most of the transport of POW's was accomplished by railcar.

Following his capture by German soldiers at the Italian farm on the Rapido River in mid-December 1943 Gerry Muldoon was taken to the prisoner of war camp designated PG-54 (prigionieri di guerra No. 54) located near the central Italian town of Passo Corese about 25 miles north of Rome. The prisoner population at that time was still largely British, New Zealanders, Australians and Indian Gurkhas from the

North African campaigns but there was a growing contingent of Americans from the more recent campaigns on Sicily and along the Gustav Line. The landings at Anzio and Nettuno had resulted in the Germans instituting an accelerated timeline for moving POW's back to Germany.

The POW camp at Passo Corese consisted of twelve barracks style wooden buildings in three rows of four, spaced about 20 feet apart. The prisoners' side of the compound had an open area in front of the prisoners' barracks that was about 200 feet by 50 feet. This area served as the assembly for twice daily roll call and announcements from the guards as well as a general exercise area. The barracks were designed to hold about 40 prisoners each but with the large influx of captured soldiers from the Italian campaign they were packed in at about 50 to 60 prisoners per barrack. The German side of the compound had a headquarters building, several soldiers' barracks and a variety of other outbuildings including the kitchen.

Meals were served outdoors in a single file line served up by the ladleful by a work crew of sullen Bulgarian workers who spoke no English. Water was available from three or four large water tanks along the side of the row of barracks. The transient nature of this camp did not lend itself to organized attempts at large scale escape such as tunneling and in fact the ground was so rocky that tunneling would not have been feasible at all. On the other hand, the frequent intake and export of prisoners allowed occasional opportunities for one or two man bolts. By February Gerry had been at the camp almost as long as any other POW.

The barracks buildings were each heated with a single coal burning stove located in the center of the single large room. In the cold Italian winter of 1943-44 the drafts that came in through gaps in the siding sent a chill down the outer reaches of the room. A single thin blanket did little to provide warmth, and many of the soldiers spent part or even all of the night huddled on stools close to the stove. The bunks were stacked three high with only about 12 inches of clearance between the lower and upper bunks. Due to Gerry's seniority in the camp he had graduated to one of the top bunks closer to the center of the room. The hardest part of being a POW for Gerry was the endless waiting for something to happen. Each day blurred into the one before and the one after in a steady stream of sameness.

During his two months at the camp Gerry had received exactly one letter from home in a Red Cross Christmas shipment that arrived in mid-January. His mother's letter had been heavily redacted by U.S. military censors. He learned that the winter wheat crop was progressing nicely back home and that Mom and Dad Muldoon had some help on the farm in the form of two German POW's from the nearby POW camp at Greeley, Colorado. The irony of this particular arrangement struck him as peculiar in his wry way of looking at things. As far as news of his brothers Seamus and Eddie there was none as those sections of his mother's letter were blacked out. All he could tell was that Seamus was still in [redacted] and Eddie had been moved to [redacted]. He guessed that meant Seamus was still in Chicago and that Eddie had been transferred to Anzio since their meeting in Naples back in December.

The fifth of February dawned cold and clear. As the POW's milled around in the exercise yard at PG-54 following morning roll call Gerry kept his ears open. Rumors had been

119

travelling far and wide since the beach landings at Anzio the previous month. The guards' side of the compound had seemed busier than usual the last 10 days or so.

In the seven weeks since Gerry's capture his normally long rangy form had become almost gaunt. He reckoned that he had lost about 30 of his original 185 pounds. The twice daily meals usually consisted of a thin gruel or broth with green leafy vegetables of dubious provenance accompanied by a hunk of dry black bread. On good days the boys could vaguely distinguish a piece of meat or gristle floating in the watery mix.

The rumor mill on this particular morning contained tidbits about the Anzio beachhead. Alternative versions of the scuttlebutt had the Allies rolling up the German lines like harvest-ready wheat or the Germans pushing the Allies back onto the thin line of the actual beach and into the Tyrrhennian Sea. The truth was actually somewhere between those two extremes. The beachhead had become basically an arm wrestling match with small incremental gains and losses of ground usually pivoting around the crossroads cluster of buildings at Carroceto known as "The Factory". The hoped-for breakout of Allied troops was not yet visible on the horizon.

Gerry had taken to loitering as close to the fence line as the guards would allow, near the German side of the compound. From here he could sometimes engage certain guards in conversation. In yet another strange quirk of fate one of the guards at this camp was the same soldier who had captured Gerry at the farmhouse in December and confiscated the Randall knife. At the time of Gerry's capture this man, Hermann, had been a sergeant in the infantry. Now he was a private manning a guard post at a POW transit camp. During one of their conversations Gerry learned that he had been demoted for reporting for duty one morning drunk on cheap Italian wine. It seems that puking on your commanding officer's highly shined dress boots is not a good career move no matter which army you've joined.

On occasion the German would flip Gerry a cigarette from across the roughly six foot gap between the prisoner's fence and the guards' compound. This morning Gerry casually asked Hermann how much longer he expected to remain on guard duty. Hermann let slip that he expected this would be his last week, as they had received orders to prepare to move north. Gerry mimed two fingers to his lips and Hermann reached into his pocket. Lighting the cigarette Hermann flicked it across the gap. Gerry picked it up and inhaled deeply. Exhaling the thin stream of smoke smoothly he asked, "You still have that knife you took off me back at the Rapido?"

Hermann smiled and chuckled, "Yes my friend I still have that knife. And a wonderful knife it is. The fine wood handle fits my hand like it was intended specifically for me. What is that wood? Walnut?"

"Maple. Red Maple," Gerry replied. He lifted a hand in a half-hearted wave and strolled back across the exercise yard to rejoin the main group. He walked casually up to the senior officer in the compound, an Air Force Captain from Ohio.

"Cap'n. I think we may be on the move this week. One of the guards just let slip that they have orders to relocate north. Might explain the increased traffic the last few days."

The Captain replied, "We've been hearing similar snippets of info. I want you to start spreading the word to the boys to be on the alert and to have their traveling shoes laced on tightly. If we're on the move it might present a chance to make a break for it."

Feb 6, 1944- EZ Dog Diaries
Docked about 1030. Moved down to Nettuno, VI Corps HQ. Shells dropping in town all day. Put up for night in a pink house in Nettuno. Quiet night

The harbor at Nettuno and the beach between there and Anzio was covered by a thin pall of smoke. The rear areas of the beachhead including supply and ammo depots, a large field hospital, rest and refit areas and various headquarters groups were jammed into a very narrow strip of land along the shore. This fairly concentrated area of troops and equipment was a prime target for German artillery. Several measures served to limit the effectiveness of German artillery barrages and air attacks. The Allied forces did enjoy a remarkable level of air superiority. Other than occasional harassing raids by small enemy squadrons or single aircraft the Allies ruled the air. Secondly, the Allies kept visibility limited as much as possible by burning smudge pots along the beach. This accounted for the hazy sky that Eddie Muldoon saw as their LST approached the docks. This limited the Germans' visual access to the beachhead and prevented detailed forward observation and direction of artillery strikes. As time went by the Allies also added barrage balloons. The large blimp-like balloons that were tethered to the ground by cables created obstacles to approaching enemy aircraft.

The actual landing was not a dramatic splashing into the surf and a charge up the beach in a hail of enemy fire. The harbor at Nettuno more closely resembled a busy modern airport terminal. In a scene reminiscent of a military-style minuet LST's approached the docks, lowered their ramps and vehicles drove straight off onto the dock and into the swirl of an olive drab dance floor. Under the direction of the Military Police the vehicles twirled and spun either left toward Anzio or right toward Nettuno. As the new arrivals debarked and entered the stream of traffic a line-up of empty trucks and other returning vehicles curtsied and rumbled down the dock onto the ships. All the scene needed to be complete was a five-piece string quartet providing the soundtrack. Typical length of time at the docks for an individual ship was under 90 minutes.

As LST #403 cruised to the docks an occasional waterspout marked the arrival of a German artillery shell. The explosions were few and far between and really came nowhere near hitting an actual target. Rolling off the LST with the General's jeep EZ Dog could feel the acrid taste of the smudge smoke in his nose and the back of his throat. This was to become his constant companion during the duration of his stay on the beachhead. They headed down the beach to Nettuno to hook up with VI Corps HQ. The first order of business for today was to find a suitable spot for Division Artillery HQ. Within a couple of hundred yards from the VI Corps HQ Eddie spotted a vacant two-story house. The stucco walls were painted a light pink color and the house stood out among the otherwise drab buildings. He and his men staked their claim and began organizing the interior. They cleaned out some miscellaneous debris and clutter and set up some field desks in one of the downstairs rooms. The front windows of the house were almost all missing but the view out to the harbor was unimpeded.

They converted another one of the downstairs rooms into a communication center. Eddie made a note to have the Signal Corps provide land lines for phone communications to VI Corps. The battery's little cave was a smaller scale version of VI Corps HQ. The Corps HQ was housed in a rapidly growing network of tunnels that the Corps of Engineers had started carving out of the hillsides outside of Nettuno in the first days of the invasion. The total length of the growing network of underground tunnels at VI Corp was now close to two and a half miles.

Settling in for the night the men each found a corner of a room and unrolled a gunny sack. Despite being keyed up with excitement from the events of the day EZ Dog Muldoon was able to drop into a sound dreamless sleep. As he drifted off to sleep he idly wondered how they had been fortunate enough to score such a prime location for their HQ. The next day he found out the answer.

Feb 7, 1943- EZ Dog Diaries.

General decided to set up HQ in Nettuno so we started cleaning a house for it. Bombing raid across port and VI Corps HQ blew in our house. Luckily only one of the Sgts was there and he was only scratched. Shelling continued during morning so we moved to area about a mile out of town. Feels safer. Sunny weather so far.

Being in an eye-catching pink house that stood out among its drab neighbors turned out not to have been the wisest choice. Apparently an enemy artillery observer's eye had also been attracted by the pretty color. Fortunately nobody was seriously injured when the shell took out half of the downstairs in the little pink house in Nettuno. The remainder of the day was spent scouting out a safer location. Learning quickly from their mistakes EZ Dog and the enlisted men settled on a technique that had been adopted by many of the Allied forces along the beachhead. They found a smaller building tucked up against the shallow hills on the edge of town and excavated a little half cave from the back of the building into the hillside. Reinforcing the gap with scraps of timbers and downed logs and topping the whole thing off with sand bags they were able to create a safer space that was both less visible and less vulnerable to artillery shelling or bombing from the air.

While the men worked on the new HQ location EZ Dog accompanied the General to a high-level briefing at VI Corps. A major focus of the session was the issue of counter-artillery. The General assured the VI Corps brass that they would quickly have an operational counterbattery plan in place for the entire beachhead.

The following day was windy and rainy as the rest of the battery arrived on the docks. The gun crews with their howitzers in tow quickly deployed to assigned spots strategically located along the beachhead. The relatively shallow extent of the Allied position at Anzio allowed the guns to be brought to bear around the entire perimeter. This was the purpose of a centralized Division-level artillery unit that could support the entire Corps as needed. The eventual break out from the beachhead would come to rely on this principle.

During the next 10 days or so EZ Dog and his battery-mates worked constantly on developing the fire control procedures for the battery. Fourteen- to sixteen-hour days were the norm.

First and foremost the Field Artillery has to know what it is shooting at. The primary aim of counter battery is to suppress or eliminate enemy artillery units. In order to determine where the enemy artillery is active the battery HQ relies on information received from forward observers. Members of forward infantry units can relay information based on direct visual identification of enemy artillery muzzle flash (sight ranging) or the sound of enemy cannons (sound ranging). Ordnance personnel can also determine the azimuth and approximate range of enemy artillery by examining the angle of impact in the craters formed by incoming rounds. Combining these various sources of information EZ Dog could identify a range of potential targets on any given day.

Once the enemy unit was located and pinpointed on the map a program of fire could be relayed to the counter battery gun crews from the Fire Control Center. Knowing the position of each of your gun emplacements the Time on Target program can be calculated quickly and a barrage of artillery from multiple points of origin can be focused onto a single target area. Further adjustments to the targeting can be made during the barrage. In addition to forward observers on the ground there were two other types of observation used at Anzio. One of these was the small observer planes flown by EZ Dog's buddy Ace and the other pilots. These planes could take off and land from relatively short stretches of flat surface. At Anzio they usually landed right on the beach.

One of the sergeants in EZ Dog's unit came up with the other means of observation that they utilized. The constant ground haze that was meant to stymie enemy observers also hampered visibility from the beach head into the surrounding hills. This became a constant gripe of the gun crews. One day EZ Dog was sitting in the bunker going over some calculations when the sergeant came in excitedly. "Hey Captain, you've got to check this out."

Pulling EZ Dog by the shirt sleeve he hurried down to the beach a couple hundred yards away. Laying on the beach was a tall pole. EZ Dog thought it looked like a 40-foot telegraph pole. "What is that?" he asked.

"A 40-foot telegraph pole," the sergeant replied. Looking more closely EZ Dog saw that the men had secured four stout ropes near the top of the pole. On the very top someone had mounted what looked like a seat off of a tractor.

"What's that on the top?" EZ Dog queried.

"A seat off of a tractor," the sergeant clarified.

EZ Dog was starting to get exasperated. He didn't have time for such frivolity. "Get to the point, Sergeant!" he barked.

Without another word the sergeant gave a hand signal to the men. Propping the butt end of the pole into a small depression in the rocky ground two men grabbed each of the ropes. The seasick private from Kansas grabbed the tractor seat with a pair of binoculars hanging from his neck. On cue the men strained at their ropes and the pole rose slowly to a vertical position. Anchored at four points by the men holding the ropes the top of the pole was barely visible through the haze. EZ Dog could just make out the private on the top of the pole scrambling into the seat. Perched high above the beach he raised his binoculars to his eyes and began scanning the horizon.

"From that height we can see pretty clearly for several thousand yards," the sergeant explained. Johnson has even spotted enemy muzzle flashes up in the hills. We thought we could use this to help adjust fire."

"Well, I suppose that's all well and good but what if the enemy sees him sitting up there in the crow's nest?" EZ Dog asked.

"Oh, we thought of that," the sergeant replied. Looking up he yelled "Incoming!" In unison the men holding the ropes let go and scrambled for cover. Almost as if in slow motion the Kansas farm boy began to brace himself. The pole headed toward the ground as if felled by a team of lumberjacks. Just before impact the boy pushed off the seat, hit the ground with both feet and executed a nearly perfect shoulder roll. As EZ Dog rushed over the young soldier leaped to his feet, brushed some sand from his blouse and grinned, "I'm okay Captain! We've got the landing pretty much perfected. The hardest part is hanging onto that seat when we first raise the pole. We're getting pretty good at it though!"

"Carry on, sergeant." EZ Dog shook his head and chuckled to himself as he walked back to the HQ bunker.

Feb 15, 1944—EZ Dog Diaries

   Clear and warm. Shells started kicking up the dirt around the Brig CP. Makes me glad for a cave to sleep in, even though we do have air raids every night. Surprising how casual one becomes over such things. Still little change in the situation.

The second half of February 1944 began with the much anticipated German counterattack down the center of the Allied front. It seemed that the small cluster of buildings known as "The Factory" at the small crossroads village of Carroceto was to be the focus of a wrestling match between the two sides. Having withstood the initial Allied attack the

Germans hoped to now push the invading force back and force a withdrawal. The German High Command saw both strategic and psychologic value to being able to expel the invaders from their flank. On the American side the role of this second front in ending the stalemate in Italy was vital. In the days leading up to the German pushback the Allies sought to secure their position. EZ Dog Muldoon and his unit prepared a series of contingency plans for counterbattery artillery support of the front. As reports of German activity filtered back to HQ the Allies had to try to anticipate German intent and be prepared at a moment's notice to provide supporting fire.

Feb 16, 1944—EZ Dog Diaries

The "hot" beachhead suddenly became "hotter". Gerry hit with all the artillery he had at 0600 this morning. Our work here in CB ran wild. All the CPs and batteries seemed to be shelled at once.

Brig CP and rear area quite heavily shelled. Chaplain W******, M******, P****** and M****** were all killed by a single round. Irony of fate. Three out of the first four killed in the battery were listed as non-combatants.

Gerry probed our line with inf and tanks all day long. We fell back slightly in a few places but generally held. Knocked out about 25 tanks. Look for a big push tomorrow A.M.

The "grapevine" worked at lightning speed within the Anzio beachhead. The problem was not so much getting information as it was knowing which information to believe and which to disregard. The dramatic increase in German air raids and incoming artillery in the rear areas told EZ Dog that the enemy was on the move. A quick review of the situation maps along with tracking the incoming requests for supportive artillery let him quickly form a mental picture of the battlefield. In some ways the Field Artillery may have been able to understand the rapidly changing situation better than anyone else on the battlefield, being a clearinghouse of sorts for this information. At the same time whispers often grew into rumors and the mere fact of not knowing the minute-by-minute situation at the front led to a certain unease among the cannoneers. Was it true that the center of the line had broken? Was it true that German tanks were about to roll into Nettuno? EZ Dog found himself repeating the advice that he had given the young soldier on the LST when they were inbound to the beachhead. "Do your own job and let the rest fall as it may. We are part of a bigger whole and you have to trust in that."

The news of the deaths at the Brigade Command Post hit EZ Dog hard in the gut. He had known the Chaplain since the early days in North Africa and had grown to rather like him. Sunday services were usually well-attended in the battery and EZ Dog appreciated the Chaplain's plainspoken straightforward homilies. The style had rather reminded him of the pastor in the little one-room church he and his family had attended back home in Colorado. The family's Christian faith was not of the fire and brimstone variety. Rather it was along the lines of salt of the earth. "Work hard, be productive, pray and be thankful for your blessings" was the tone that had permeated his upbringing. Part of the irony EZ Dog felt when he learned of the Chaplain's death was the irony that they were all now facing real life fire and brimstone. The sheer randomness of it all once again struck him.

At the bottom of it all though was the fact that EZ Dog and the others simply did not have much time to stop and mourn their fallen comrades. The urgency of the continued calls for counterbattery support pulled them right back to the table. The next three days would turn out to be critical.

Feb 18, 1944—EZ Dog Diaries

Attack continues. German infantry have pushed ours back about three thousand yards on the main salient below Carroceto. He seemed to be rushing in reserves (est at 14 Bns) at that point. Our artillery laid down a terrific barrage. All attacks repelled. Plans for CA tomorrow made up.

Feb 19, 1944—EZ Dog Diaries

Our Counter Attack and a new German attack started almost simultaneously at different points. The Germans down the center of their salient and our tanks on their left flank. Situation clearing somewhat. Germans forced to withdraw with heavy casualties. Much artillery fire and bombing on both sides.

Feb 20, 1944—EZ Dog Diaries

Situation considerably better. Our line held at all points. Germans withdrawing at lower point of salient. Gerry had terrific casualties. About 500 PW's taken in attack, some of whom reported whole Co's wiped out. Both sides very tired. Big artillery duel started about 1900 with heavy counter-battery and barrages laid down by both sides. Gerry seems to have taken a lesson from us.

By the beginning of the fourth week of February it was becoming apparent that the German counterattack was going to be unsuccessful and the fragile toehold on the side of the Italian "boot" was going to hold. Substantial numbers of German prisoners of war had been brought into the rear areas and the word was that the German timeframe called for completely pushing the Allies off the beach by February 28. By the 21st it was obvious that was not going to happen.

Feb 24, 1944—EZ Dog Diaries

Still tight. PW report has it that Gerry will push us off the beachhead by the 28th. Somehow I think he forgot to include Gen. Truscott in his planning conference.

As the pressure from the German counterattack began to decrease EZ Dog began to get back into a routine of sorts. Duty days were still long and intense but the junior officers in the battery were able to provide a schedule that allowed an occasional day off. In a "field-expedient" sort of way the rear areas had some amenities that although simple were much nicer than the front line troops had. For example a hot bath was occasionally available. On one particular day in late February EZ Dog and one of his buddies headed off to the shower facility. The Engineers had installed a system of large holding tanks full of water that were brought to near boiling temperature. Through a gravity feed this water was distributed to a row of shower heads where the troops could grab a hot (albeit short) shower. As the two entered the changing room they heard the air raid alarm sound followed by the crescendo drone of aircraft engines. They heard a couple of explosions in the near distance. Considering prudence to be a vital part of wartime survival the two men quite literally dove to the ground seeking cover along the edge of the room. As the "All Clear" sounded they picked themselves up off the wood planks of the floor. Only then did EZ Dog look up and realize that they had taken cover beneath two giant tanks filled with boiling hot water.

CHAPTER 8- GERRY VS. GERRY

And finally he put the hand down, and then reached up and gently
straightened the points of the captain's shirt collar, and then he sort of
rearranged the tattered edges of his uniform around the wound. And then
he got up and walked away down the road in the moonlight, all alone.
--Ernie Pyle, The Death of Captain Waskow

February 28, 1944- Passo Corese, Italy

The prisoner transit camp PG 56 at Passo Corese was
bustling with activity the last week of February. The rumored
transport to the north was finally taking place. In groups of
twenty to thirty men the POW's were transported by truck to
a railroad siding to the south of town. A group of four small
enclosed boxcars sat waiting on the rails as the trucks pulled
alongside. During the truck ride from the camp two British
soldiers made a run for it by jumping from the back of their
truck as it rounded a curve, briefly out of view of the trailing
truck. Unfortunately for them a motorcycle patrol spotted
them in the brush by the side of the road before they could
make it into the nearby woods and the convoy came to a halt
while German soldiers surrounded the two men. They were
handled roughly by the guards who brought them back to the
trucks and one of them got the butt of a rifle to the face for
his trouble. Gerry continued to bide his time.

At the tracks the POWs were hustled aboard the waiting boxcars. About a hundred men were put into each car. They had room to sit on the floor or they could take turns lying down and trying to rest. The men in this car were a mix of Americans, British, Australians several Poles and about ten of the Moroccan Ghoumiers. Gerry managed to position himself near the sliding door as it clanged shut. Scant light filtered in through a small gap along the top edge of the sides of the car. In addition Gerry was able to work a small broken piece of siding loose and push it aside enough to create a small peephole.

The boxcar sat in the semidarkness for about three hours. Finally they heard the sound of an old steam locomotive pulling alongside. The boxcars jostled noisily as the locomotive bumped up against them and latched on to the boxcars. The train lurched forward and started toward the west. Gerry watched the rolling countryside passing by from his vantage point. He could not make out any towns or recognizable landmarks. As the afternoon wore on the train chugged on toward the northeast side of Rome. Twice they pulled off onto a siding while another train passed headed in the other direction. At one of these stops the guards threw open the door and gave the prisoners a couple 10 gallon containers of water and several buckets to serve as toilets. The prisoners fashioned one corner of the boxcar into a semblance of a latrine area for some small measure of privacy.

The train halted for the night just after dark. Gerry was unable to see much but they could hear a lot of train activity. One of the prisoners who had spent time around Rome before the war speculated that they were at the rail yard in Ciampino near Rome. Through the night the men huddled together for warmth. Most slept only in increments of 15 to

20 minutes at a time. Gerry was not blessed with Eddie's ability to sleep anywhere and anytime and actually stayed awake throughout the night.

Just before sun up Gerry was leaning against the wall with his eye to the peephole watching the darkness. In the distance he could hear sounds of the rail yard coming to life. Muffled voices were made incomprehensible by the growling of some type of electric motors. Gerry could hear the sound of an electric locomotive moving something. The motors fell silent and Gerry heard a Teutonic voice barking something sharply in the night. Suddenly the entire boxcar shook to the sound of a thunderous explosion. Just before the shockwave knocked him to the floor Gerry caught sight of a huge muzzle flash. This was much bigger than any of the artillery field pieces he had seen during the campaign near Cassino. He scrambled back to his feet and once again put his eye to the peephole. In the vague predawn he was barely able to make out the cannon smoke billowing around the barrel of the biggest gun he had ever seen. He estimated the barrel to be at least 70 feet long.

Over the next few minutes Gerry listened to the renewed whirring of the electric motors and watched as the gun's barrel was lowered down to almost horizontal from its elevated firing position. He heard the screeching of a locomotives wheels scrabbling for purchase on the rails and was just able to see that the huge gun was mounted on a flatbed railcar. The locomotive pulled the flatcar along what looked like a long curving section of track and Gerry could see the entire apparatus disappear into the mouth of a tunnel in the side of the hill next to the railroad yard. He watched as several men lowered a camouflage curtain of some sort over the mouth of the tunnel making it virtually invisible. Gerry described to his fellow excited prisoners what he had seen.

Based on the location of the railroad yard and the general direction of fire Gerry surmised that the intended target was most likely the Allies on the beachhead at Anzio. He said a quick silent prayer for the safety of his brother Eddie, imploring him by force of willpower to keep his head down for crying out loud.

As the sun came up Gerry continued to work on the small opening in the side of the boxcar. By picking at the wood around the edges he was able to gradually enlarge the hole to a size that he could reach through with his lean lanky arm. By stretching to the maximum extent he was able to just barely feel the heavy padlock that held the sliding door closed.

By 7:30 the boxcar lurched and began to roll again. Moving from the siding out onto the main track they headed toward the north. By 8:00 they had left the buildings of the area around Rome behind and were moving jerkily through a countryside of rolling hills and farms.

The train began a long sweeping curve up a slight incline. Ahead and to the right Gerry could make out the trestles of a railroad bridge. Approaching the bridge the train slowed to a crawl. In the distance Gerry heard an explosion followed by the sound of an airplane engine. Pressing his eyes to the peephole he scanned the skies. The single airplane sound was joined by several others in a mounting crescendo of engine whine. One of the planes came in low parallel to the train tracks then pulled up and banked steeply to the right.

"Spitfires!" Gerry yelled. "It's the Brits!"

An enthusiastic cheer rose from the men in the boxcar. "Give 'em hell boys!"

The Captain asked Gerry, "Are they trying to take out the bridge? What are they attacking?"

Gerry continued to watch what he could of the action. Off to the right he saw one of the British planes headed straight at the train. It was a great shock to Gerry when the Spitfire's wing-mounted Browning machine guns opened up. He yelled, "Ah hell! They're attacking us!"

The splats of sound as the machine gun bore down on the boxcars threw the men inside into a panic. As a group they surged toward the door and men began yelling frantically. Gerry had not seen any planes other than the Spitfires but the sound of two sharp explosions from the front of the train announced the arrival of some sort of bomber. The train came to a full stop.

Gerry looked down at the inside of the door and saw two large caliber holes at thigh level just inches to his right. He reached out the hole in the side of the boxcar and felt for the padlock. Unbelievably one of the machine gun rounds had demolished the padlock. Gerry quickly lifted the hasp and threw the bolt open. Several of the men threw their shoulders against the door and it slid open. The men piled out of the rail car onto the ground and began to scatter as another pair of bombs exploded off to the left. Singly and in groups of two to three the prisoners ran, hobbled or crawled away from the train.

Gerry chanced a backwards glance and saw the German guards either running toward the bridge or hunkering down under the locomotive for cover. Just as he started to turn back around the second box car took a direct hit from an Allied bomb. The devastation was instantaneous and complete.

"Spread out!" "Scatter!" "Into the woods," men were yelling. "Make them work to catch us. Split up and head south toward friendly lines!"

About two dozen men made it from the train into the tree line. Two of the boxcars were intact and still contained their human cargo. Nothing but platform and wheels remained of the car that had been hit. The car Gerry had been in sat empty except for half a dozen corpses of men who had been killed in the air raid.

The air attack ended as quickly as it had begun. The German guards began to regroup and gathered up a few stragglers from Gerry's car before they could make it into the woods. As he paused to catch his breath Gerry felt a pain in his right leg. He looked down and spied the hole in his trousers with fresh blood beginning to soak into the fabric. It seems one of the thigh-high holes in the boxcar had had his name on it. In the adrenaline of the moment he had not even noticed the wound until now.

He scrambled into a thicket of bushes and pulled a kerchief from his pocket. Using this he was able to fashion a crude tourniquet. He explored the wound with his fingers and found that it was a through and through wound. Entrance and exit wounds were both in the outer meaty portion of his mid-thigh from front to back. It did not feel like the thigh bone was injured.

Gerry quickly surveyed his surroundings. He had reached the tree line a couple of minutes behind the lead group of his fellow escapees. By now they had scattered into the thick woods and none were to be seen. He dared not call out. With his leg injury he could not hope to outrun the searchers. He crawled as deeply into the thicket as he could and tried to camouflage himself with branches. He figured that his best chance was to lay up, stop the bleeding from his leg, avoid the likely German search teams until dark and then double back across the field and head in the opposite direction. Surely the Germans would pursue the escaped men in the direction they had fled.

The warming spring sun shone brightly as the day wore on. Gerry kept very still under cover of the brush. His adrenaline surge began to wear off and the pain from his leg throbbed intensely. The active bleeding had stopped but there was still a slow ooze. He kept pressure on the area as well as he could. Finally, weakened by the loss of blood and exhausted from the lack of sleep the last two days and with the faint warmth of the sunshine on his face Gerry fell asleep.

Two or three times during the remainder of the afternoon Gerry partially awakened to hear the sound of German soldiers calling out. "American soldiers! You cannot hide! You cannot run away! Come out and we will give you food and water!" One of the searchers passed by no more than 20 feet away from Gerry's hiding spot but did not see him.

As evening wore on Gerry moved cautiously to the edge of the woods and looked out at the scene. A group of about twenty recaptured POWs was moving across the field in bedraggled formation under the watch of several German soldiers. He watched as the men were loaded into several transport trucks that had arrived on the scene. It appeared that the prisoners in the two intact box cars had already been moved by truck. A railway repair crew was already on the scene preparing to replace the damaged track.

Gerry began to move as darkness descended. He made his way along the edge of the tree line toward the river. At the water's edge he drank greedily. In his great thirst he disregarded the muddy appearance of the water. He released the kerchief from his leg and rinsed it out. He was able to clean up the wound and in the pale moonlight could make out the edges of the wound. He considered himself fortunate that it was a pretty clean entry and exit.

Gerry broke off a fairly straight branch about two inches thick and fashioned a crude walking stick or crutch. "Time to get moving," he told himself. The leg injury slowed him down and he had to move quietly but by morning he had moved perhaps two miles through the rugged unfamiliar terrain. He stopped to rest near a narrow dirt road and found a place in the woods for concealment in the daytime. Gerry figured that the Germans wouldn't spend more than 24 hours searching and that most of the search would be concentrated on the east side of the tracks where the prisoners had bolted. By doubling back to the west he hoped to avoid the German searchers entirely. Now he settled in and tried to get some rest.

The barrel of a German rifle poked in his ribs wakened Gerry. He had seen enough strange things in this war that he didn't figure anything could ever surprise him again but he wasn't prepared for this remarkable coincidence. Of all the German soldiers who could have found him it turned out to be the same soldier that had captured him along the Rapido River and had guarded him at the PW camp in PG 56 in Passo Corese. "Hermann you big dumb son of a gun! How nice to see you!"

Hermann was not in the mood for any banter. His superiors had come down hard on the guards yesterday for allowing over fifty prisoners to escape. They were under strict orders to recapture every single one of them. "Stille! Silence! Auf! On your feet!" he commanded brusquely.

Gerry struggled to his feet and looked around. For some inexplicable reason Hermann was by himself. The German soldier ordered Gerry to move on down the road while he trailed several steps behind. Gerry made a point of exaggerating his injury. He walked with a decidedly pronounced limp and feigned not being able to put any weight on his right leg at all, using the walking stick for support. He had no desire to spend the rest of this war in a POW camp deep inside Germany. He knew that if he allowed Hermann to return him to the prison train that his best opportunity for freedom would be gone. It had to be now.

He didn't have to pretend very much because his leg really did hurt. As they came to a stretch of road with a steep drop off on one side Gerry turned a slight misstep into a stumble. He fell to his knees in the road. Hermann approached him and nudged him with the barrel of his rifle. As Gerry started to stand he whirled violently to his right pushing off with his uninjured left leg. He swung the walking stick up in a sweeping arc and caught Hermann flush on the jaw. With a grunt and a grimace Hermann dropped his rifle. Gerry lunged forward tackling Hermann around the waist like it was the fourth quarter of the regional football championship game. The two men tumbled to the side of the road and in a flurry of arms and legs they careened down the steep slope. Both men had the wind knocked from them momentarily as they bounced to a halt at the bottom of the slope. Before Hermann could gather himself Gerry was on him again. Arm in arm and hand to hand the two men struggled.

Hermann fought because that was what he had been taught. He fought with the cold efficiency of a single cog in a huge war machine. He fought without passion but with deadly intensity.

Gerry fought for survival. He fought with the image of his home and family in the back of his mind. He fought with a fury born of righteous anger that this foe had dragged him into this war. He fought against this one man because he could not fight back against the shells that rained forth from guns like the giant rail gun in the yards at Ciampino. He fought with a passion born of love and desperation.

Teeth gritted with determination the two men rolled back and forth on the ground. The struggle began to tilt in Gerry's favor. Gaining the upper position he found his hand slipping inside the German's field jacket. His hand closed around the handle of the knife on the German's belt, the Randall knife, his Randall knife! The knife that his mother had gifted to his brother and that his brother had hidden among his luggage when he left home for the war.

Flipping the strap with his thumb Gerry pulled the Randall knife from its sheath. He straddled the German's chest and pinned his arms to the ground with his knees. He pushed the soldier's head back and exposed the neck. Gerry breathed deeply as he brought the blade up against the right side of the German's neck. He felt the tension slip from man's body and saw the fight go out of his eyes. The man stared blankly as if looking right through Gerry with a look of pure resignation on his face. Gerry tossed the knife aside and stood up. As he looked down at Hermann he muttered half out loud, "Screw it! You're not worth it. Go home to your family and try to look at yourself in the mirror every morning for the rest of your life!"

Gerry turned away and wiped a dribble of blood from the corner of his mouth. Before he had taken two steps the German soldier lunged to his feet and threw his arm around Gerry's neck in a chokehold. Flail as he might Gerry could not dislodge the man's grip. His thrashing began to subside as he slipped into unconsciousness. Just before his vision faded completely to black Gerry saw an apparition. A mirage of sorts rose above him, a ghostlike figure dressed in billowing pantaloons, a sleeveless vest and a great turban.

Gerry blacked out. The Ghoum warrior scooped up the Randall knife and stepped up behind the two men on the ground. With a single fluid movement he drew the blade across the German's neck neatly severing the carotid artery and windpipe. The German sputtered his dying breath in a gurgle of frothy blood and went limp. The Ghoum rolled Gerry's unconscious form away. He placed the handle of the knife in Gerry's hand and stepped away from the two bodies on the ground. As if a puff of wind had moved the leaves on the trees he quickly disappeared into the woods the same way he had arrived.

Gerry awoke to find a dead German soldier lying next to him on the forest floor. In his right hand he held his brother's Randall knife with the soldier's blood drying on the blade. He would never know the full truth of what happened in that clearing on the first day of March 1944 but his sleep would forever after be haunted by the image of the Moroccan "Gooms". He also wondered if his parents had known when they bought it and gave it to Seamus that the unforgiving Randall knife was meant not for whittling wood but for darker things.

March saw the Anzio beachhead settle once again into a static sort of stalemate with little net gain on either side. Some unknown wag somewhere along the way dubbed this phase of the campaign "The Sitzkrieg". On the front the troops dug in for what would become almost three months of a return to World War I style trench warfare. At Headquarters however once the main German counterattack had been thwarted the Allied focus began to shift from defense to offense. The hoped-for link-up with 5th Army forces moving up the Italian mainland remained an illusory mirage as the Germans, weather and geography (but mostly the Germans) continued to stymie the Allied advance in the south. Various contingencies were put forward including a push toward the south to link up with the 5th Army, a push inland to cut supply lines to the Germans along the Gustav Line or a push toward the Alban Hills and Rome without joining up with the Fifth Army. Every time a new proposal was floated the counterbattery team was tasked with developing a fire support plan.

On February 22, 1944 General Lucian Truscott took over command of VI Corps. The Allied High Command had expressed disappointment in the failure of Major General Lucas to exploit the initial beachhead. Granted, the original landing force was undermanned (two divisions rather than the three originally allocated) and woefully short of landing craft. Ultimately General Lucas' decision to stand pat and regroup after the initial invasion may have been the only realistic decision to make. Pushing forward without well-established reinforcements and resupply may well have proven disastrous.

At any rate, General Truscott brought a renewed sense of purpose and energy to the beachhead including personal visits to various units. In particular as March wore on into April Truscott was putting more and more pressure on the counterbattery unit to provide relief from the continued German barrages. These attacks were perhaps as much harassing as they were damaging but were inhibiting Allied progress nonetheless.

EZ Dog Muldoon was often amused by the creativity of American GI's. A sort of dark humor permeated the ranks. One particular example was a penchant among the troops to tag enemy weapons with creative nicknames. The cannon crews told EZ Dog of semi-regular nighttime attacks by a single German plane with a distinctive engine sound as if it weren't firing on all cylinders. This distinct sound set this one plane apart from the other German aircraft. This particular pilot had a penchant of flying low over Allied positions at night dropping antipersonnel bombs. The gun crews started calling this particular plane "Benzene Betty". Betty was another example of the harassment received in the rear areas. She didn't really do much damage but she did cause some jitters among the gun crews.

Another distinctive weapon that caused headaches for EZ Dog's crew was "Mechanical Joe". Mechanical Joe was a self-propelled artillery piece that was able to fire very rapidly although fortunately without much damaging effect. Because of the mobility of the self-propelled guns it was difficult for counterbattery units to neutralize Mechanical Joe. Mechanical Joe may actually have been more than one weapon acting in concert.

The most famous pet name for enemy weaponry on the beachhead at Anzio however was "Anzio Annie". This was the awe-inspiring gun that Gerry had witnessed in action from the POW boxcar in the rail yard at Ciampino on that morning at the end of February.

After finding himself alone with the dead German soldier Gerry took stock of his situation. He rifled quickly through the dead man's pockets and liberated two packs of cigarettes, a box of wooden matches, a sheet of paper with passwords for the week of March 1st and 45 Deutschemarks. He removed the man's belt with the Randall knife's sheath and put it around his own waist. He wiped the blood from the blade as well as he could and sheathed the knife. After removing the soldier's canteen of water and a pouch with spare rifle ammunition he limped his way back up the slope to the dirt road. He retrieved the man's rifle from where it had fallen to the ground and checked the magazine. There was one round in the chamber and two rounds in the magazine.

Gerry estimated that he was 30 miles or so north of Rome. He figured that his best bet was to work his way south, skirting the periphery of Rome itself and make his way toward the Allied lines outside of Anzio. As the crow flies the closest Allied troops were probably 60 miles away. As the wounded American escapee limps it would turn out to be a trek of closer to 100 miles.

Gerry slung the rifle over his shoulder and set a course in a south by southeasterly direction. He decided to hole up during the day and move mostly at night. For the moment though he had to put some distance between himself and the German search patrols. He tried to ignore the throbbing from his leg wound.

As boys the Muldoon brothers had spent countless hours out in the countryside near their parents' farm. Trees are a rare sight in the grassy plains of northeastern Colorado so the boys had learned to use the terrain to their best advantage. Although the prairie lands look flat to the untrained eye they had learned to use shallow dry creek beds for cover as they stalked the jackrabbits, prong-horned antelopes and occasional mule deer that they hunted for meat to put on the supper table. They would lie patiently in wait with very shallow breathing hearing only the sound of their own heart beat as they waited. The learned how not to move for 15 to 20 minutes or longer at a time as they slowly made their way within shooting range of the wily and wary antelope. They learned to use small clumps of grass as cover by making themselves look incredibly small and hugging the ground.

During camping trips out to the Indian tepee circles Gerry and his brothers had played a game of their own creation. One of the boys would get a one hour head start and take off into the gently rolling grasslands. Going to ground and traveling as stealthily as possible he would then try to elude the other two as they set out in pursuit. All three boys had become self-trained experts in the art of camouflage, stalking and evasion. None of Gerry's Army training had prepared him for what he must now do. Thankfully though his brothers were right beside him in spirit as he put their grassland skills to good use. Food, water, shelter from the elements and avoidance of enemy troops were his top priorities. It would take every ounce of Gerry's strength, endurance and cunning to survive the coming days.

CHAPTER 9- MEET ANZIO ANNIE

First Close Shave Since Anzio—"Am happy to relate that I am the proud owner once more of the famous Rolls Razor, the first one since Anzio, Italy. Guarded the last one proudly and zealously throughout North Africa, to Salerno and Anzio, where it finally met its Waterloo in combat after I was seriously wounded for my second time on 29 February 1944. No razor since that fateful day had given me the complete satisfaction of a truly gratifying smooth shave."
-John A. Matovsky, 1ˢᵗ Lt., U.S.A.
(Advertisement for Rolls Razors, Life Magazine, 1952)

April 1944, Nettuno, Italy

Although Eddie Muldoon had the ability to sleep under even the most challenging circumstances the sleep was not always dreamless. One dream in particular recurred with some frequency. In this dream Eddie was standing in the middle of a broad expanse of prairie with knee-high wheat stretching as far as the eye could see. To the west he could see his brother Gerry far off in the distance waving both arms over his head. To the south he could see his brother Seamus running in slow motion. Far to the north he could make out the very vague figures of his mother and father in classic

American Gothic pose except that his mother was holding the pitchfork and his father had on a giant broad-brimmed straw hat. To the east was nothing but darkness. In the middle of the eastern darkness he was able to see a pinpoint of light. As the pinpoint of light grew steadily larger he began to hear the sound of a far off locomotive engine. The locomotive sound grew steadily as the light got bigger and bigger. Bigger, louder, churning, burning. The train was heading straight for Eddie. He looked down at his feet and saw that they were made of clay. He was unable to run. He was unable to walk. He was utterly unable to move. He looked to his left and his parents were waving goodbye. He looked over his shoulder to the west and Gerry had his hands covering his eyes. He looked to his right and Seamus was fading into the distance. He looked back to the east and the freight train was bearing down on him with a roar. He closed his eyes tightly in the final instant as the headlight flashed bright white and then the sound abruptly stopped. There was a faint ringing in his ears. When he opened his eyes he was once again standing in the field of wheat all alone. Eddie awoke with a start.

In the waking world Eddie found that it was still 1944 and he was still in a semi-dugout bunker on the beachhead at Anzio. With another 14 hour day facing him he pulled himself out of the cot and started his morning ritual. Pulling out one of the few personal amenities he had brought to Anzio he set up his Sterno camp stove and started heating the percolator for coffee. Splashing cold water on his face he lathered up with an old hand-me-down shaving brush he had gotten from his dad and a mug with a bar of G.I. soap in the bottom. He heard the crunching and felt the drag of the single-edged razor blade as it scraped yesterday's stubble from his face. He applied styptic to a couple of nicks on his chin then toweled off. Brushing off yesterday's accumulated dust from his blouse he finished getting dressed and poured his first cup of coffee. Inhaling deeply of the fresh morning air he stepped out to meet the day.

During periodic lulls in the action EZ Dog on occasion would travel by jeep to one of the forward infantry positions and give briefings to the troops on various aspects of Field Artillery and its role in support of the fighting men. Today was one of those days.

4 Apr 1944—EZ Dog Diaries

School teacher again! This morning I went to a British Inf Brig (13th) to give a lecture on counterbattery. Rather dry I know, but after all I only had a very short notice to make it up. Maj W****** decided at the last moment he would not be able to make it.

Visiting the front line troops always gave EZ Dog a renewed sense of perspective about this war. Despite the frequent shelling of the rear areas the actual damage inflicted by the German guns was really quite manageable. In a game of hit or miss it was much more 'miss' than 'hit'. In his entire four months on the Anzio Beachhead EZ Dog Muldoon did not have anything that could properly be considered a close call. Entering the British infantry bunker near the front lines EZ Dog saw a different story written on the faces of the soldiers. Holding the left flank of the Allied position at Anzio the British troops had been engaged in some frankly hellish action. Entire units had been killed or captured. In some places an undermanned platoon held a company sector. These men had withstood wave after wave of German counterattacks and held on by the barest of margins. Their eyes had a faraway almost dreamlike stare. They blinked at a noticeably slower rate. Their smiles were lopsided and fleeting. The overall sense the EZ Dog got was almost one of wry shame as if they were apologizing to their fallen comrades for having survived. However bad he and the cannoneers back at Anzio thought they might have had it these Tommies had seen much worse.

Giving a canned lecture on counterbattery techniques always seemed like the most boring thing in the world to EZ Dog in these circumstances but he gave it his best effort. On this morning he cut the briefing short after ten minutes and broke out a carton of cigarettes. "That's enough about me, fellas. What's happening in your neck of the woods?" he asked.

The group breathed a collective sigh of relief as they lit up their cigarettes. To a man they all smoked. EZ Dog let them talk on their own time. Gradually the men loosened up and began to regale the American officer with war stories. Withering machine gun fire and onrushing Panzer tanks cut into their lines. Plucky grenadiers and British anti-tank guns pushed back.

One soldier told of a farmer's pig that rooted unperturbed in the muck in the no-man's land between his unit and a platoon of German soldiers with bullets flying mere inches over its head. On a dare one of his mates had crawled along an irrigation ditch, reached out to grab the pig by its hind feet, slit the animal's throat and dragged the carcass back to the safety of the British lines. The platoon ate well that night for sure.

Toward the end of the hour-long session one of the soldiers approached EZ Dog. "Here's what the Krauts have been showering us with," he said, pulling a sheet of paper from his tunic pocket. Taking the paper from the young man Eddie recognized it as a propaganda leaflet. The Germans sought to demoralize Allied troops by any means possible. This particular sample was printed on cheap paper.

151

On one side labeled "The Girl You Left Behind" was a pin-up quality drawing of a beautiful and buxom young woman standing in front of a swarthy, fat, balding, implicitly Jewish businessman at his desk. The woman's dress is hiked up exposing the tops of her silk stockings and her panties as she tries to modestly cover herself. The businessman's hand is high on the woman's inner thigh and he leans in toward her crotch leeringly. On the reverse side of the flyer the text read:

> *"Sam Knows What He Wants. Two years ago comely Joan Hopkins was still a salesgirl behind the ribbon counter in a New York 5 & 10 cent store getting 12 dollars a week. Today she is pulling down 60 bucks as the private secretary to Sam Levy. Business is excellent and Sam is making a pile of dough on war contracts. FOR HIM THE SLAUGHTER CAN'T LAST LONG ENOUGH. Sam has no scruples about getting a bit intimate with Joan. And why should he have any? Tall and handsome Bob Harrison, Joan's fiancé is on the front, thousands of miles away, fighting for guys like Sam Levy. Joan loves Bob but she doesn't know when…or if…he will come back."*

"Here's the really funny bit though, mate," the British soldier continued. "My real name is Robbie Harrison just like the bloke in the flyer! Ain't that a pip?" Eddie didn't know quite how to react but the room erupted in laughter. "But the stupid Krauts don't know what they're talking about. Me girl's name ain't Joan, it's Gertie innit?!" EZ Dog joined in as another gale of laughter filled the bunker.

April 4, 1944—Chicago

As Seamus arrived at the Special Warfare Animal Group on this gloomy Tuesday morning Smythe pulled him aside in the hallway.

"Bad news, Muldoon! They pulled the rug out! We're officially suspended." Smythe whispered.

"Crap, I knew it!" Seamus swore as he slammed the heel of his hand against the wall. The sound echoed up and down the narrow hallway and people all along the hall turned their head toward the disturbance. Smythe led Seamus by the arm down the hall and into his office.

Seamus shook his head vigorously as he paced back and forth at great speed, pivoting on the ball of his feet every three steps, "So, everything we've worked on for the last year and a half is right out the window? What in the blazes is wrong with those eggheads in the War Department? This project will work! I just know it."

"My orders are to disband the Unit. I talked to the Two Smiths yesterday and they are both already on their way back to New York. We just can't keep you on here any longer Seamus. I wish I had better news. I have to tell you that I am really grateful for all your hard work and your inventiveness. To be honest I didn't have much faith in the project when we first started. Watching the way you work with your hamsters and the things you can get them to do has been one of the most amazing things in my entire life. You made a believer of me."

"Thanks Smythe," Seamus replied while making a show of examining the fingernails of his left hand. "Well I suppose I'll head back to Colorado. Mom and Dad could use my help on the place. You know, Smythe, when my brother Gerry and I signed up for the Army after Pearl I was about as happy as a kid could be. When they told me my flat feet disqualified me from serving and I watched my brother climb aboard that bus without me I felt like I had been punched in the gut. Then when you recruited me for this project I was on top of the world again. Now standing here in this room I just feel exactly the same way I did when they booted me from the Army. I guess it just isn't in the cards for me to do anything useful in this war. Looks like I'm destined to be a dryland wheat farmer after all."

As Seamus turned to leave the office Smythe cleared his throat. "Hey, Muldoon. I did hear one additional piece of information from the War Office that I am not authorized to brief you on. This is strictly off the record you understand but heed me when I suggest to you that even though you are heading back out west it would behoove you to keep your hamster in top physical shape. There may come a time…" Smythe's voice trailed off. "I'm not saying anything, I'm just saying."

Seamus raised one eyebrow in typical Muldoon fashion and started to reply. Catching himself just in time he closed his mouth and merely nodded. Within the hour Seamus and his hamster were out the door at S.W.A.G. Neither Seamus nor the hamster cast a backwards glance as he walked away.

5 Apr, 1944—EZ Dog Diaries

The "bee" is on CB, with an increase of ammo Gerry is bouncing more and more into the port. General Truscott came into our office today to see what we are doing. Somehow I don't think he was satisfied with the picture.

Back in Nettuno EZ Dog and his pals in the counterbattery section continued to work on a seemingly unsolvable task. Since mid-February the Allies along the

Italian coastline had received sporadic but persistent visits on more days than not from a particularly unwelcome visitor. The largest artillery piece in the Allied arsenal at Anzio was the 8 inch howitzer followed by the 155 mm Long Tom (6 inch caliber). EZ Dog knew that the Germans were employing some 170 mm long guns which easily outdid the Allies artillery in terms of effective range. Even more intimidating was a much larger gun. The sound of the incoming shells from this larger gun sounded just like a freight train. This resulted in many of the Allied troops referring to the behemoth as the Anzio Express. The sound of the shell passing overhead seemed to last for half a minute although in reality it was probably just a few seconds. The initial impact of the huge shells shook the surrounding earth noticeably even preceding the actual explosion. The amount of high explosive in the large shells was enough to create a crater as deep as a house.

EZ Dog knew what this weapon was from the sound alone. There was only one gun in the entire German arsenal like this. It had to be the Kruppwerks 280-mm railway cannon. It wasn't known how many of these weapons the Germans had in operation but it was probably on the order of one to two dozen throughout Europe. Designated the K5 Railway Gun these long-range cannons were designed to be easily moved over long distances for deployment at the far reaches of a continental battleground. They had been used quite a bit on the Russian front and had been deployed along the French coast targeting shipping in the English Channel. Now since at least the middle of February there was one (or maybe two) somewhere in the Albano Hills north of Anzio. Whether it was one or two the identity of these massive guns came to be known as "Anzio Annie".

As demoralizing as the pornographic propaganda leaflets may have been on Allied troops the psychologic effects of Anzio Annie was potentially even more paralyzing. The big guns were usually hidden during the day and fired at night. The incoming freight train sound and the thunderous explosions would disrupt even EZ Dog Muldoon's usually sound sleep. Many of the Allied troops came to dread the sound of the damn thing.

When General Truscott took command of the invasion force he placed top priority on neutralizing the highly effective German artillery. As time wore on and the inertia holding the Allies in place seemed to become almost paralyzing General Truscott increased the pressure on EZ Dog's unit.

The Germans and the Allies engaged in a deadly game of cat and mouse. Although the Krupp 280 mm Kanon was a formidable weapon it did have some limitations that the Allies hoped to use to their advantage. First of all the sheer size of the weapon hampered its mobility in actual battle. The length of the barrel was 70 feet. The recoil when the gun was fired was so powerful that it would tip over a rail car. This meant that the gun could only be fired in line with the section of tracks it was on. In order to provide for a full range of fire the Germans used one of two techniques. They either built a roundabout turntable for full 360 degree rotation or they chose a curved section of track that would allow the weapon to be positioned in line with the eventual target along an arc of up to 180 degrees.

The projectile fired from this gun was over eleven inches in diameter, three feet long and weighed over 500 lbs. It was massive and it could be thrown up to 40 miles.

In the country surrounding the beachhead there were only a limited number of places with suitable geography and suitable stretches of track for firing such a weapon. The Allies knew that the big guns had to be in one of those few locations but they had been unable to zero in on the exact location. The Germans used a variety of measures to avoid detection. They parked the guns inside tunnels or caves when they were not firing. They wheeled them out for actual firing pretty sparingly. They also constructed several railcars with decoys constructed from telephone poles to give the appearance of a long barrel and intentionally under-camouflaged these decoys to keep the Allied bombers occupied. They utilized simultaneous flash simulators so that Allied observers could not be sure which flash was the actual location of the firing weapon.

EZ Dog estimated that due to the topography of the terrain above Anzio the likely location of the big rail guns was within 20 miles distance from the beach rather than the full 40 mile range of the weapon. This meant that there was a chance that the rail gun could possibly be targeted by a 155 Long Tom positioned at the extreme northern extent of the beachhead. This might provide an opportunity for the counterbattery to do its job if they could attain enough accuracy. The bad news was that the situation would preclude the American unit from using a concentration of fire. It would probably come down to a single American gun.

Apr 8, 1944—EZ Dog Diaries

*Maj W****** was called back from Naples. Pressure is really on CB now. We are making a nice set-up with two sub-sections, one for west and one for east halves of the beachhead. B******, RA, has the west sector. I have the east. Major W****** is a super coordinator.*

To EZ Dog this rearrangement of the organizational structure of the unit was both an honor and a disappointment. It felt somewhat like rearranging the deck chairs on a sinking ship. Ultimately it was a superficial change when he would rather be doing something more substantial to take out Anzio Annie. His opportunity came sooner than he could have anticipated.

On the very same day the unit realignment was announced they caught a tremendous break. The Anzio Express came roaring in from the north as usual. Most of the troops along the trajectory of this incoming shell ducked as they heard the sound of the shell splitting through the air and braced themselves for the massive explosion. But on this day the explosion never came. The massive German shell had failed to explode; a dud. Troops in the vicinity of the impact were grateful that the shell did not explode for the obvious self-preservation reasons. EZ Dog was also grateful that the shell did not explode but for a decidedly different reason. The opportunity to examine one of these artillery marvels could well be worth its weight in gold. A lot can be divined about the nature of a weapon by looking at the projectile that comes from it. Divisional Ordnance crews located the deeply plowed furrow on the beach and began excavation to uncover the unexploded shell. The excavation took three days.

Apr 11, 1944—EZ Dog Diaries

Bomb Disposal brought in an unusual specimen today, a 280mm dud. It has 12 longitudinal rotating strips instead of the usual band. Length: about 3 ½ ft. Wt.: over 500 lbs. Range is unknown but it is bound to be a very long range gun.

In addition to the very useful ballistics information about the nature of this German superweapon EZ Dog was able to gain some additional very useful knowledge from this dud. The pattern of rifling on the shell gave them a sense of likely muzzle velocity and rate of spin and an estimation of likely range. Scrapings from the surface of the shell gave them some information about the metal configuration of the barrel itself.

More importantly in conjunction with the Ordnance crew he was able to plot the angle of impact and the direction of travel of the shell based on the marks of its impact on the beach. Shooting a back azimuth along this line of travel EZ Dog plotted a line on his map. Of the two dozen or so possible gun locations that had been identified by the Allies in the region surrounding the beachhead the azimuth that EZ Dog plotted on his map passed through two. One, a railroad tunnel in the Alban Heights was 28 miles north of Anzio. The other possibility was the rail yards at Ciampino a mere 23 miles due north of Anzio. Eddie circled these two spots in red on his map and began to ponder the possibilities.

April 15, 1944 Muldoon family farm, northeastern Colorado

Seamus made it to Denver on the train, hopped a bus to Greeley and then hitched a ride on the back of a flatbed truck with a family of migrant workers. They arrived in the early evening. He tapped on the roof of the truck as they neared the driveway and the driver pulled to a halt. Shaking the man's hand Seamus said, "Thank you sir!" Turning toward the house he slung his bag over his shoulder and walked briskly the last quarter mile. Mom must have seen him from the kitchen because she came out the front door of the house drying her hands on a dishtowel and fussing with her apron.

"Oh Seamus!" she exclaimed, smothering him in a motherly hug. "Oh Seamus! Come in, come in. Your father's out at the milk barn finishing up. Come in. Have you eaten?

You look like you haven't been eating? Can I get you something to eat? We have a little fried chicken left over. I can heat that up and some mashed potatoes with gravy. I can probably find some fresh corn. Come in."

Seamus chuckled to himself, "Good ol' Mom!" Settling down at the kitchen table Seamus was soon digging into a plate heaped high with Mom's good cooking. Mom waited patiently while he satisfied his hunger. As he cleaned the last bits of gravy from his plate with a piece of bread Mom placed a full quarter of an apple pie in front of him. He did not miss a beat as he dug in once again. He finished the pie by licking his finger and using it to pick up the last few crumbs of crust on the plate. Opening his breast pocket flap he offered a few crumbs to Houdini who peeked out just long enough to grab the pie before ducking back down.

By the time Seamus finished supper his father had come in from the barnyard. Night was falling. The three talked late into the night under the light of a single kitchen overhead bulb. Seamus told them about his work in Chicago, leaving out the Top Secret elements. He asked if there had been any word of Eddie and Gerry.

Mom went into the bedroom closet and pulled down the shoebox from the shelf. This box was her link to her sons. Mom updated Seamus on the latest news from Eddie in Anzio by reading his latest letters out loud. Eddie's letters were always pretty dry and he was spare in his use of language but Mom cherished the mere sight of his handwriting on paper and read with a good degree of emotion.

Eventually Seamus excused himself. He settled Houdini back into the hamster cage and headed for the tenant house. He barely got his shoes off and flopped on his bed before falling to sleep. He slept for 16 hours straight.

Over the next several days Seamus silently joined his father at the farm tasks. He and his father did not talk very much. Just being together in the familiar routines of running the farm seemed to be sufficient for both father and son.

Seamus also met the two young German prisoners who had been performing as day laborers on the farm. The POW camp at Greeley was about 20 miles from the Muldoon farm. Opened in June of 1943 it currently housed about 2500 German and Austrian prisoners mostly from the African campaigns. The surrounding farms of the region had sent many of their young men to join the military after Pearl Harbor and in a small way the POWs were used to offset that agricultural labor shortage. Each weekday morning a truck would make the rounds of the local farms. One or two prisoners of war would be dropped off to help local farmers with various tasks. The farmers' families would provide lunch. In the afternoon the truck would come back around to pick up the Germans and return them to the POW barracks in Greeley for the night.

The two young men that had been working at the Muldoon farm were both from southeastern Germany and had both grown up on farms themselves. Peter had been a driver and Reichardt had been a tank mechanic with Rommel's Afrika Korps and had been captured in Tunisia by American troops almost a year ago. Since early January the two men had been coming to the farm regularly. Peter was a capable field hand and Reichardt's mechanical skills had proven very useful a time or two helping to keep Old Man Muldoon's farm machinery functioning.

One afternoon about a week after his return Seamus and his father were mucking out the gutters in the dairy barn. As Seamus hosed down the concrete floor Dad took a seat on a bale of hay and wiped his brow. It seemed to Seamus that his father had aged fifteen years since that day in December 1941 when they had listened to the radio broadcast of the President's address to the nation after Pearl Harbor. He seemed physically diminished. His shoulders were more stooped and he walked with an almost shuffling gait. The weight of running the farm by himself was sitting heavily on the old man. Although he was barely 50 years old the thin wisps of hair along the famous Muldoon high receding hairline were snow white. Liver spots populated his face and arms after years in the high prairie sun.

"It's nice having you home again son," he said awkwardly. "Nice having you back home. Won't be long before Eddie and Gerry get back too I reckon."

As the two men headed back toward the main farmhouse Mom was driving down the driveway toward the house after running errands in town. She slid to a halt throwing a cloud of dust into the air. She jumped out of the truck and came running out to meet them in the middle of the barnyard. Seamus knew from the look on her face that something had happened. "We've got word of Gerry," she said simply. She handed her husband the official-looking envelope with the War Department return address. "This was in today's mail."

Dad pulled the single sheet of paper from the envelope and fished his reading glasses out of the breast pocket of his overalls. Settling the glasses halfway down the bridge of his nose he tilted his head backwards to find the right angle and began to read. Seamus peered over his right shoulder and tried to read along with him. Dad dropped his arms to his side and his shoulders drooped even more than they had just a few minutes before. The paper dropped from his fingers to the ground and Seamus scooped it up. Lifting it up to catch the afternoon sunlight he read out loud without realizing it.

"Dear Mr. and Mrs. Muldoon,

The President of the United States and the Secretary of the War Department regret to inform you that your son Gerald F. Muldoon while imprisoned by military forces of the German Republic on or about March 1, 1944 was involved in an air raid incident. A prisoner of war transport train carrying American and British soldiers came under attack by air forces of Great Britain in the belief that the train was a German military troop transport train. During this air raid at least 47 Allied servicemen lost their lives. As of March 20, 1944 the latest report from the International Red Cross indicates that your son Gerald was in one of the rail cars that came under fire. His current official status is Prisoner of War, Missing, Presumed Killed in Action."

Dad Muldoon took his wife gently in his arms and held her as she began to cry. All of the emotion that she had held inside for the last 2 years came bubbling to the surface. The two stood unmoving as the sun lowered into the west. Her body was wracked with silent sobs. Seamus stood by helplessly.

The following morning Seamus rose early as usual. His parents did not. Seamus waited quietly for half an hour before figuring out that he would be on his own this morning. He fried a couple of eggs and buttered his own toast. A big glass of cold milk finished his breakfast. After tidying up the kitchen he headed out to the barn where the herd stood impatiently waiting to be milked. The sun was up when Seamus emerged from the milking shed. The flatbed truck from the POW Camp pulled in at the driveway. Stenciled on the side of the green canvas covering was "POW Camp 202, Camp Greeley, CO".

Seamus met the truck at the end of the driveway and told the driver the news about Gerry. "I don't think it's a good idea to have you boys here for a while," he explained to Peter and Reichardt. "Nothing personal you understand, it's just that my folks are pretty upset and might say something in the heat of it all. You'd better give it a week or two."

The old truck turned around and headed back up the long driveway. Seamus watched the truck turn out onto the main road. At the same instant a black sedan coming from the south turned into the driveway in a cloud of dust and motored up to the house. Climbing out from behind the wheel in his usual dark leather jacket Mr. Smythe removed his aviator style sunglasses and looked around the farmyard.

"So this is the renowned Muldoon family farm!" he proclaimed. "This explains so much about you, Seamus."

"Cut the crap Smythe, I'm not in the mood for it," he said. He pulled the folded up letter from his pocket and handed it to Smythe. Smythe read quickly and nodded.

"Fair enough, Muldoon," Smythe opined. "I can see how that would be upsetting. But here's the thing. I've read a lot of government-ese during my time with the Special Weapons group and you have to learn to read between the lines. You also have to remember that the Germans are sticklers for record keeping. If the Germans had found your brother's body he would be listed as 'deceased'. If they had recaptured him he would be listed as 'prisoner of war'. This designation here, 'missing, presumed killed in action' is bunk. All this means is that they didn't find him. There's a good chance your boy is on the loose, somewhere out there in Italy

164

behind German lines. If he has half a head on his shoulders he stands a good chance of getting back to friendly forces. If I were you I would stop pulling the long face and concentrate on doing my job."

Seamus gave Smythe a long hard look. "I seem to recall that you terminated my job a few weeks ago. Look around you Smythe. This place is my job now."

Smythe replied, "And I seem to recall that I told you to keep your hamster training active. Well I hope that you have my friend because we're going to get our shot after all. We need to be on a plane to the East Coast by 8 o'clock tonight. We're headed to Europe."

"I'm afraid not. My parents need me here more than ever. That damn war has no use for me and I have no use for it," Seamus replied angrily.

Smythe pulled Seamus by the arm and they walked as they talked. Smythe briefed him on the special request that had come down from the War Department to the commander of the Special Warfare Animal Group. The S.W.A.G chief in his turn had looked at the prototypes that were currently available and had decided to dust off the mothballed Section H. This was to be a one-off operation. Although the hamster project was not well suited for general field deployment this particular request seemed tailor-made for the hamster team.

Smythe outlined the stalemate situation on the ground at Anzio and the peril that the Allies faced from the intense shelling from Anzio Annie. He pleaded the case that a breakout at Anzio would be the decisive factor in breaking the psychologic will of the German military, the beginning of the beginning of the end so to speak.

It took about 15 minutes of intense lobbying on Smythe's part but by the time they had circled the outbuildings twice Seamus was sold. "I'm in," he declared firmly and shook Smythe's hand. "Now I just have to figure out how to break this to Mom and Dad."

The two men clattered in at the front door, wiped their shoes and clomped up the stairs to the main level of the house. Mom and Dad Muldoon were sitting at the kitchen table over a cup of coffee. When they looked up Seamus noticed that his mother's eyes were reddened. They both pushed their chairs back and rose to their feet as Seamus introduced Mr. Smythe. Mom busied herself with making a fresh pot of coffee and conjuring up a plate of her world-famous fresh cinnamon rolls. It always amazed Seamus that when he was looking for a snack he could never find one of Mom's rolls but if a houseguest showed up she could always come up with a plate that smelled as if it had just come out of the oven. He had often suspected that she had a secret hidden compartment somewhere in the kitchen. He had gone so far as moving every canister and box of baking soda trying to find the hidden trigger that would pop open the secret stash of cinnamon rolls. To date he had been unsuccessful.

Sitting back down at the kitchen table the four talked through the rest of the morning. After some small talk about the weather Smythe regaled the two older folks with stories about Seamus and his time with Smythe in Chicago.

Eventually the topic of conversation turned to Gerry. Smythe explained his interpretation of the notification letter and his thought that Gerry was likely alive. Mom Muldoon began to nod.

"I prayed on this last night. I asked the Lord 'Why?' Then I opened my heart and listened. I did not receive any answers but this morning something deep inside me tells me that Gerry is still alive. Somehow a mother knows these

166

things. Call it a mother's instinct or a message from God or just a gut feeling, but until I get confirmation I am going to hold on to the belief that he is still alive," she said.

"Mom…Dad? I've got something to tell you," Seamus began hesitantly. "Mr. Smythe has asked me to reopen our project. We have been given a specific mission and I can't give you any details. I might have an opportunity to find out what has happened to Gerry. All I can say is I'm going to Italy."

Seamus almost winced while bracing himself for his mother's wrath. Instead he was surprised to see both Mom and Dad nodding their heads in agreement. "All right son! Go do what you have to do! If you have it in your power to perform some small act that will bring this damned war to an end we want you to do it," Dad said frankly. Mom silently gave her assent.

With the tension easing out of the room Seamus ventured a more lighthearted comment, "Besides, Gerry still has my Randall knife. I really love that knife. I think I'll go get it back from him."

Smythe slapped him on the shoulder. "Good! Go pack. We have a plane waiting for us in Denver. Oh and thanks for the cinnamon rolls Mrs. Muldoon!"

Mom smiled appreciatively, tilted her head modestly to one side and said cryptically, "Seamus still doesn't know how I do it."

Apr 12, 1944—EZ Dog Diaries

Spring is here for sure. The swallows came to town and now hundreds of them are wheeling and winging around. I wonder if they will stay with all this shelling. For the first time we had our own bombers over the enemy arty area. Results are not known.

In some ways the battlefield at Anzio greatly resembled the trench warfare of the First World War. The front line Infantry units dug in and held their ground. There was very little movement along the entire sector. There were skirmishes but no major engagements. Meanwhile in the rear areas the Field Artillery on both sides continued their macabre dance of cat and mouse, battery and counterbattery. One of the biggest difficulties that EZ Dog and the rest of the counterbattery had to overcome was target acquisition and fire direction. Unlike battlefield tanks the Field Artillery cannoneer does not have a direct line of sight from his gun to the target. Identifying mobile targets on a fluid battlefield such as Anzio first of all required spotting and determining the map coordinates of an enemy unit or emplacement. This information was relayed by observers to the Fire Control Center by radio or land line. The FCC decided which cannon resources to use for the particular fire mission while calculating range and azimuth to the target. The FCC also determined how much of a powder charge to apply for that particular battery for that particular projectile for that particular targeting. All of that information was then relayed to the battery.

At the battery the gun crew would load an empty casing with the correct number of pre-measured powder bags, then attach the projectile packed with high explosives and the correct fuse. At the gun mount itself the crew would set the proper direction and barrel elevation for the called shot. The rear breech would be opened, the shell rammed home and seated. The breech was then closed and the gun cocked. The crew would stand clear and the gunner would take hold of the rope lanyard attached to the trigger mechanism. At the command of "Fire!" the cannoneer would sharply pull the lanyard and the weapon would fire.

Meanwhile back at the target the observer would make note of the single explosion relative to the target. Estimating how far short or long and how far left or right of the target the observer would relay this observation back to the FCC. Adjustments in range and azimuth would be recalculated and relayed back to the battery for adjustments on the barrel. Once the battery zeroed in on the target they could open up a full barrage with the order "Fire for effect!"

Of course, when the enemy moved to a different location the whole process had to be repeated.

During April and into early May Anzio Annie continued to visit the beachhead on a regular basis. In contrast, the biggest artillery piece in the Allied arsenal at Anzio was a 240 mm howitzer known as the Black Dragon. Since being deployed to Anzio early in the campaign the 240's had become a key tool in the counterbattery operations for VI Corps.

Apr 14, 1944—EZ Dog Diaries

Arty tried a new wrinkle today. A precision adjustment on three heavy guns. A P-51 adjusted the 8" howitzers with devastating effect. Those guns shouldn't fire for a while.

Apr 15, 1944—EZ Dog Diaries

Precision shoots have now graduated to the 240's. Gerry's arty must be getting a bit on the touchy side. It's bad enough to have those things drop in helter-skelter but it must be literal hell to know that someone can see you and is adjusting right on the point where you are.

Smoke pots on the beachhead keep all the rear areas under a continual haze. Gerry tries to shoot back into it but since he can't see his results are somewhat ineffective.

EZ Dog spent some time during the third week of April touring the entire Nettuno-Anzio rear areas. The young private from Kansas drove the jeep while they surveyed damage along the beachhead. The acrid smoke from the smudge pots irritated the back of EZ Dog's throat. High in the sky over the harbor and along the beach, barrage balloons anchored by long cables hovered over the scene. The jeep reached the large field hospital known as Hell's Half Acre. The hospital facility was too large to burrow underground and had been targeted a number of times by enemy artillery and air strikes. As the two drove along the perimeter of the hospital they saw crews of medics and nurses out filling sandbags and piling them waist high along the outside of the large field tents. The large red cross on a white square background clearly marked this area as hospital but that did not deter the harassing German fire. Rumor among the troops was that many soldiers downplayed or frankly lied about injuries in order to avoid being sent to the hospital. They felt safer on the front lines than at the hospital. The hospital compound was constantly in a state of turmoil and movement. Troops who were deemed suitable to return to the lines were treated and stabilized. Those who had more severe injuries were stabilized and then moved down to the harbor at Nettuno to await loading on one of the LST transport ships for evacuation to Naples for further treatment. Eventually the more severely injured would be shipped back to the States. These men had done their duty under the most difficult of circumstances and for them the day-to-day war was over. The scars of war however would stay with them for the rest of their lives.

All along the beach EZ Dog could see the craters left by the daily enemy barrages. Despite the damage trucks full of supplies and troops continued to move up and down. EZ Dog and his driver passed an ordnance recovery depot. Here a process similar to the triage system used at the hospital was at work. Spent shell casings were piled 10 to 15 feet deep over a half acre. Crews were hard at work salvaging those casings that could be re-used and separating out the ones that were damaged. These shell casing would be shipped back to Naples as well. Eventually the scrap metal, unlike the soldiers, would be recycled and re-used. The sheer mass of spent casings gave a hint of the massive amounts of armaments that had been deployed on the beachhead since January.

The final stop on today's tour was the Division Artillery Flash and Sound Observation unit. The members of this unit were responsible for locating enemy artillery positions by visual spotting of enemy muzzle flashes from the hills above the beachhead and by sound ranging of artillery pieces. A series of microphones were arrayed at intervals to allow a rough triangulation process. When an active enemy battery went into action these ranging systems went to work. The command tent was set up with an array of collapsible field tables staffed by specialists with phone and radio contact to forward units. The plotters were constantly marking azimuths and lines of intersection from various reports in order to pinpoint locations for forwarding to the Fire Control Center. In conjunction with reports from forward observers this information was the central nervous system of the Field Artillery. EZ Dog reviewed the latest reports with the officer in charge. Over a cup of field expedient coffee the two men talked about the possible location of Anzio Annie. The younger man reported that they also had been focusing on the area around the Ciampino rail yards. EZ Dog learned that the Germans had been employing a new decoy tactic. Every time the Anzio Express left the station for another run at the beachhead several decoy units would simultaneously carry out simulated firing with explosive charges meant to mimic the sound and flash of Anzio Annie. This confounding information made it more difficult to pin down the precise location.

Poring over the charts together they determined that the only site common to all barrages was a quarter mile stretch of railroad track adjacent to the Ciampino yards. The two men agreed that this was the home of Anzio Annie. As before though, the distance to Ciampino was outside the effective range of even the largest Allied guns. Air raids had resulted in a decrease in the frequency of activity of the big guns but the air crews had not been able to put Annie out of commission. The Germans chose nighttime and cloudy days for the main activity and continued to pound the beachhead. The almost random timing of attacks added to the general anxiety in the Allied positions. That rumbling roar of the freight train could come at any time and everyone at the rear was ill at ease.

Returning to the HQ bunker EZ Dog pulled out his own maps again. He reviewed the daily situation report to determine the status of the front lines. He considered the weapons available to him.

The 105 mm howitzer was a short range piece used primarily in direct combat support. It had neither the range nor the shell size to engage the enemy's "heavies".

The 155 mm Long Toms were the workhorse at Anzio. The maximum official range of the Long Tom was about 13.7 miles but during his time at Fort Sill EZ Dog had seen a Long Tom Crew fire an accurate round at over 14 miles.

The biggest gun deployed at Anzio by the Allies was the 240 mm Black Dragon. The Black Dragon had a stated range of about 14.7 miles and was almost as accurate as the Long Toms. At first blush this might have seemed the most likely candidate to take on Anzio Annie, meeting size with size. However the 240 mm piece had a distinct disadvantage compared to the Long Tom. It was not nearly as mobile. It had to be dismantled before it could be transported. The disassembly and reassembly times alone made it a poor choice for deployment in a rapidly changing scenario.

EZ Dog put a draftsman's compass on the map, set for a radius of 14.5 miles. He figured that this was the approximate maximum range of a 155 mm Long Tom gun. He centered the compass on the rail yards at Ciampino and drew an arc. At the southern extent of this arc the line came within a half a mile of The Factory at Carroceto. This cluster of buildings had been the focal point of the British sector at Anzio. During the early days after the invasion British and American troops had captured this location and pushed several miles beyond. The big German counterattack in late February had been directed along this line of approach toward the beach and the Germans had pushed the British back in this area. When the counterattack stalled the Allies had been able to reestablish the front line in this vicinity but were still about a mile and a half below Carroceto. The Factory was still under German control as of the third week

173

in April. If the Artillery was going to have a realistic shot at Anzio Annie it was going to have to come from the vicinity of The Factory. As things stood now the Long Toms were not within striking distance and Anzio Annie ruled the beachhead.

In addition to touring the beachhead rear areas in a jeep EZ Dog toured high above the battleground in a "Flying Jeep". The main observation plane in use by Allied artillery units during the Italian campaigns was the Stinson L-5. Modified from a civilian aircraft for a diverse series of roles in combat the L-5 was a two-seater unarmed plane. The pilot's seat was forward and the passenger's seat to the rear. Both seats had a control stick. In the event of the pilot being disabled the rear seat crew member could fly the plane. The L-5 was slow and unarmed. In the air it was certainly vulnerable to enemy aircraft or ground fire. The frame was made of welded hollow steel tubing and the covering was made of fabric. This offered zero in the way of protection on the battlefield. The single engine and wooden propeller could push the plane at a top speed of about just about 100 mph. The rear side windows of the plane had been modified to tilt outward allowing the rear passenger to have better views of the ground below. In addition to observation roles the L-5's ability to land and take off from improvised landing strips enabled it to serve a role in rescuing troops from behind enemy lines or communicating with isolated units.

EZ Dog's friend Ace touched the L-5 down on a makeshift landing strip along the beach just northwest of Nettuno. Spinning the tail-dragger around at the end of the strip he waited for EZ Dog to sprint across the open ground and hop into the rear seat. They bounced along the beach quickly gaining enough speed to lift off. Ace banked smoothly out over the harbor and weaved his way among the barrage balloons as he gained altitude. They reached their cruising altitude of about 8,000 feet and headed northwest parallel to the coastline. Swinging inland Ace guided the plane smoothly over the battlefield below. EZ Dog was able to pick out the occasional flash of an enemy artillery battery firing. He plotted the position on the map spread awkwardly in his lap and radioed the information back to the fire control center. He was able to observe and correct the incoming Allied fire for a couple of minutes until ground haze and low-lying clouds obscured his vision.

Occasionally as they flew along on a straight and level course they could hear a distinct buzzing sound over the engine noise. The first time he heard this noise he didn't realize what it was. Ace later told him that the buzzing sound was the noise of an artillery shell passing by on its arching trajectory towards its eventual target. Ace sometimes was able to actually see the shells as they reached their acme. The shells would come almost to a halt before descending back toward earth. Back in late March an observation plane of the 1st Armored Brigade had been downed inadvertently by a 155 mm artillery shell. Both men on board had been killed.

It always amazed EZ Dog how they could fly along the front lines and remain unmolested. They cruised too high for small arms fire but too low to be seen as much of a threat or draw anti-aircraft fire. The Allied air superiority in Italy kept the German fighter airplanes so busy that they didn't have much spare time for worrying about a little observation plane. At the end of the day the L-5 was pretty small potatoes. EZ Dog usually felt like a mouse walking across the street during a circus parade. He hoped that the elephants wouldn't step on him.

Reaching the southeastern extent of the beachhead Ace signaled EZ Dog to 'take the stick'. This was always Eddie's favorite part of flying with Ace. If conditions were fair Ace would let Eddie steer the plane on the return trip. Banking smoothly back out over the sea Eddie imagined he was back home in Colorado. He had taken some flight training back during college and used to really get a kick cruising high above the eastern Colorado prairies. There was nothing quite like enjoying planes and plains at the same time.

Ace took over the controls as they cruised back down into the harbor area. Once again he weaved his way through the barrage balloons and dropped down onto the landing strip with a thud. EZ Dog clapped him on the shoulder and hopped out of the plane. "Thanks, Ace," he hollered over the engine noise.

Ace hollered back, "Hey, by the way, I'm supposed to pick up a special package in Naples sometime in the next few days. Something to do with Brigade Artillery. Do you know anything about that?"

EZ Dog shrugged and yelled, "Nope! You'll just have to surprise me. Look me up when you get back!" He gave a thumbs-up sign and trotted up the slope while Ace taxied back out.

Apr 18, 1944—EZ Dog Diaries

Cloudy and rainy. Another quiet day except for some 'heavies' in town. That's always distracting. The C[hief] of S[taff] gets on the phone immediately and wonders, why? A new plan is under way. Quite extensive and somewhat involved. I only hope it works. There is some indication of Gerry pulling out.

A new plan was under way indeed. Seamus and Smythe made the drive from Fort Collins to the airport in Denver in record time. Waiting for them on the tarmac was a military version of the DC-3 passenger plane with propellers already turning. Before the two men had secured the hatch and settled into their seats the plane was rolling out to the runway where it received priority clearance for take-off. Once in the air headed east Seamus took note of the wooden crate secured at the rear of the passenger cabin. Smythe informed him that they had the only two working prototypes of the guided shell packed carefully in padded packaging material in that crate. The two men huddled together under a single small lamp reviewing the final prototype sketches from the H-Section project.

The plane touched down briefly in Chicago to refuel and to take on one additional passenger. During the next leg of the flight this Army officer briefed the two men on the situation in Anzio and the specific mission they had been assigned. Neither of them had heard the term "Anzio Annie" before. As the officer filled them in on the size, range and destructive power of the German big gun Seamus let go a long slow whistle. He knew very well that his brother Eddie was stuck on that beachhead along with thousands of other men.

Along with a few personal belongings in a small suitcase Seamus had brought the small carrying case that he used for transporting his hamsters. Following Smythe's instructions he had brought two hamsters along. Of course he had his number one guy, Houdini. The second hamster in Seamus' portable carrier was somewhat of a surprise. At four years of age Hammie the Second was quite a geezer as hamsters go. He was from the last litter ever produced by Seamus' state champion homing hamster Hammie. He had been the lowest performing hamster during the H-Section physical trials and his speed performance had always been suspect. Hammie the Second actually had been more accurate than Houdini in the steering test runs. Seamus just had a gut feeling about him as his second choice. He had that intangible 'something special'.

The hours crept by. At a small military airfield in upstate New York they changed flight crews and refueled again. Back in the air again the plane followed the North Atlantic route hopping to Newfoundland, Iceland and Scotland. They had a brief chance to stretch their legs at each refueling stop. Burnt coffee and stale cigarettes were available in the hangar area. Seamus began to lose track of time as the plane droned on through the North Atlantic skies.

They laid over at an RAF air base somewhere in Scotland for two days. Besides catching up on their sleep the two men used the time on the ground in Scotland to reinforce the two hamsters training. They rehearsed the entire sequence from loading the hamster into the shell through simulated firing and steering maneuvers to the final trip to the rear escape hatch. Seamus had every confidence in the ability of his hamsters. He worried more about glitches in the mechanical functioning of the prototypes.

The next day they were on the move again. They skirted the mainland of Europe by hopping down to Gibraltar then across the Mediterranean to finally touch down in Naples.

Apr 19, 1944—EZ Dog Diaries

Counterbattery was put on the spot for sure. [Margin note: Met Gen Truscott, CG VI Corps, on this deal.] A notice was given to do something about the firing and all Div Arty Cmdrs were called in on the session. Nothing in the way of a decision made except to enlarge the CB section. We now will have 9 officers and 12 men.

General Truscott was all business this morning. As the various artillery men filled the small conference room deep in the underground tunnels of VI Corps Headquarters there was very little small talk. As the general entered the room EZ Dog barked, "Atten-shun!" The chatter stopped instantly.

"At ease men. Be seated. Let's get started," General Truscott uttered in his typical no nonsense fashion. A quick series of briefings followed. Each presenting officer had 5-10 minutes to make their presentation after which General Truscott would ask one or two pointed questions that were almost always right on point. EZ Dog anxiously awaited his turn on the hot seat. One officer who presented a briefing on close-in artillery support of armor and infantry units lurched from the room bordering on tears after a particularly harsh query from the general. EZ Dog's turn came after about 20 minutes and followed a brief presentation by the Ordnance section describing the 280 mm dud and Anzio Annie's devastating capacity. The general showed a keen interest in the photos of the shell and whispered something to his aide who scribbled furiously in a notebook as he nodded.

EZ Dog stepped briskly to the large wall-mounted photomap of the entire Anzio theater of operations. Wooden pointer in hand he gave a quick rundown of German artillery positions and assets followed by an update on Allied counterbattery assets, locations and areas of responsibility. He then moved to a description of the varied sources of intelligence that pointed toward the rail yards at Ciampino as the likely location of Annie. He ended by quickly outlining his plan to position a Long Tom battery at the most forward extent of Allied lines near The Factory at Carroceto in order to launch a decisive strike against Anzio Annie.

General Truscott stroked his chin thoughtfully as he digested EZ Dog's briefing. "Captain Muldoon, we are not going to sit on this damned beachhead forever. Within the next two to three weeks we will be committing all of our resources into advancing and breaking this impasse with the Nazis. I cannot expect to do that with this pain-in-the-ass German heavy gun breathing down our necks. If our boys can push forward far enough at Carroceto and we get you your position for the 155's can you promise me that you can eliminate the threat of that infernal gun?"

With a barely perceptible gulp Captain Eddie Muldoon replied, "Absolutely yes, sir. If we get our shot we can take out that bastard! One shot is all I ask!"

"Fair enough," the general said. He sized up young Muldoon with a critical eye for several long seconds before adding, "You ask for one shot? One shot is all we are going to have. The entire Corps is going to have our britches around our ankles and our ass sticking out in the breeze on this deal. You'd better not let the Gerries shoot it off or there will be hell to pay. Understood?"

EZ Dog nodded almost imperceptibly.

"What's next?" the general stated brusquely.

EZ Dog slowly let out his breath and hoped that nobody would see him wiping his sweaty palms on his trousers as he stepped to the side and a briefing on ammunition logistics ensued.

With April drawing to a close anticipation continued to build on the beachhead. Troops and equipment continued to move in at the harbor. Rumors of the 5th Army making progress on the Cassino front created a buzz. The long-awaited breakout would surely begin at any time.   Meanwhile EZ Dog waited for the special delivery from Naples.

CHAPTER 10- A MESSAGE FROM GARCIA

[These] are things I have no special desire now to tell in detail. The point I wish to make is this: McKinley gave Rowan a letter to be delivered to Garcia; Rowan took the letter and did not ask, "Where is he at?"
--Elbert Hubbard, A Message to Garcia 1899

It was mid-April in the Italian countryside. "Muldoons were never very good at growing beards," Gerry mused to himself as he stroked the skimpy six weeks' worth of facial hair covering his lower face. He nibbled on the last few scraps of a plump Italian rabbit that he had roasted over a small open fire. His current position was high on a rocky hillside a few miles east and south of the outskirts of Rome. He was at least a half a mile from the nearest road and had chosen this site because it was not on the usual routes frequented by German Army troops.

Since his escape from the Nazi prisoner train in the aftermath of the friendly fire incident at the end of February he had been living the life of a recluse hobo fugitive. He had moved mostly at nighttime and hidden during the day. His original plan had been to move roughly due south in order to intersect the Allied lines outside of Anzio. That plan was hampered by the more heavily populated eastern outskirts of Rome which forced him to circle well out and around to the east. In addition the German army was constantly ferrying men and equipment back and forth between the Gustav Line and the Anzio beachhead although Gerry did not know this at the time. What he did know was that there was an amazing stream of nearly constant road and rail traffic through the region that he was trying to traverse. His leg was slowly healing but still decreased his mobility. What with taking time to find food and avoiding Italian farmhouses and their ever present barking dogs in the night he was lucky if he averaged a mile a day. He had been hiding out at his current location for the past five days. The fresh spring water that flowed nearby and the availability of edible green leafy weeds and small game animals made this a good oasis for a respite.

Every day as the sun came up and Gerry burrowed into hiding for the day he stopped and took inventory from the ground up. His army shoes and gaiters had held up nicely and kept his feet well protected. The single pair of socks was wearing thin but he kept them clean by washing in spring water and drying in the sun every several days. The pants he wore had been liberated from an Italian farmwife's clothes line late one moonless night and although they were about 4 inches too short for Gerry's long legs the woolen fabric was warm and durable. These pants had replaced the pair that got torn during his escape. On his right flank he wore the Randall knife secure in its sheath. On his left flank he carried the German canteen. His army tunic still served well as a shirt. He had a bedroll consisting of a thick wool blanket that had been generously albeit unknowingly donated by a roving tinker in a donkey cart whose camp Gerry had run across three weeks ago. While the tinker bathed in a nearby stream Gerry had snuck into his camp and helped himself to the blanket. In his pockets he had his cigarette lighter and a length of twine that he had picked up along the way. He still had his handkerchief. He had smoked his last cigarette over a month ago. On his left wrist was his father's old wrist watch with the mother of pearl inlay around the outside of the dial face.

He no longer needed the improvised crutch but he did carry a walking stick along with the German rifle and the unfired ammunition. He had not been willing to use the rifle for hunting in order to avoid being discovered. Instead he had fashioned snares and woodland traps in the low brush to capture small game (mostly rabbits) for food. He had augmented the game and wild vegetables with fruit from farmers' orchards. One particularly lucky day he had actually scored a fresh baked apple pie that was cooling on the kitchen windowsill of an Italian farmhouse. He had cut that pie into four quarters using the Randall knife because he didn't know a pie could be cut into more than four pieces. He ate one piece per day for each of the next four days. He ate one for himself, one for each of his two brothers and one for his father. On the last day he set aside a small sliver of his dad's quarter for day number five. This small sliver was for his mother because that was all she ever wanted.

Gerry knew that if he didn't get back on the move soon that one of two things would happen before he reached the Allied lines. Either the war would come to an end or he would utterly lose his sanity from the solitude and lack of human contact. He already spent way too much time having two-sided conversations with himself. He knew that if he reached the point of having three-sided conversations with himself that he would be around the bend with no coming back.

In order to keep himself alive he had resorted to the mental discipline that he had acquired as a youth in the

184

rugged prairie lands of Colorado and honed during basic training. In addition to his daily inventory of assets he performed regular assessments of his physical condition. He tried to wipe his teeth with the cleanest part of his handkerchief every day, even if he had not had much to eat that day. He inspected his feet every day for blisters or open sores. He kept a mental note of survival priorities. Water, nutrition and shelter from inclement weather as well as direct sun ranked high. Avoidance of enemy patrols was also a major priority. He forced himself to survey his surroundings several times a day for movement, noise and signs of human activity. After his experience being turned over to the Germans by the Italian farmer on the Rapido River back in December he decided not to trust any locals. He avoided any and all contact with the local population. He stayed away from any structures. Even if he thought a barn looked abandoned or a shack was unoccupied he preferred to sleep on the ground with a simple shelter made of branches as deep in the woods as he could get. He also maintained a sense of place and time, carefully keeping track of direction of travel and how far he had come each day. He preferred to stick to the higher ground when possible. The final tool in his survival kit was prayer. He made a conscious point at the beginning and end of each day to recite the Lord's Prayer. He usually included an addendum asking that the Lord look after his parents back on the farm and his two brothers wherever the war had taken them. He always finished with, "And Dear Lord grant me the courage to see me through this ordeal that you have placed upon me. I know you have kept me alive for some reason. I don't ask you to show me the reason unless that is your will, but dwell within me so that I have the strength to be your vessel and fulfill your plan, in Jesus' name, amen."

From his current vantage point on a high knoll in the Alban hills he was able to see the buildings of Rome to the northwest. He kept track of his position on a mental map in his mind. By cross referencing the track of the sun and moon with identifiable landmarks such as the dome and spires of St. Peter's Basilica in the center of Rome or the waters of Lake Albano he was able to calculate his general position and progress across the countryside.

With darkness Gerry once again gathered himself and set off toward the south. He planned to skirt around the western side of Lake Albano and drop down toward the Anzio battlefield from there. He surprised himself by covering almost 2 miles this night by moving steadily throughout the night. At around three o'clock in the morning he began looking for a spot to hole up for the day. Settling on a suitable location he took care to camouflage his position to avoid being spotted from the surrounding countryside or from the air. He always tried to stop near a spring or creek so that he would have fresh water.

In the faint light of the setting half-moon Gerry found a brushy area and set out a couple of snares. He had found that early morning was the best time to catch a rabbit. Retreating to his hiding spot he settled in to await the coming of daylight. Gazing off to the northwest at the darkened center of Rome he listened for any sounds that would indicate nearby houses or sentry posts. As his eyes traversed the dark horizon a sudden flash of light from the low land about three miles to the northwest lit up the sky. Counting to himself, "one one-thousand, two one-thousand…" he waited for the loud rolling rumble of sound. It echoed up the hillsides like the sound of thunder in a rainless Colorado summer thunderstorm. For the next half hour the flash and roar of the big gun continued about every four to five minutes. It was joined by smaller flashes and smaller concussions from multiple sites between Gerry and the outskirts of Rome. Round after round were flung in the direction of Anzio. Finally at about 4:30 a.m. the activity came to a halt. Gerry made note of the approximate location then settled down to try to sleep.

When Gerry awoke it was mid-morning. The first sound he heard was songbirds in the surrounding trees. There must have been two or three hundred of them. The second sound he heard was the engines of a German convoy making its way across the slope below him. A narrow dirt road crossed the ridge line and dipped down toward the southwest. A staff car and three troop trucks rolled along kicking up dust as they went. Gerry's position was about 100 yards uphill from the road at its closest point.

After the convoy had passed he checked his snares...empty. He looked off toward the northwest where he had seen the big gun firing earlier. He could vaguely make out what looked like several trains moving parallel to each other in a very small area. He was not able to see the fearsome weapon.

After taking his morning inventory he moved to a spot within a dozen yards of the road and concealed himself again. He waited. After about an hour he sensed movement off to the right. Peering carefully around the side of a tree trunk he saw a young girl pedaling an old red bicycle up the road. The sound of faint singing wafted up to him. He recognized the tune and much to his shock he also recognized the voice. The tune was 'Lili Marlene' and the voice belonged to the young Italian singer he and Eddie had met during their rendezvous in Naples last December, Miss Giannina Marie. Gerry did a classic double take and then shook his head to clear his thoughts. Surely he was beginning to hallucinate.

187

Just a few nights ago he thought he had heard Seamus calling to him from the top of a tree. He had begun to worry about his sanity.

After clearing his head he thought the hallucination would disappear. Instead the singing seemed to get louder and louder as the girl on the bicycle came closer. At the spot where the small brook crossed under the road the girl coasted to a stop. She stepped down to the water and splashed a little on her face and arms. Gerry could not see her face at first. As she took off her kerchief and brushed the dust from her hair she turned toward Gerry. At the very instant that he recognized that it was indeed Giannina Marie she spied him. Six weeks' worth of facial hair and general grime gave him a frightful appearance and she most certainly did not recognize him from their brief encounter four months earlier.

Her eyes wide with alarm she managed to remain calm. She did not scream. She did not flee. She started to slowly inch her way back up to the road and her bicycle.

Gerry felt a desperation born of six long weeks on the run behind enemy lines. There come times in life where great things turn on a single decision. After having been turned over to the Germans by an Italian family in December and after six weeks of scrupulously avoiding contact with Italian civilians for that very reason Gerry decided on the spot that this was more than just a mere chance encounter. Didn't his mother always say that God works in mysterious ways? Didn't his father always tell him to lick his finger and check the wind? The thought also passed through his mind that Giannina had been using the English lyrics to "Lili Marlene" rather than the German lyrics.

Gerry stepped out from behind the tree and held his open palms out toward the girl. He pleaded, "Please, don't be frightened! I'm not going to hurt you. You know me,

Giannina! It's Gerry Muldoon. We met in Naples back in December."

At the sound of her name Giannina looked up sharply. The name Gerry Muldoon was not registering with her. She looked intently at his face, "I don't know you. Leave me alone!"

Gerry's shoulders sagged with disappointment. "Look, if you can't help me I understand. I'm just trying to get back home," as he spoke Gerry reached up to wipe his forehead. His wristwatch caught the sun and the reflection flashed across the girl's face. She stepped a couple of steps closer and looked hard at the watch.

"I've seen that watch before! That mother-of-pearl," she mused. "Wait, at the Parc Hotel. You were with your brother, the handsome one, Eddie?"

Gerry breathed a sigh. For once in his young life he was happy that his younger brother Eddie had always been considered the better looking of the two. "Yes, yes, Handsome Eddie. That's what we always called him back home. Handsome Eddie indeed!" Gerry had never called his brother Handsome Eddie but for now he was willing to do whatever was necessary.

The two lapsed into silence for half a minute. Laughing awkwardly they both started to speak again at the same time, blurting out simultaneously, "What are you doing way out here?"

Gerry quickly explained about being taken prisoner and his escape. Giannina quickly explained that her family lived on a nearby farm and that she had returned home in January when her father had been injured in a farm accident. She was helping her mother on the farm while he recovered.

Just then Gerry heard the sound of an automobile engine. Giannina pushed him toward the trees. "Hide!" she commanded.

Gerry scrambled back behind the trees and hugged the ground. Giannina calmly set her bicycle upright and hopped aboard. She began to sing "Lili Marlene" again. This time she used the German lyrics because coming around the corner was the same German staff car that had accompanied the convoy earlier. An older sergeant and a younger enlisted man were the only two in the car. The car halted opposite Gerry's position so that the open top car was now between him and Giannina. Gerry reached down at his side and pulled the Randall knife from its sheath. He coiled his arm and leg muscles and waited, poised to leap if he had to. He could not quite make out the conversation that Giannina was having with the two Germans but it was obvious the younger man was trying to make time with her. During her days entertaining in Naples Giannina had become quite practiced in the art of rebuffing young soldiers' advances. She had a way about her that made most young men feel privileged to have been rejected by a woman as beautiful as she was. She was good at letting them down easy.

Eventually the older man nudged the younger man and gestured down the road. The younger man put the car into gear and eased on down the road. He tossed an "Auf wiedersehen Fraulein!" over his shoulder as they drove away.

She waited until the car was out of sight and then spit in the dirt dismissively.

Gerry stepped out from behind the tree. "I must be getting along or my mother will worry," she said. "Where are you staying? It is not safe for you here. The Germans are everywhere. How can I help you?"

Gerry told her he had been holed up in the nearby hills. She told him it was too dangerous for him to come to her parents' farm because German soldiers were using their barn as a barracks.

Remembering the barking of Anzio Annie from the early morning hours Gerry had a sudden inspiration. "Are you able to move freely along these roads?" he asked. "Would there be any way to get a message to my brother at Anzio?"

Giannina thought for a moment. "My cousin lives a few miles from Nettuno near the Pontine Marshes. My mother and I have been down there twice in the last two months. When I travel with her the Germans usually leave us alone. We have local travel papers."

She pulled a tattered notebook and a stub of a pencil from her dress pocket. Gerry whittled the pencil tip to a sharp point with the Randall knife and began to write.

"Quickly, go now! I will stay in this general area while you are gone. I will look for you right here at 9 o'clock every morning and 4 o'clock every afternoon. I don't know how I can ever thank you. Please stay safe," Gerry implored her.

She folded the message up and slid it inside her blouse for safekeeping. Gerry blushed a little bit. She reached up on her tiptoes and gave him a quick kiss on the cheek. "Eddie is not the only handsome man in his family. I shall call you Handsome Gerry," she said flirtatiously, "but you will have to shave this ugly stuff off your face before I will consider you truly handsome!" Turning briskly she climbed aboard her bicycle and pedaled on down the road. Gerry blushed a lot.

Apr 21, 1944—EZ Dog Diaries

Still more big ones. He seems to have changed tactics from concentration on troops to heavy harassing. 34 Div made a little gain of about half a mile tonight. 3 Div had a field day with artillery on about 150 Krauts. 10 are said to have gotten away.

Apr 22, 1944—EZ Dog Diaries

Rather cloudy today. Gerry must have been mad about the 34th drive, He cut loose with everything at 2100 with a repeat performance at 2200. All our firing seemed to do very little good. Lots of heavy stuff dropped into town.

The daily repetition was becoming tedious to Eddie Muldoon. Every few days brought word from VI Corps HQ of a new breakout plan. The counterbattery section would hunker down with their maps and charts and protractors. Poring over the latest aerial reconnaissance photographs and intelligence reports of enemy troop movements they would set up a prioritized list of targets and potential targets. They would try to anticipate possible scenarios in different sectors of the beachhead. Contingency after contingency piled up on EZ Dog's desk. To him it always seemed most plausible that the push would come along the Carroceto sector. All roads to Rome led through The Factory became his new adaptation of the old saying.

The more difficult task for EZ Dog was trying to guess how the Germans would deploy their artillery. It could be safely assumed that in a fluid battlefield scenario that highly mobile artillery units would be able to operate from hundreds if not thousands of possible sites. Pre-targeting would really not be an option. The counterbattery would have to rely heavily on real time reporting from forward observers in the field and in the air. The sheer pace of activity would create a scene of seeming chaos at the Fire Control Center and the gun crews would be scrambling to keep up the rate of fire and the rapid adjustments.

Just as EZ Dog and the rest of the section wrapped up their three days of work new word would come down from VI Corps of a different plan with different troop movements and the section would begin their calibrations anew.

With May just around the corner spring was definitely in the air. The flocks of swallows flew up and down the coast swooping in and out among the shelled out buildings of Nettuno. The peony bush outside the latrine was in full bloom and the fragrant white petals fought a scent battle of their own against the more earthly odors of the latrine. The days were growing longer. Additional Allied troops and equipment continued to filter into the port. Anzio Annie continued her sporadic but effective harassing fire. The more seasoned soldiers would sometime lay bets with each other on which newcomer would have the worst reaction to their first encounter with the freight train roar of the heavy shells.

Amid all of the counterbattery's contingency plans one constant remained. Anzio Annie was still unmolested and still lobbing shells with devastating effect against the beachhead. EZ Dog was growing an intense hatred of that gun and everything it stood for. He was fed up with having to be in this foreign country, living in a bunker eating dirt. He was fed up with being away from his family. He was fed up with the constant reminders from the Chief of Staff that something needed to be done about the big gun. So he was not in a good mood when Ace burst into the bunker one morning. EZ Dog was only half listening and caught just the tail end of Ace's excited announcement, "...another message from Gerry!"

"Dammit Ace! I know!" EZ Dog yelled. They send us a message every damn day!" EZ Dog winced visibly at himself with this second swear word in a single sentence. He could see the sharp nonverbal rebuke he would get from his mother back on the farm any time he banged his thumb with a hammer and let loose a string of profanity.

"Not THAT Gerry you knucklehead. Your brother Gerry!" Ace laughed.

As they walked over to the HQ compound Ace explained, "A sentry with one of the forward units caught her trying to sneak across the lines on a bicycle if you can imagine. They decided she was not a threat and tried releasing her but she insisted on coming to Nettuno. She said she had a very important message but refused to say anything more unless she could talk to Handsome Captain Eddie Muldoon of the United States Army. So they handed her over to the MPs who brought her down here. They searched her and found a written message with your name on it. She's in here." They approached a small holding cell in one of the myriad hallways of the extensive underground HQ facility in Nettuno. A single MP stood on guard outside the door. As he checked the ID papers of the two artillerymen a faint smile crossed his lips. "Handsome Eddie, eh?" Eddie looked at him quizzically.

A thin bespectacled captain who Eddie recognized vaguely as being with the S2 section emerged from the room. Seeing the man's nametag Eddie remembered him as Charlie Cooper. "You're Muldoon?" Cooper asked brusquely. "Thanks for coming in. So, this woman claims to be a local and claims to know you and claims to have a message from your brother. How cuckoo is that?"

"My brother is a POW somewhere back in Germany," Eddie mused. "And I don't know any local women except for that old lady who still lives down on the main road through Nettuno. What's this girl's name?"

"Gina something-or-other," the intelligence officer replied. "We think she's spreading misinformation for the

194

Germans. We've been seeing a lot of that going on lately. The Krauts threaten these kids' families and send them out to tell a bunch of lies. Basically just trying to muddy the waters. We've gotten pretty good at sorting them out though. But since your name came up we felt obligated to look into it a little more. You're artillery right? Tell me what you think of this. She had it stuffed in her bra as if we wouldn't think to search there," he leered.

Reaching into his shirt pocket Captain Cooper pulled out a scrap of notebook paper and handed it to Eddie. As he began to read the note EZ Dog's eyes widened and his jaw dropped, "Well, I'll be! This really is from Gerry!"

The handwritten note read "Ed, escaped PW train early Mar. Living 'backwoods' style. Now SE of Rome. Good view of Gmn 'big boy'. Can stay here. Rmbr antelope hunt in '39? I'll spot it if you'll shoot it. Need map/radio. – Gerry"

"Captain, can I get a look at this girl?" EZ Dog muttered. The captain led him over to the door and opened the small speakeasy window. Inside the room seated at a bare metal table sat the singer Giannina Marie. Her face was a blend of icy resolve and fiery resistance. She tapped her foot impatiently as she waited. Even without make-up and smudged with dirt the natural beauty of her face shone through.

"My brother and I met her in Naples last fall. She was a singer at the Parc Hotel," he explained to Cooper. I have no idea how she ended up in this part of the country or how she met up with my brother again or how he got away from the Germans, but I can tell you beyond a shadow of a doubt that note is real. It is real and it may just contain the key to getting off this damned beach!"

"I'm afraid I'm going to need more than just your say-so, Muldoon," Cooper desisted. "We can't go running off after every little piece of information that comes in. The Germans are experts at this kind of thing."

"Listen up you egghead!" Eddie glowered. "There's no German on the planet that would know about my brother and me hunting antelope back in '39. That was the time Gerry stalked up to within 30 yards of a big ol' buck antelope that was hiding out along a dry creek bed. Gerry sent me hand signals indicating where that old boy was heading and I was able to zero in for a kill shot from 250 yards. The buck came out from behind cover for all of 10 seconds, but thanks to Gerry I was ready and popped him cleanly. No other way I would have been able to make that shot."

Cooper shrugged noncommittally. Eddie reached up and grabbed him by the collar. "Don't you get it, man? We're talking about a kill shot on Anzio Annie! Now get me in that room. And while you're at it get me someone from General Truscott's staff on the wire. Oh and a couple cups of joe."

Something in the intensity of EZ Dog's manner caused the intelligence man to hesitate. EZ Dog's leaned in and his fierce unblinking gaze convinced the man to act. He barked some orders to the MP at the holding room door and then gestured for EZ Dog to proceed into the room.

Giannina looked up as the door opened and when she saw Eddie she jumped to her feet. Although her hands were cuffed she managed to throw her arms around Eddie's neck in a joyous embrace. "Oh, Handsome Eddie!"

Somewhat sheepishly Eddie managed to peel her arms away and lead her back to her chair. "Tell me about Gerry!" he asked excitedly. "How did you find him? Or how did he find you? Where is he? What did he tell you?" The questions poured out in rapid sequence.

Giannina recounted the circumstances of her chance reunion with Gerry. The intelligence officer had a map brought in. As the three drank their coffee and talked he made notations on the map and scribbled furiously in his notebook. Giannina told of the German staff car and Gerry's heroism. She described how thin he looked but that he still had a passionate fire in his eyes. She sadly told him how Gerry had described the British attack on the POW train. She told Eddie how ugly Gerry's beard looked and that she hoped he would shave it soon so that he could be handsome like his brother. Captain Cooper neglected to include that particular bit of information in his notes.

They talked late into the night. The MP's scrounged up some food for all. Eddie had run quickly back to the counterbattery bunker and scooped up his own maps. They pored over the aerial surveillance photos and cross-referenced them with maps of the area. From Gerry's position as Giannina pinpointed it on the map Eddie drew a straight line to the northwest. It intersected with the back azimuth line he had plotted when the 280 mm dud had landed on the beach. The point of intersection was the railroad yards at Ciampino. EZ Dog sat back and thoughtfully tapped his front teeth with the eraser end of his pencil.

The next day Ace told EZ Dog that he was heading down to Naples. "That special package I was supposed to pick up finally came in. Do you want anything else while I'm down there?" EZ Dog asked him to bring back a couple packs of cigars if he had the time. General Truscott's adjutant stopped by the counterbattery section and huddled with EZ Dog for about 45 minutes. In the afternoon he said his goodbyes to Giannina. Before the MP's escorted her back to the countryside along the eastern sector of the front Eddie verbally gave her a message to pass on to Gerry. She was to tell him that Eddie was sending some gear including a map and a radio along with some food and a bedroll. He was to check in by radio every day at 1800 hours for an update. Until the offensive actually kicked off though, he was to lay low and stay out of sight. "Tell him we're coming to get him!" he exhorted.

Seamus Muldoon and the taciturn Mr. Smythe sat in a small flight operations room at a grass lined airstrip south of Naples. For the hundredth time Smythe walked Seamus through the procedures for the launch of their pet project. Due to time and space considerations Smythe would not be accompanying Seamus on to Anzio. It was all in Seamus' hands from this point on.

Smythe intoned the instructions, "Now remember you've only got two shells. The first is the target indicator shell. Once you have contact with your forward observer he will relay final target coordinates back to the Fire Control Center. The gun crew will load this shell into the weapon and send it downrange. On impact this shell will release a dense cloud of blue smoke. The observer will report back the location of the impact with distance and azimuth corrections to put you right on target with the guided projectile. When that information comes back to the gun crew they will load the powder charge into the canister. You will then step up, load the hamster into the projectile and hand it off to the gun crew. They will mount the projectile on the canister and load it up. Then, God willing, all of the training you've done over the last year and half will pay off. You got it?"

"Yeah, Smythe. I've got it, I've got it." Seamus replied wearily. As the two men talked Seamus could hear the distant drone of a small airplane approaching. Shading his eyes with his hand he picked up the inbound path of the Stinson L-5 coming from the east.

"Wait a second. You mean I'm flying in that?" he asked incredulously. "That thing is tiny! What if someone starts shooting at us?"

The plane touched down with a couple of extra bounces for good measure and rolled over to where the two men were stepping out to greet it. Ace cut the engine and hopped out as the propeller spun to a halt. "Which one of you is Muldoon?" he asked. Smythe indicated Seamus with a slight tilt of the head. Ace extended his hand and offered Seamus a firm handshake. "Pleased to meet you, son. I work with your brother, Handsome Eddie. Name's Ace! Are you ready to go?" Seamus raised one eyebrow at hearing Eddie's new moniker but did not respond.

Seamus and Smythe readied the crate with the special artillery shells and Ace helped them load it into the narrow cargo area behind the rear seat of the L-5. Seamus grabbed his suitcase and the hamster carrying case and placed them in the rear seat. He turned back and gave Smythe a quick goodbye. "Thanks Smythe," was all he said.

"All right Seamus. You'll do fine. Give 'em hell!" Smythe returned simply.

"Let's go," Ace called. "There's some weather moving in and I want to get into Nettuno ahead of the storm. Besides, the Germans don't like to fly so much during bad weather. It's a good way to avoid those Messerschmitt fighter planes. Seamus cast a worried eye back at Smythe who smiled and gave him a 'thumbs-up'. As soon as Seamus was settled into the rear seat with the suitcase in his lap Ace closed the hatch doors and fired up the engines. Taxiing out to the strip he turned left and accelerated quickly into the wind. The L-5 lifted off smoothly and banked toward the northeast. Ace set a course about a mile off the coast and flew parallel to the shoreline at about 7,000 feet.

Once they were on a straight and level path he shouted back over his shoulder at Seamus, "Do you want to take the stick for a bit?" Seamus hunkered down even lower in his seat and shook his head. He hoped Ace didn't recognize the fear in his face.

"Eddie is always badgering me to let him fly the darn thing," Ace hollered back at Seamus.

Seamus mustered enough gumption to yell back over the engine noise, "Yeah, well my brother is crazy!"

A little over an hour later Ace got Seamus' attention and pointed ahead and to the right of the plane. "There's Anzio!"

Despite his trepidation Seamus looked down at the scene unfolding below. The entire coast line from northwest of Anzio to a couple miles east of Nettuno was bathed in a dark grey haze. He could only vaguely see that there were two towns along the beach. He could not make out any activity on the ground through the haze. Floating serenely above the smoke from the smudge pots were a dozen or more barrage balloons. He reached forward and tapped Ace on the shoulder, "What are those blimps?"

Ace shouted something but his reply was drowned out by the prop wash. Within a few minutes he had descended to a point level with the barrage balloons and began the now familiar weaving course down to the narrow landing strip just outside of Nettuno. As Seamus' eyes adjusted to the haze he suddenly saw the ground rushing up at them. He closed his eyes tightly and inadvertently ducked just in time to miss the plane's smooth nose up maneuver and touchdown on the ground. He opened his eyes and let out a long slow breath.

As the L-5 came to a halt Seamus saw Eddie running out from the side of the strip with a huge grin on his face. Eddie threw open the half-door and leaned in. He grabbed Seamus in an awkward bear hug and pounded his back. "Seamus! Boy are you a sight for sore eyes! Welcome, welcome! Come on! What are you waiting for? Let's get you out of there."

Ace smiled to see the two brothers reunited. Although Seamus was not as tall as either Eddie or Gerry he definitely had a strong family resemblance. Eddie wouldn't be able to deny that Seamus was his brother. All three of the brothers had a certain presence, not that anyone in their right mind would call any of the Muldoon boys handsome.

Ace handed EZ Dog his two packs of cigars and helped unload Seamus and his gear. The brothers gave him a wave and made their way up the beach to the waiting jeep. Within a couple of minutes they pulled up at the counterbattery bunker.

"So how was your trip? When did you leave the States? How are Mom and Dad?" EZ Dog once again fired off questions one right after the other.

"Slow down big brother. Let me catch my breath first," Seamus held him off temporarily. "First things first. Mom and Dad took the news about Gerry pretty rough. Mom in particular."

"Wait, what news about Gerry?" Eddie asked anxiously.

Seamus continued somberly, "The day before I left the farm we got word from the War Department that Gerry had been killed at the end of February during a POW breakout somewhere up above Rome. I thought you had heard."

"Aw hell, Seamus. You know the War Department never gets anything right. Half the time they don't know their rear end from a hole in the ground," Eddie rejoined. "Gerry's not dead!"

"Hot damn! I knew it!" Seamus shouted. "How do you know? What's the story, Ed? Have you talked with him? Where is he?"

Now it was Eddie's turn to pull in the reins on Seamus' rapid-fire questioning. He calmed Seamus down and filled him in on Gerry and the escape and his chance meeting with the beautiful Italian songstress and the big German artillery piece.

Seamus did not want to hear about the German artillery just yet. "Wait just a stinkin' minute. What? Gerry's got a beautiful Italian songstress looking after him? That sly dog! Man oh man! I am sure glad to hear he's okay. That just made my day! Um, is she really beautiful? And she sings? Man oh man! Gerry always was a lucky stiff!"

May 1, 1944—EZ Dog Diaries

May Day—and such a beautiful day I decided to take a hop with [Ace] in his L-5. We flew for over an hour—around the lines, over town, up and down. He let me have the stick most of the time. After the flight I watched the 240 fire a few rounds. A beautiful gun— if guns can be called that.

May of 1944 arrived at Anzio with cloudy weather and an air of anticipation. Both sides seemed to be taking a collective deep breath before the inevitable push by the Allies. Speculation continued about the specifics of the attack but that there would be an offensive was not in doubt. Would it happen this week or next? Would it push toward the southeast and the hoped-for link up with the 5ᵗʰ Army or would it push inland to cut rail and highway lines of communication?

The ongoing artillery duel continued but at a reduced pace. Anzio Annie still made her presence felt on most days. The cloudy weather hampered aerial observation and the Allies still could not bring an effective airstrike against the big rail gun. Even though field artillery does not have a direct line of sight requirement you still have to be able to see it in order to shoot it.

EZ Dog's contingency plans were drawn up to cover every possible scenario so the day by day workload eased up a little bit. Seamus and EZ Dog spent a lot of time together both on the job and off. At work they gave briefings to the Long Tom gun crews explaining that they were going to be launching a new weapon that had not been field tested. The hamster-guided aspect however was kept in the strictest confidence. The two brothers spent time going over maps and selecting possible spots from which to fire the hamster shell.

May 3, 1944 —EZ Dog Diaries

I've been more or less loafing today—a sun bath for an hour and a half—a real bath later in the afternoon.

Gerry must have been as lazy as we were. It was the quietest day on the beachhead yet.

Outside of work the two brothers took advantage of the occasional break in the weather to sit down by the water's edge and talk. When they were not working they did not talk much about the war. They preferred to reminisce about happier times back home in Colorado. They laughed talking about the time they had gone trout fishing with Dad and Gerry up on the Cache La Poudre River. Gerry had hooked a nice trout in a deep hole beneath a large boulder. While crowing proudly as he reeled in the fish Gerry had lost his footing and tumbled into the water. In all his flailing around he managed to drop Dad's fine bamboo fly rod into the creek. Dad had jumped to the rescue. Just as Gerry was struggling to his feet the old man had plunged into the icy water where he elbowed Gerry aside sending him splashing to the seat of his pants in knee deep water while Dad groped along the bottom of the creek for his fly rod. Unbelievably he actually was able to locate the rod and pulled it out of the water triumphantly. To everybody's surprise the line was still taut and the boys all cheered as Dad reeled in the 14-inch rainbow trout.

EZ Dog laughed until his sides ached watching and listening as Seamus acted out the incident in great detail portraying both of the major parts in the drama. Seamus even did a sitz splash in the Tyrrhenian Sea when showing how Dad had elbowed Gerry to the side. When he stopped to think about it Eddie realized that he hadn't laughed that genuinely since December of 1941.

In addition to time with EZ Dog Seamus spent an hour or more each day working with Houdini and Hammie. They usually spent about a half hour on conditioning which in this Spartan setting consisted mostly of running on the hamster wheel. Seamus rigged up a spent shell casing with a length of parachute cord so that he could twirl the shell around to

204

create centripetal force to mimic the G-forces the hamsters would experience. They then spent perhaps twenty minutes on the small steering device simulator that Smythe and the two Smiths had built back in Chicago. The two hamsters settled in nicely in their travel case which Seamus kept under the head of his cot in the counterbattery bunker. The occasional impact of a nearby artillery round did not seem to bother the two rodents in the slightest.

Gerry sat on a steep hillside high in the Albano Hills. He had established a well-hidden campsite deep in a grove of trees at the top of a narrow canyon. It was about 150 yards away from the road and provided him with good fields of view to the northwest. He could see traffic along the road for close to a mile in both directions and when the weather allowed he could see the dome of St. Peter's Basilica in the hazy distance.

He had met with Giannina twice since her return from Anzio. His spirits soared when she gave him Eddie's message. He thought to himself, "Okay Gerry, you're back in the war. Let's give 'em hell!" Giannina had taken a considerable risk to bring a basket of food right past the German troops housed in her father's barn.

The two sat quietly in a shady grove next to the brook. They talked quietly about their lives. She told him what it had been like growing up on a small farm in the Italian hills. He told her what it had been like growing up on a dryland wheat farm on the Colorado plains. They found more similarities than differences. He watched the dappled sunlight through the leaves dance across her cheeks. He listened to the sound of her laughter mingle with the sound of the water flowing down the stream. He could not remember ever having been happier. He told her of the time he had been fishing in a mountain stream back home when his father had fallen into the water and dropped his best bamboo fly-fishing rod. Gerry had dove into the water and rescued his father while simultaneously reeling in a 22-inch rainbow trout while his brothers Eddie and Seamus had stood by helplessly.

In the middle of the bloodiest war in human history these two young people carved out an hour of happiness. As Giannina prepared to leave Gerry stood awkwardly. She leaned forward and whispered that she had one more thing to give him for now. Reaching into the basket she pulled out a stainless steel double-edged razor. "From your handsome brother Eddie," she explained. "So you too can be handsome.

She gave him a quick kiss on the cheek and said, "Ciao bella!" He watched her turn and scramble up the incline to the road and her waiting bicycle. As she crested the top of the slope she was silhouetted briefly by the sun and he realized just how thin the fabric of her dress was. Then she was back on her bicycle and the momentary vision faded.

For the next three days Gerry waited near the stone bridge over the brook as Giannina had instructed him. On the third day he heard a faint engine drone off in the clouds. The engine sound came and went in a zigzag pattern. He wondered if Ace would be able to locate the road with all the cloud cover. All of a sudden he saw the L-5 swoop down out of a cloud bank and zoom by about fifty feet above the ground. He saw Ace's hand reach out the half window and drop a bag toward the trees. The plane then climbed steeply back into the clouds.

The bag arced gracefully toward the ground as Gerry watched. He cursed silently under his breath when the bag landed squarely in the boughs of a birch tree, about 25 feet above the ground. He checked the road in both directions and then scrambled across. Scrabbling for a foothold he began to climb up into the tree. As he reached out to try to free the bag's tangled straps from the tree limbs he heard a different engine noise approaching from the east. Over the crest of the hill came a single German soldier on a motorcycle. Gerry hugged the tree as tightly as possible and tried to make himself disappear right into the trunk. He almost dared not to breathe. The motorcycle pulled even with the birch tree and Gerry cursed silently under his breath again. The motorcyclist set the kickstand and climbed off the bike. He walked around the bike a couple of times swinging his arms and stretching. He bent over and touched his toes five times and then did five deep knee bends. He performed some sort of Teutonic deep breathing ritual—in/out, in/out, in/out—with an audible "Hoo, hoo, hoo," as he exhaled. Gerry felt his grip beginning to slip and a fly landed on the tip of his nose. He shook his mustache trying to shoo the fly without making any noise. The fly refused to budge. He thrust out his lower lip and tried to blow up to chase the fly from his nose. Finally he rubbed his nose against the bark of the tree.

Meanwhile the German soldier walked over to the base of the birch tree twenty five feet below Gerry's perch. He unzipped his own fly and began to whistle tunelessly as he relieved himself on the base of the tree. Endless seconds dragged on. Gerry marveled at the man's bladder capacity. Finally with a hitch and a zip the soldier finished his business and returned to the motorcycle. Kicking it to a start he pulled back onto the dirt road and puttered on out of sight around the bend.

Gerry climbed back down the tree and headed back to his campsite. From the sack that Ace had dropped for him he pulled a small field radio, several maps, a pair of binoculars and a .45-caliber army pistol with ammunition. There was a canvas pouch with some army rations and a canteen full of water. Eddie had also included a packet of cigars and a small flask of whiskey. These were two vices that Eddie hoped his mother would forgive Gerry given his current predicament. The last item in the packet was a small metallic box with a couple of dials and a directional antenna. Reading the 3 X 5 card taped to the side of the box Gerry chuckled. "Seamus and his darn hamsters, eh?"

Gerry relocated his camp to a north-facing slope of a ridge that was just to the north of a large lake. From a rocky prominence nearby he could command a panoramic view of the countryside in a 180 degree sector to his north. Using the dome of St. Peter's Basilica and a prominent peak to his east as landmarks he determined that he was near the village of Marino on the north shore of Lake Albano. Downtown Rome was a little over 13 miles to the northwest and the peak two miles to his east was known as Rocca di Papa. Locating the site of Anzio Annie in the railyards at Ciampino he determined the range to be about 3.5 miles to his northwest, almost in line with St. Peter's. With cigar in hand Gerry settled in to wait for the cavalry.

CHAPTER 11- ALL ROADS
LEAD TO ROME

Your task will not be an easy one. Your enemy is well-trained, well-equipped and battle hardened. He will fight savagely.
Gen. Dwight D. Eisenhower- Order of the Day June 6, 1944

"Rome, just yesterday trembling for the lives of her sons and daughters, for the fate of her incomparable treasures of religion and culture, having before her eyes the terrifying spectre of war and unimaginable destruction, looks today with new hope and reinforced confidence at her salvation."
-Pope Pius XII, Words to the Roman People June 6, 1944

Inflow of troops and equipment into the Anzio beachhead continued during the first ten days of May. All signs pointed toward the long-awaited push but D-Day was not yet set. Eddie and Seamus talked nearly every day. They tried to put the war on hold for an hour or two at a time. Seamus told Eddie how worn down Dad had looked last month. The German POW's helped some with physical labor but the morning and evening milking fell entirely to Dad. One of the neighbors had been stopping by every morning to pick up the milk to take into town. This helped a bit but the physical wear and tear on top of the uncertainty of Gerry's situation was taking its toll on the folks. In addition the wheat crop was looking pretty meager this spring. The brothers both agreed that the only way around it was to get this war over with. News from England suggested that the big push into France could come any day.

On May 11 things began to happen.

May 11, 1944—EZ Dog Diaries

This started out to be a quiet day. [Margin note: Met Gen Tate, 34 Div Arty Cmdr.] Then G-3 ordered a psuedo-preparation for 2330. Fifteen minutes with everything on the beachhead shooting.

Word came that the Cassino front had shoved off at 2300. Things are looking up now.

Part of the Allied strategy was to make a series of feints at different locations to keep the Germans guessing. Every so often the artillery batteries would lay in a barrage at some location along the Anzio front signaling that a push was coming. The German artillery response to these pseudo-preparations was useful for gauging their preparedness in different sectors. In addition the threat of a push at Anzio kept the Germans from moving troops to the Cassino front to bolster the situation there. Over the next several days the Allies at the Cassino front made some slow but steady progress in the treacherous mountain terrain. Moroccan Ghoums, New Zealanders, Poles, French and others joined the British and Americans.

May 14, 1944—EZ Dog Diaries.

Another quiet day on the beachhead. The Germans seem to be concentrating their efforts on the other front. 5th Army has taken over 1000 prisoners in the attack. This is apt to prove a definite factor in

German defenses. The French and New Zealanders have crossed the Rapido and Garigliano in some strength.

Anzio Annie continued to put in an occasional appearance. General Truscott's adjutant was in constant communication with the counterbattery with instructions to be ready to take out the big gun. Allied air attacks on the Ciampino rail yards had still not been able to put her out of commission due to the Germans' ability to pick and choose when they trundled her out of the cave and the fact that the Allied air crews had not yet identified the specific tunnel entrance where Annie was hiding. The big gun was used sporadically enough that aircraft were not able to get on site quickly enough to strike a blow when she was out in the open.

Eddie communicated only very sparingly with Gerry during this time. He was however able to find out that Gerry's vantage point did not allow him to see the actual tunnel entrance. It looked more and more like they would have to use the artillery plan at a time when Annie was out in the open for that brief period of time. As the situation stood currently none of the Long Tom batteries could be positioned far enough forward to bring the rail gun into range. This would have to happen "on the fly" once the breakout had actually begun. Truscott rightly was concerned that neutralizing the rail gun could be a decisive factor in breaking the stalemate. Until they actually gained enough territory to position the Long Toms near The Factory at Carroceto Eddie and Seamus were on hold. The waiting was the hardest part.

May 15, 1944—EZ Dog Diaries

News from II Corps and FEC [French Expeditionary Corps] still looks promising. Both corps have moved well forward—as much as 4-5,000 yds. Several key points taken. Also quite a number of prisoners.

Our front will remain static for a while it seems, but we are ready.

Two 8" guns are expected tomorrow. They will be a welcome addition to outrange Gerry's 170's.

May 16, 1944—EZ Dog Diaries

Goums [Moroccan troops] on the other front have progressed 8-10,000 yds in front of everyone else. II Corps is moving steadily. Lots of PW's being taken. Polish Corps unable to move far.

Finally on May 18th British and Polish troops surrounded and captured the Italian town of Cassino which had been the key point in the stiff German resistance along the Gustav Line. This critical victory highlighted the beginning of the end for the Germans in Italy.

Back at Anzio reinforcements continued to pour into the port and rapidly moved to forward positions. May 19th brought the word EZ Dog and Seamus had been waiting for.

May 19, 1944—EZ Dog Diaries

Rainy but not sloppy yet. Business is picking up on the beachhead. Advance elements of 36 Div came in today. We are starting to compile a program for D-Day which would indicate that day not too far off. "E" CB section will move to the field May 21. Most of the units of Corps Arty and lots of Div Arty units moved to battle positions ready for the start.

May 23rd at 0630 the much anticipated breakout from the Anzio beachhead began. The initial thrust of the assault was in a northeasterly direction toward the town of Cisterna which lies due east of Carroceto. As the U.S. 36th Division and 1st Armored Division pushed to Cisterna in the first 24 hours of the attack EZ Dog's unit followed close behind. Choosing a location midway between Carroceto and Cisterna the designated Long Tom battery set up in a shallow valley. The majority of their shelling was done in support of the main assault, but EZ Dog had been given one gun for the special mission against Anzio Annie.

EZ Dog and Seamus bounced along the rutted road in the jeep with Seamus' special crate and hamster cage strapped tightly in the back seat. While EZ Dog coordinated with the communications officer and the battery commander Seamus double checked the two shells for the thousandth time. The gun crew set up the gun in firing position and set a preliminary range and azimuth for the center of the rail yards at Ciampino.

In the communication center the staff handled an astounding amount of radio and telephone traffic. Calls for artillery support were coming in from around the battlefield as fast as the communications crew could handle them. The earth shook with mighty salvos from the other Long Tom crews. Meanwhile EZ Dog and Seamus waited impatiently. Finally the call they were waiting for came in. A tank battalion in the vicinity of Carroceto reported incoming shells of the Anzio Express. Annie was up and barking!

Eddie tried raising Gerry on the radio using the call sign they had given him. "Antelope One this is Hunting Lodge, over." There was no response. "Antelope One this is Hunting Lodge, over," Eddie repeated. After readjusting the antenna and fine tuning the frequency he tried again. "Antelope One, Hunting Lodge, over."

213

The radio crackled to life and Eddie heard Gerry's voice. "Lodge this is Antelope One. How do you read?"

"Weak and distorted, Antelope One. It will have to do. Do you have target in sight? Over."

Gerry was sitting in his observation site on the rock outcropping overlooking the area surrounding Rome. The day was clear. Activity along the local roads had been noticeably increased yesterday and today as the Germans scrambled to reposition troops to critical areas. For the last twenty minutes he had been watching the big gun in Ciampino fire its massive shells to the south.

"Hunting Lodge, Antelope One. I have visual on target. Coordinates as previously reported. Fire when ready. Over."

Anzio Annie typically made use of the same stretch of tracks. Assuming she followed her usual patterns the general map coordinates were known. Gerry had just confirmed this. Back at the battery Eddie and Seamus went into action. Seamus pulled out the unmanned 155 mm target indicator shell. This shell was intended to get them into the ball park so that the guided round could be pinpointed onto the target.

Eddie called out the firing program—powder charge, range and azimuth. The gun crew smoothly loaded the powder bags. One of the loaders took the shell from Seamus and fitted it to the canister. Another member of the crew opened the breech. The loader pushed the shell into the breech and seated it firmly. The breech was locked into position. The gun crew commander yelled, "Ready, Fire!" The cannoneer pulled the lanyard briskly and the gun roared. Flame and smoke erupted from the muzzle as the gun recoiled. The gun bounced back to its starting position and the crew threw open the breech and extracted the spent canister.

Seamus shuddered from the mighty commotion. Houdini and Hammie the Second cowered in his breast pocket. Although they had been sound-conditioned to loud bangs back in Chicago the simulators did not match the intensity of the artillery up close. Seamus ran through his final pre-deployment checklist. He said a quick "Eenie, Meenie, Miney, Mo" and selected Houdini. He gave the hamster a half a hamster treat for good luck and leaned down to whisper something in Houdini's ear.

Gerry had his binoculars trained on Anzio Annie. The big German gun barked again with a thunderous roar of fire and sound. After a seeming eternity Gerry saw a puff of blue smoke about fifty yards south of the flat car that held Annie. He keyed his radio talk button, "Hunting Lodge this is Antelope One. Smoke spotted, drifting slowly southeast from impact point. Add fifty due north, fire for effect! Over."

Back at the Long Tom battery the radio spewed static and all Eddie heard was, "…Antelope …southeast …add …north."

"Antelope One say again. Over!"

Gerry was able to see the gun crew scrambling around the flatcar preparing to lower the barrel and retreat into the tunnel. He radioed frantically, "Hunting Lodge, smoke drifting southeast at target. Add fifty due north, fire for effect! It's now or never Eddie!"

Eddie and Seamus looked at each other. Seamus said, "I heard add fifty north. How about you?" Eddie nodded and ran back over to the Long Tom doing mental calculations in his head as he ran.

Seamus popped open the rear hatch of the shell and loaded Houdini inside. He visually checked through the transparent nosepiece and saw that Houdini had crawled into proper launch position inside the hamster wheel. He thought it was probably his imagination but it almost looked like Houdini extended his paw in a "thumbs up" gesture. "Nah, couldn't be," Seamus muttered to himself.

Eddie called out the firing program for the gun crew once again with a slight adjustment of the barrel to add fifty yards to the north. The crew loaded the powder bags. Seamus handed over the shell with Houdini inside. The crew loaded the shell into the breech. "Locked and loaded!" the gun commander said quietly to EZ Dog.

EZ Dog reached over to the gun and made a minor adjustment of the elevation hand wheel. "Old Man Muldoon's fudge factor!" he exclaimed as he nodded to the gun commander.

"Ready, Fire!" As the gun barked and the shell accelerated down the barrel Houdini's world came to a standstill. Initially flattened like a pancake by the sudden acceleration the hamster immediately recoiled to his original shape. He leaped onto the wheel and began running in the opposite direction of the shell's rotation. Soon he was able to counteract the rotation and settled into stable trajectory through the air with the hamster wheel holding steady as the shell rotated around it. He reached up and put his paws on the steering control levers. As the shell reached its highest point it actually seemed to hesitate briefly before arching over and heading toward the ground. The seconds ticked by. Houdini was able to briefly see Anzio Annie on the ground far below. The shell accelerated toward the ground and the big gun grew larger in the transparent nosecone. Houdini made one last tweak of the controls which centered the muzzle of the big German gun in his viewfinder. He jumped out of the wheel and scrambled his way to the rear of the projectile. The little hamster popped open the escape hatch and jumped out into mid-air. As his parachute deployed and he began to drift toward the southeast he watched the scene below.

Gerry was watching the same scene through his binoculars three miles to the south. The German gun crew had the barrel almost completely lowered and the electric motors that powered the flat car were beginning to move the car slowly toward the tunnel.

I wish I could report that the 155 mm projectile had dropped straight down the barrel of Anzio Annie with pinpoint accuracy thereby ending her career but that's not what happened. Nobody had anticipated that the action of opening the rear escape hatch would create an asymmetric airstream at the back end of the projectile. This resulted in a slight last second deviation. Instead of striking the gun directly the shell hit the side of the rail car right next to the rear wheels. The brunt of the explosion did not cause even the slightest damage to the gun itself but it did completely knock the wheels off the undercarriage of the rail car. As it turned out the Germans were unable to move the big gun for several days. They attempted to camouflage the gun in place but it was exposed and vulnerable now that the Allies knew it was in the open. Anzio Annie had fired her last. Official war historians would later determine that an Allied airstrike on May 29th, 1944 disabled the German Kruppwerks 280 mm railroad cannon commonly known as Anzio Annie as it sat exposed in the rail yards at Ciampino just southeast of Rome after having been lightly damaged by a random artillery round. Only a select few men would know the truth.

The light breeze carried the hamster several hundred yards to the southeast before he landed in an open field. He quickly scrambled out of the parachute and tried to recover from the effects of the rapid acceleration and the high-speed rotation of riding in an artillery shell. Once he got his bearings he tilted his ears toward the south. Over the distant rumblings of war he could faintly make out the sound of his mother calling him. Gerry had turned on the homing beacon.

Meanwhile the Allied assault continued. I will leave it to the war historians to do the armchair quarterbacking analysis of command decisions. The original plan of the attack called for the main thrust led by the 1st Armored Division to push toward the northeast toward the middle of the Italian peninsula. If successful this maneuver would cut off the two main highways connecting north and south along with their accompanying railroads. This would bring pressure to bear on the Germans' right flank and threaten to eliminate their main routes of resupply. More importantly it would give the Allies a chance of entrapping the main German force and potentially take several German divisions out of the war entirely.

Despite some heated battles at Cisterna and Cori lead elements of the 1st Armored Division had pushed forward into the Velletri gap within a few days of the onset of the campaign. The main objective was the town of Valmontone sitting astride Route 6. The Germans were in disarray and were scrambling to stem the tide at Valmontone. Surprisingly the Allies failed to exploit the momentum. In a controversial move General Truscott was ordered by General Clark not to proceed further toward Valmontone and to redirect the thrust of the attack in an abrupt ninety degree turn to the northwest toward the Alban Hills and Clark's ultimate goal of Rome. This left Field Marshall Kesselring enough of an opening to withdraw the bulk of his forces to the north of Italy rather than see them trapped and either annihilated or captured. Over the coming week and a half the Allies were able to fight their way through what remained of German resistance in the Alban Hills and advance on Rome. Toward the end the German resistance melted away and it became an all-out sprint toward Rome. The Field Artillery scrambled to keep up with the front line troops and the situation on the ground became very chaotic.

As the Long Tom battery moved on in support of the attack EZ Dog and Seamus were left to find their own way. EZ Dog tried raising Gerry on the radio again but was unsuccessful. Traveling to Gerry's position by jeep was out of the question given the fluid nature of the battlefield during these days. He began to formulate a different plan to rescue Gerry by air. In order to do that however he would have to locate Division Artillery Headquarters which was on the move as well.

Gerry had decided to stay put. From monitoring radio communications he had been able to discern that the Allied breakout had been successful and that the situation was definitely in flux. He thought it would be best to remain in hiding and not go on the move. At 1800 hours on May 25th about 24 hours after the strike on Anzio Annie Gerry powered up the radio and keyed the mike. "Hunting Lodge this is Antelope Hunt 1 over." Nothing. He tried again with no response. As he continued to fiddle with the knobs and adjust the signal the sound of static and faint snippets of other radio conversations began to fade. Slowly the radio went dead. Once again Gerry was on his own. This time however the area behind enemy lines had become like a hive of angry bees. Trucks, tanks and foot soldiers zipped this way and that on the surrounding country lanes. He would have to hunker down once again and wait.

CHAPTER 12- BUZZ THE POPE

"We had massed all our strength to take Rome. We were keyed up. We not only wanted the honor of capturing Rome, but we felt that we more than deserved it…"
General Mark Clark, Commander of VI Corps, U.S. Army

May 1944- The Velletri Gap, central Italy

The morning of May 27th EZ Dog awoke with a sore neck. Although he had once again been able to sleep well in a makeshift lean-to with Seamus snoring alongside him the rocky ground had provided little comfort. His 24-year-old body ached like that of a man twice his age. After a quick wash-up he and Seamus hopped back in the jeep and headed toward the northeast hoping to catch up with the HQ Section. The roads were crowded. At first the U.S. troops that they encountered were moving quickly up toward the vicinity of Valmontone. Occasional groups of German POWs were being marched back toward Anzio where they would be loaded aboard ships for transport to the rear. By noon they began to notice a shift. More of the U.S. troops were heading back toward the south and west. EZ Dog spotted an Ordnance officer that he recognized from one of their baseball games at Nettuno last month.

"What's the poop?" EZ Dog called.

"We're redirecting the attack up toward Albano. I guess we're going to Rome!" the man hollered back.

"Any word on Corps Artillery HQ?" EZ Dog asked.

"Last I heard they were up around Cori, you might look for them up there," was the reply.

EZ Dog and Seamus continued on toward the northeast and started to feel like a salmon swimming upstream against the current of major troop movements. Time after time they had to divert the jeep almost into the roadside ditch in order to allow a troop convoy or group of tanks to pass by in the other direction.

May 27, 1944—EZ Dog Journals

The axis of attack was changed with the main effort now going towards Lanuvio and up the railway towards Albano. 1 AD was pulled from the Artena sector and put in with the 45th.

I took a jeep ride up through Cori to see the havoc. At least 12 Tiger tanks (and they are really big) are knocked out along the road. Trucks, SP's, motor-cycles and command cars are smashed up all through the area. Guns are blown up—from 150's to AT [antitank] guns. Gerry hurt awfully bad on that retreat. Even a few of those "good" Krauts are laying around yet, too.

The destructiveness of the war was astounding to Seamus. Nothing in his previous life had prepared him for the scene that was unfolding before him. One German Tiger was a burned out shell, blackened by intense fire. Seamus fought back the urge to vomit when he realized the clump of blackened material hanging from the open hatch was the charred remains of a German soldier.

As they passed through a small cluster of buildings at an intersection of two dirt lanes the two brothers saw three elderly Italian civilians sitting on the stoop of a stone house, the only building of the village that still had an intact roof. The three men's heads swung back and forth slowly as they watched the comings and goings of the raucous American GI's. Pulling to the side of the road EZ Dog consulted his map once again. Gesturing at the map he asked the Italians, "Cori? Cori?" but got no response. "Valmontone?" No response. Finally one of the men shrugged slightly and inclined his head wordlessly indicating the road to the left. The expressions on the three men's faces did not change at all. Just as EZ Dog put the jeep into gear and before he drove away the front door of the building swung open. A little girl of about seven with dark hair, rosy red lips and a smudged white dress skipped down the steps and ran over to the jeep. From behind her back she pulled a single white and yellow daisy that she proffered shyly to EZ Dog. Her eyes were wide and her head was tilted down while she clutched the flower in her tiny fist. EZ Dog held her gaze for several seconds before he reached out and accepted the proffered flower.

"Grazie Signore Americano!" the girl said in a crystal clear voice. EZ Dog's face relaxed for the first time in days and he broke into a crooked smile.

"Well, you are very welcome, young lady!" he proclaimed with mock seriousness. "Very welcome indeed." He reached over and patted the side of her head gently. Then he reached over to his brother and tucked the stem of the flower into the lapel of Seamus' field jacket at a rakish angle. The jeep bucked a little as he released the clutch and headed off toward Cori.

When they reached Cori a beleaguered MP was able to direct them to the center of town where the Artillery HQ had been temporarily established in what used to be the town hall.

The building was a flurry of activity. EZ Dog and Seamus walked up a broad flight of stairs to the second floor where enlisted men and officers alike were scurrying here and there. Dodging clerks carrying folding tables and footlockers the two men were finally able to locate Ace. The pilot had his feet up on a small ornately carved side table in a room the size of a postage stamp. He was leaning back in his chair balancing a mug of steaming black G.I. coffee on his belly. A half-smoked cigarette hung from his lips and he managed to take a sip of coffee without removing the cigarette. "Ace!" Eddie exclaimed, "You're just the man I've been looking for. Gerry's in trouble up in the hills above Lake Albano."

Ace replied laconically, "Boy, I'll say! Gerry's in trouble all over the damn country! Our fellas have been kicking butt all over the place. Those Krauts are running around like a bunch of chickens with their wings cut off."

Seamus scratched his head. "Don't you mean 'with their heads cut off'?" he asked.

Ace scoffed, "Heh, yeah. Heads, wings, whatever. They're on the run and that's a fact!"

"Not THOSE Gerries you dummy! My brother Gerry!" EZ Dog huffed. "He's stuck up behind the lines somewhere up near Marino. Hopefully with a hamster in his pocket and a pretty Italian girl on his arm. Problem is we've lost radio contact with him. We were hoping we could get to him on the ground but the whole situation's just too fluid. It's like a hornets' nest out there." EZ Dog quickly updated Ace on the hamster shell mission and Gerry's role as forward observer. Ace was especially interested to hear how Gerry had managed to get together with the attractive Italian singer from the hotel in Naples.

"So where's the Stinson, Ace?" EZ Dog asked. "Let's go see if we can find him."

"Well the plane is in a farmer's field a half a mile west of town, but No Can Do my friend. I'm grounded." Ace replied as he pulled up his pants leg to reveal a heavily bandaged calf area. "Took a bullet a couple of days ago while I was out spotting up near Valmontone. Damn rifle slug came right up through the floor of the plane and caught me square in the leg. A few inches to the right and I'd be singing soprano right about now." It amazed Seamus to hear these Army men joke about near death. After months hunkered down on the beach at Anzio Ace and EZ Dog understood all too well the dark humor that became one's constant companion when a random artillery shell could ruin your day very quickly.

EZ Dog shook his head, "So you're telling me you can't fly?"

"Yeah, no! I can't fly." Ace said. "Not for another week the docs tell me. And the other L5's are already off toward Rome. I don't expect any of the boys will be coming back this way. Maybe you can jeep it on over to the new front and hitch a ride with Moose or Skandowski or one of the other pilots."

"Well crap, Ace. I was counting on you. Guess we'll head over by jeep and see what we can scrounge up. You take care, y'hear?"

Exiting the building Seamus turned to Eddie and said, "Now what?"

"I've got an idea," Eddie replied slowly.

Gerry stayed well out of sight in the thicket of trees on the crest of the hill overlooking Rome to the north. Over the last few days the amount of German military traffic on the little dirt road had increased dramatically. Everybody seemed to be in a hurry to get somewhere, but the movements were chaotic at best as if there were no overreaching plan. One afternoon he watched a small convoy storm past heading northeast only to see the same three trucks rumble by heading southwest a half hour later.

He had decided that he would give the hamster one more day. If he had not arrived Gerry would set out on foot once more and head toward what he hoped were Allied lines toward the south and east. Poring over his maps he identified a peak south of Rocca di Papa that overlooked the Velletri gap. From what he had gathered by monitoring radio chatter before his radio went dead the Allies had pushed well up toward Valmontone. From the high ground there Gerry figured that he could spot enough activity on the ground to have a better idea of how to get back to friendly lines. It also would give him an opportunity to signal an Allied airplane somehow. He gathered his meager supplies and prepared to leave first thing in the morning.

The sun was low in the west when Gerry spotted Giannina pedaling her bike along the now-familiar road. He had hoped she wouldn't risk getting caught and arrested by the Germans but at the same time he had hoped she would come see him before he left. She hid her bicycle in the bushes and the two made their way to the little clearing by the brook. She spread a cloth on the ground and opened her basket to reveal a skimpy meal of two small apples, a slab of white cheese, some wine and a small loaf of crusty farm bread. The young American soldier and the beautiful Italian singer spoke little as they ate. Their eyes said everything to each other that needed to be said, more than compensating for the verbal silence. Reaching across the cloth to pick up the small bottle of red wine Gerry found his face within a few inches of hers. She awkwardly brushed her hair back from the side of her face and lowered her gaze in that incomprehensible way that women do. She reached up and touched his now clean-shaven cheek. "Handsome Gerry," she murmured.

Shy and yet provocative the glance and flutter of her eyelids gave Gerry the permission he had been hoping for. Their lips met tentatively at first, then searchingly and then passionately. She lunged into his arms and the warmth of their embrace chased away the cool night air. "Oh, handsome Gerry," she sighed. "I hate this war oh so very much."

Gerry lightly touched her lips with his finger. "Shh, shh, shush," he murmured. "Don't say anything. One day soon this war will be over and I will come back and find you. For now just holding you in my arms is all I could ever want or need. Tomorrow will come and I want you to be part of all my tomorrows!"

Reluctantly the two young lovers separated. "You must go now, before the Germans come by on their nightly patrol. Go my love," Gerry implored.

Gerry watched from the depth of the trees. Giannina mounted the bank and retrieved her bicycle from the bushes. She pushed it out to the road and hopped onto the seat. Just then a German army motorcycle came around the bend. It was ridden by the same young soldier who had accosted Giannina in the same place last month. He pulled up in front of her with his motorcycle blocking her way. He pulled his goggles off his face and smiled a toothy smile that reminded Giannina of a rabid dog.

"Guten abend, Fraulein!" he leered. "You remember me don't you? You promised me a kiss last month if I remember correctly."

Giannina lowered her gaze to avoid spearing him with the anger of her eyes. The young German soldier reached

226

out toward her shoulder, "Come on fraulein! Just one little kiss, eh?"

She jerked her shoulder away and her eyes flashed angrily toward the German. His cold smile froze and his eyes turned mean. He grabbed her roughly by the upper arm and tried to pull her toward him. "Why you little Italienisch bitch!" he spit.

Giannina yelled, "No!" and kicked him in the shin as hard as she could. She broke away from his grasp and turned to flee. She scrambled for footing on the loose gravel surface and fell to one knee. The soldier grabbed her in a choke hold and forced her into the bushes by the side of the road. Her strength was no match for his and she struggled vainly to free herself from his crushing grasp. As the young man forced her to the ground she tried to curl up into a ball. He pushed her onto her back and straddled her hips and pinned her wrists to the ground above her head with one hand. Reaching down he roughly tore her blouse and began to grope her chest. He leaned forward. She smelled his hot stale breath and felt the scratch of his five o'clock stubble on her cheek.

As the soldier pushed himself onto her Giannina closed her eyes and steeled herself. Neither she nor the German soldier saw Gerry step from the woods with the Randall knife flashing in his left hand. Neither of them saw him step behind the German. Gerry threw his right arm around the German's neck and jerked back. He plunged the Randall knife into the left side of the German's ribcage piercing the back wall of the heart. The man died almost instantly and his body went limp. Gerry tossed the body into a crumpled heap on the ground beside Giannina.

He swept Giannina up in his arms and held her close. He carried her to the stream and helped her to clean the blood from her clothes as well as they could.

Giannina looked at Gerry oddly with the image of the bleeding dead soldier still fresh in her mind. She wondered how a man could be so tender and loving in one moment and calmly stab another man in the heart the next moment. What kind of man was this American?

As if reading her thoughts Gerry said, "He would have killed you, Giannina. I only did what I had to do."

Once Giannina had calmed herself and pulled her shawl tightly around her they went back to the road. Gerry took the German motorcycle and pushed it over the roadside berm and down the embankment and into a thicket of bushes. He then sent Giannina quickly on her way down the road toward her parents' farm. He watched her form ride off out of sight and felt an overwhelming sadness growing within him. He dragged the soldier's body and hid it alongside the motorcycle.

He knew that the Germans would come looking for their man. He knew he could not stay here any longer. He returned to his camp and gathered his things in preparation for leaving. Looking at the homing beacon transmitter he was surprised to see the bedraggled and half-starved form of a small hamster curled up asleep on top of the casing. Houdini the homing hamster had covered the three and a half miles from just outside the railyards at Ciampino to the top of the ridge near Marino in four and a half days. This was nearly two full days slower than the all-time U.S. record but when considering that he had tracked a sound signal from among the cacophony of war while traversing a hostile war-torn countryside after striking a crippling blow at one of the biggest cannons in history the achievement was still noteworthy.

Gerry scooped the hamster up and dropped him into his left breast pocket along with a few crumbs of leftover Italian bread. "Well I suppose Seamus will be glad to see you," he muttered to himself.

Houdini opened his eyes briefly and looked up at Gerry before falling back into a deep sleep. Gerry turned his thoughts away from Giannina Marie and started off toward the southeast. He moved quickly but kept away from roads to avoid being seen. The night was clear and cloudless as he hiked toward what he hoped would be a rendezvous with the U.S. Army.

May 29, 1944—EZ Dog Diaries

...as we circled the town to land the Italians started pouring out into the field. By the time we stopped rolling at least a couple hundred were gathered around shaking hands and raising a fuss in general. We broke out a carton of cigarettes and had a great time giving them away. On the way back we toured the front lines - saw a lot of 3d Div doughboys moving up and quite a number of our tanks maneuvering.

The front as a whole is moving quite slowly. Mines, wire and suicide squads account for most of the delay.

Seamus and Eddie left the HQ building in Cori and climbed back in the jeep. "Come on, Seamus Let's go find Gerry!" EZ Dog said with a curtness Seamus was not used to. The two men took the first road heading west. After clocking half a mile EZ Dog pulled over. Just as Ace had said, there was the L5, tucked mostly out of sight behind a small wooden barn.

Eddie flashed his lopsided grin. "What do you say, Seamus? Want to go flying?"

"Whoa, Eddie! What are you talking about? You don't know how to fly an airplane!" Seamus said incredulously.

"Well, not officially anyway," Eddie replied. "Ace has been letting me fly when we go spotting. There's really not much to it. Besides, this is Gerry we're talking about. We don't have time to drive all over Italy looking for a pilot. Come on!"

Seamus hesitated, then said, "Oh hell, Eddie. Why not?"

The brothers grabbed their gear, including maps and a pair of binoculars and headed for the plane. They lifted the tail end and rotated the plane so it was headed toward the field. Ace had left several Gerry cans of fuel in the shed. Eddie topped up the tank with fuel and climbed aboard. Seamus hopped into the back seat and they pulled the door and window closed.

Eddie settled into the cockpit. His lanky legs straddled the single stick. He reached up with his left hand and opened the fuel valve, adjusting the mix as he had seen Ace do so many times before. His right hand hit the starter switch and the engine sputtered to life. He revved the engine and then released the brake. The angle of the plane with its single rear wheel meant that the nose of the plane was higher than Eddie's head. He could not see the ground directly in front of him. He steered the plane back and forth to get a view of the field in front of him. He picked a cluster of trees at the far end of the field and headed straight toward it. The plane picked up speed as it bounced across the field. When the speed felt right he eased back on the stick and the plane bounced one last time before lifting off the ground. He climbed steadily, clearing the trees at a comfortable height and then banked gently to the left and set a course toward the northwest. As they reached an altitude of about 1500 feet he leveled off and glanced back over his shoulder at Seamus.

Eddie hollered back at his brother, "Not bad for a first time, eh?"

Seamus' eyes widened in surprise. "First time? You numbskull! I thought you told me you had flown this thing before!"

"Well, I have! All except for the take-off and landing part," Eddie laughed.

Seamus shook his head in disbelief. The last they had heard from Gerry was while the Allies were pushing strongly up toward Valmontone to the northeast. Trying to place himself inside Gerry's mind Eddie figured that Gerry would head toward the Velletri Gap in an attempt to hook back up with the Allied lines. Although the attack had swung around toward Rome to the northwest Eddie decided to focus the search more to the east. They set up a zig-zagging search pattern as they headed over the Velletri Gap.

The small plane droned steadily through the mid-morning air. Scattered clouds lay placidly across the sky. Looking down on the Italian countryside from an altitude of about a thousand feet Seamus and Eddie could make out the small villages and towns dotting the landscape. Here and there they were able to see isolated groups of military vehicles, some German, some Allied moving to and fro. In the hills south of Lake Albano they could see muzzle flashes of German artillery positions firing off toward the Allied troops to the south and west. The engine noise sounded like an old jalopy with a constant putt-putt. The propeller spun rapidly in a blur of motion pulling them through the air. The rush of wind noise against the cockpit windows almost drowned out the engine. Eddie smoothly banked the plane back and forth while Seamus scanned the roads and tree lines looking for any sign of their brother.

After about 45 minutes of searching Seamus tapped Eddie on the shoulder. "Over there on the left. Isn't that an American jeep?"

On the top of a narrow ridge Eddie saw the jeep that Seamus had seen. It sat about a half a mile from a small village that was perched on the edge of the ridgeline overlooking the Velletri Gap. A man was standing on the back seat of the jeep waving his hands over his head at the small plane. Eddie waggled the wings to signal that they had seen the soldier. Circling around he saw that the road was fairly straight and level at that particular spot. He eased the plane around for a gradual approach and headed in for a landing. The plane hit hard and bounced up about five feet in the air before coming back to earth and rolling out to a stop a mere hundred yards from the closest building.

"Don't tell me. That was your first time landing an airplane, right?" Seamus opined sarcastically.

Almost instantly a sizeable crowd of villagers appeared from the nearby town. Seamus looked nervously as the crowd encircled the plane, shouting and gesticulating excitedly. "What are they saying, Eddie?"

Eddie shrugged, "I can't understand Italian very well, but I think they are happy to see us. Why don't you reach behind your seat and see if Ace has anything stashed back there? He usually keeps a couple cartons of cigarettes and some K-rations. Don't forget to smile!"

Eddie and Seamus clambered out of the plane and tried to clear a space in the crowd. Seamus quickly calculated that there were about forty people ranging from school aged children to octogenarians. The people were all shouting and cheering as they reached out to shake hands and pat the two

Americans on the back. Eddie broke out a carton of cigarettes and began handing them out to the lively crowd. From somewhere in the small cargo hold Seamus extracted a box of hard candy. He quickly drew a small crowd of children as he sat down on the ground and began distributing the candies. He made the children laugh happily by making funny faces and whistling Yankee Doodle Dandy. He then had a brainstorm and reached back into the plane. Seamus pulled out his hamster case and brought out Hammie. Holding the hamster gently in his hands he showed the children and let them each reach out and carefully pet the hamster. Hammie delighted the children when he scampered up Seamus' sleeve, ran across his shoulders and jumped into his breast pocket. When he poked his head out of the pocket Seamus gave him a little piece of cracker from one of the K-ration boxes. The children squealed with glee.

One of the adult villagers spoke a little bit of English and introduced himself proudly as Giacomo. In a fractured fashion Eddie tried to make him understand that they were looking for a lost American soldier named Gerry Muldoon. The man smiled broadly and said, "Si signore! Many American soldiers! Very happy. We are glad for the American soldiers!" It was quickly obvious to Eddie that Giacomo did not have any information about Gerry.

As the excitement died down, the villagers began to drift back toward the village in groups of two or three. Some of the men loitered nearby enjoying their smokes.

Making their way through the thinning crowd the men in the jeep greeted Eddie and Seamus. They identified themselves as a Major in the infantry and his driver, a young private.

"Quite a welcome from these locals, eh? They mobbed us earlier but we didn't have any goodies to give them. I'm afraid we're lost. The front has been moving so rapidly that it is pretty much a free-for-all," the Major said. "We took a wrong turn somewhere this morning and ended up here. Do you have any idea where we can find the 3rd Division? They are supposed to be somewhere near Cecchina. Our map doesn't include that sector."

Seamus and Eddie dug into Eddie's bag for his maps. Spreading the situation map out on the hood of the jeep Eddie and the Major began to pore over it. Eddie located the village and the ridge line and estimated they were about three miles due north of Velletri. They located the town of Cecchina, about six miles to the west and plotted a route along country roads that would get the Major where he needed to be.

Seamus and Eddie waved as the Major and his driver headed off toward the west.

The two men climbed back into the airplane. Eddie checked the gauges and noted that they were low on fuel. "We'd better head back to Cori and gas up," he told Seamus. He fired up the engine and taxied back onto the narrow country lane. Accelerating into the light breeze the plane lifted off smoothly and began to climb. A couple of stragglers from the village raised their arms in farewell. Eddie turned the plane back toward the south and set a course for Cori.

As the L5 receded into the distance Gerry Muldoon burst from the tree line. It had taken him almost 36 hours to cover the six and a half miles from his hideout on the slopes above Marino to this hilltop village north of Velletri. Taking into account lots of backtracking, skirting around villages and avoiding German patrols in the area he had probably covered closer to 20 miles. He had forded creeks, climbed through dense vegetation, struggled over downed trees and at times had sprinted flat out across stretches of open ground in order to reach cover. He thought back briefly to his championship run on the obstacle course back during basic training and realized that the obstacle course was a mere stroll in the park compared to the real thing. His weeks in the woods had reduced his lanky muscular frame to a mere 145 pounds and he was frankly exhausted.

As he had approached the ridgeline he had heard the familiar sound of the L5 revving up for take-off. He summoned his last reserves of energy and broke into a ragged stumbling run toward the open ground. He saw the plane lift off and bank away. Shouting as loudly as his raspy voice would allow and waving his arms frantically he tried vainly to get the pilot's attention. After nearly seven weeks living off the land behind German lines Gerry was utterly spent. As he realized the plane's occupants had not seen him he fell to his knees. The heavy breathing of his last burst of physical exertion turned into sobs of despair.

He thought of his parents back home on the farm. He thought of his brothers and the many memories of growing up with them on the plains of Colorado. He thought of the Rocky Mountains that always had loomed in the distance throughout his life. He thought of fly-fishing with his dad and brothers in the mountain streams above Fort Collins. He thought fondly of the brief moments of happiness that he had shared with Giannina Marie in the middle of war. He closed his eyes and sank to the ground. This was how it would end, he thought, alone on a barren hilltop in a foreign land. He lay with his face in the dust. His mind returned to the familiar Bible verse he had learned in Sunday school years ago. "The Lord is my Shepherd, I shall not want. He maketh me to lie down in green pastures. He leadeth me beside still waters. He restoreth my soul. He leadeth me in the paths of righteousness for His name's sake…" he recited the Psalm silently.

As Gerry's breathing returned to normal he sensed movement nearby. A shadow fell across his face. He barely lifted his head as he opened his eyes. He was sure that the Germans had finally caught up with him.

Gerry was surprised to hear his name spoken with a heavy Italian accent. "Gerry Muldoon, si?" the English-speaking villager asked. "I am Giacomo. I very happy to seeing American soldiers! I just meet your brothers!"

The villagers helped Gerry to his feet and half carried him to a nearby house. They gave him water and some bread and cheese. When Houdini popped his nose up out of Gerry's pocket for a bite of cheese Giacomo laughed. "I also happy to meet your brother's…eh…how do you say? Topo? Mouse? Do all American soldiers carry a topo with them?"

Gerry managed a smile and said, "No. Just me and my kid brother Seamus." With that he fell onto the narrow bed in the corner of the room and fell into a deep and much-deserved sleep.

The next morning Gerry awoke refreshed with a renewed sense of purpose. He knew that Eddie and Seamus were looking for him. He needed to figure out a way to get a message to them in the event that they flew back this way. He talked with Giacomo and was able to let him know that he needed some paint. Giacomo quickly rounded up some white paint, a broad paint brush and a pair of oversized coveralls. Gerry climbed up a ladder with the paint while a cluster of villagers looked on bemusedly.

Gerry needed to paint a signal that would be recognized by Eddie but not mean anything to a German pilot who might happen to see it. The usual S.O.S. was out of the question. The letters needed to be big enough to be seen and the roof of this particular house was only about 20 feet long. Gerry felt his stomach rumbling with hunger and suddenly knew what he would paint.

Before he could get started a group of military vehicles roared into town; a platoon of German troops on the move under pressure from the Allied offensive. As the lead car pulled to a stop Gerry froze in near-panic. A German soldier dismounted from the staff car and looked over the assembled villagers wondering what they were up to.

Giacomo stepped up and shrugged his shoulders expressively, an ingratiating grin on his face. "Guten tag mein Herr. Ich heisse Giacomo. Ich spreche etwas Deutsch. Es macht mir froh Deutschen Soldaten zum begnegen!"

The soldier asked Giacomo in German if he had seen any Americans. "Kein amerikaneren," he answered in his heavily accented German. "Aber mein bruder ist ein Dummkopf. Er arbeitet sehr langsam!"

Turning away from the Germans and looking up at Gerry on the roof Giacomo winked broadly and yelled in rapid fire Italian while gesticulating wildly. The only words Gerry was able to make out were "Idiota" and "rapidamente, presto" which he took to mean, "Hurry up, you idiot!"

Gerry adopted a buffoonish grin and a shuffling manner. "Si, Si, presto!" he huffed in a harsh croak, hoping to mask his accent. He began to vigorously smear paint on the side of the building.

The German soldier scoffed, and said something in German to the driver. The other occupants of the car laughed as the small convoy started up again and drove on out of town.

When they were out of sight Gerry came down the ladder. His knees were shaking. "What did they say?" he asked Giacomo.

"They said that it was no wonder the stupid Italians surrendered when they did. I don't think the Germans like us very much," Giacomo spit with a hand gesture that needed no translation.

Gerry scrambled back up the ladder and onto the slate roof. He carefully painted a single word and a single number in 10-foot tall letters on the roof—"PIE-4". He then came down the ladder and settled in to wait. He figured there was no way Eddie and Seamus could resist an offer of pie.

May 30, 1944—EZ Dog Diaries

Corps Arty has moved so well up we had to displace our CP. This time to a nice forward slope about 5000 yds from Velletri our front most elements are still not within 2000 yds of the town. We can hear the MG's and machine pistols banging all times of day and night. Progress is still forward on all fronts, but very slow. 36 Div jumped off on a right hook at Velletri from a line near the 3ᵈ Div. Object to isolate and reduce Velletri. Attack was going well with very little opposition at last report.

Upon his return to Cori EZ Dog had been pressed back into duty with the artillery. Since Ace was still laid up with his leg wound and pilots were in short supply EZ Dog had convinced the higher ups that he could fill Ace's role temporarily while Ace recovered. In the freewheeling atmosphere that prevailed during this two week period he received permission with minimal resistance from the general staff. He also managed to get Seamus approval to hang around as a special attaché. EZ Dog was tasked with aerial observation and inventory of German artillery positions and damage estimates. In the 10 days since the offensive started over 6,000 German prisoners of war had been captured and untold numbers of enemy killed. Dozens of disabled German tanks and other heavy equipment were scattered across the battlefield. In the first two days of surveillance above the Velletri Gap EZ Dog and Seamus had counted over 40 destroyed or abandoned German artillery pieces.

During this three-day period EZ Dog and Seamus flew two or three times a day surveying the damage the Gerries had sustained. They also spent at least an hour of each flight traversing the area north of Velletri looking for any signs of their brother Gerry while hoping that he could survive the damage he may have sustained.

June 1, 1944—EZ Dog Diaries.

T_____ sent me on another inspection of gun locations. We have covered roughly one quarter of the E locations and so far have found 40 guns. Gerry lost far more stuff than any of us dared hope for. Velletri is completely surrounded and should be cleaned up soon. 88 and 85 Divs moved up on our right to help the 3d Div on II Corps front. They are moving well up beside our 36th Div.

The first of June was a clear, cloudless Thursday. Late in the afternoon EZ Dog and Seamus were cruising along in the L5 in the vicinity of Velletri. Looking down on the lowlands of the Gap they could see pockets of activity on the ground. Allied tanks were maneuvering. From their vantage point high in the air the shell impacts from tanks and artillery looked like miniature splashes of raindrops on a dusty field during a Colorado summer afternoon thunderstorm. They had an odd feeling of detachment from the noise, chaos and personal suffering on the ground below.

While Eddie maneuvered the plane in a predetermined search grid Seamus made notations on a map propped in his lap. After finishing their sweep over the Velletri battlefield Eddie steered the plane back toward the village on the ridge line north of Velletri.

"Hey, Eddie," Seamus said tapping Eddie on the shoulder. What does that say on that roof down there?"

Eddie squinted to make out the letters. "Looks like PIG-4. What does that mean? That doesn't make any sense."

Suddenly Seamus reached forward and grabbed Eddie by both shoulders and shook him excitedly. "Wait a second, Eddie! That's not a 'G' it's an 'E'. Now who else on this planet do you know who cuts a pie into only four pieces? That's Gerry! It has to be!"

Eddie swung around to bring the plane closer to the building. "Well I'll be a monkey's uncle. You're right, Seamus! Pie! That has to be Gerry!"

Eddie circled around and made his approach to the narrow country lane. He bounced in for a landing and taxied up the road to the village limits. He cut the engine and the two men climbed out once again. The streets of the village were empty as they walked to the center of town. Eddie called out, "Giacomo!? Are you here?" There was no response. They walked back to the edge of town. As they approached the small house with the painting on the roof the front door burst open. Gerry bounded down the steps and hollered, "Eddie, Seamus!" Eddie and Seamus broke into a run and tackled Gerry as one.

"Oh man, am I glad to see you two!" Gerry exclaimed as the three brothers embraced warmly. "Even you, Seamus, you little runt!" Gerry tousled Seamus' hair fondly.

"Boy, you look pitiful!" Eddie admonished his older brother. "Haven't you been eating? Mom is going to have my hide if she sees you looking like this! She told me to take good care of you two."

As they continued with the long-awaited reunion the villagers began emerging from their houses and gathered around. Giacomo came to the front of the group and proudly shook the hands of all three Americans. "Eddie! We found your brother Gerry Muldoon just after you left the other day. I am much glad to see you together. Gerry has quite a tale to tell you, eh?"

Eddie trotted back to the plane and grabbed a box of cigars and a couple bottles of Italian wine he had been saving for this moment. Passing the cigars out to the villagers he reserved three for himself and his brothers. Trimming the ends they hovered around as Gerry flicked his old beat up Zippo. The lighter flickered but would not light. "I've got this," Seamus said. He fired up the cigars and the three brothers puffed away in celebration. Sitting on the front stoop of the little house the three Americans basked in the glow of the happy villagers. "Hey Seamus I've got someone who wants to see you," Gerry said. Reaching in his pocket he pulled out Houdini the hamster.

Seamus grabbed the hamster and gave him a quick once over. He looked none the worse for the wear after his ordeal on the run with Gerry. He walked over to the plane and pulled out his hamster case, reuniting Houdini and Hammie. He gave them each a couple of hamster treats from the stash he always carried with him.

After about 20 minutes Giacomo pulled Eddie aside. "There have been lots of Germans coming through here. They have not been very happy. From what I can tell they are on the run and they are in a really bad mood. You and your brothers better leave now before they come back."

Eddie agreed. "Come on you two, there'll be time to celebrate when we're back on the ground within our own lines." The three men got into the plane, Eddie in the front seat and Gerry perched awkwardly on Seamus' lap in the back seat. The villagers picked up the tail of the plane and spun it around so it was headed out of town. Eddie fired up the engine and began to roll down the road. Seamus and Gerry waved out the open side window. "Grazie, Giacomo, grazie! Arrivaderci!"

"Viva la Americanos!" Giacomo yelled. The villagers waved briefly and then disappeared again as quickly as they had appeared. The L5 lifted off smoothly and putt-putted off toward Cori.

"Hey, wait a second!" Gerry yelled over the cabin noise. "When did you learn how to fly?"

Seamus laughed, "Well, it's still a work in progress it seems!" Eddie grinned his lopsided Muldoon grin.

June 2, 1944—EZ Dog Diaries

36 Div finished off Velletri. Some 250-300 PW's. Other fronts including II Corps and Eighth Army moving well forward. Official count thru VI Corps cage is well over 6,500 PW's, which is more than they took through the entire Italian campaign up to the time the present offensive started. Camino fell to our troops late in period. Mopping up continues.

The fog of battle hangs over all the country. Smoke, fog, and dust limits visibility to barely a mile. Without the war, undoubtedly this would be beautiful spring weather.

Over the next three days the three Muldoons were largely out of the war. The rapidly moving and constantly shifting front largely outstripped the Field Artillery. Tanks and infantry carried the battle forward. German artillery units were either in full retreat or had abandoned their gun emplacements entirely, some damaged and some just forsaken.

Gerry set about regaining his strength. After a quick check-up at the HQ aid station and an all-clear from the medics he and Seamus settled into a back room of the new Artillery HQ located in a spacious villa on the outskirts of Velletri. The building had been used as German Staff headquarters up until the day before yesterday. The Germans had vacated so quickly that half eaten meals sat on the large dining room table. The boys found several crates of provisions. It seems that German field officers managed to eat quite well. A generous ham and several bottles of wine had been left behind by the fleeing German Army. Gerry and Seamus set about preparing a homecoming feast while Eddie attended to some paperwork and filed some reports for Division Artillery HQ.

Just as Eddie came in that evening a couple of local women brought by a couple of freshly baked wild berry pies to welcome the liberators. After dinner Eddie pulled out one of the pies and looked around at his brothers and his buddy Ace. "What do you say, Gerry? Four pieces?"

"Absolutely," Gerry grinned. Eddie spun the pie and deftly sliced two perpendicular cuts. He lifted a slab of pie onto each of four plates and handed one to each of his dinner companions. Seamus picked up a knife and cut a thin sliver from the edge of his piece. "Just a tiny piece for the boys," he said and slipped the tidbit into the hamster case for Houdini and Hammie. "Enjoy, fellas!" he said.

June 3, 1944—EZ Dog Diaries

We moved CP to Velletri today - in a beautiful villa (running water and electric lights) on the side of a very beautiful hill. There is very little sign of war here - a welcome relief. Velletri itself is badly torn up but we are about a mile out of town. Our villa was formerly occupied by members of the German high command. They moved out day before yesterday. This morning our wire crew captured a Kraut 1st Sgt in the air raid shelter that goes with the house. The front is moving forward so fast we hear only faint sounds from the front. Lanuvio was cleaned up today and troops move on to Genzano, below Lake Nemi, and Rocca di Papa north of the lake. II Corps advanced within 7 miles and probably less of Rome. Our armor was last reported South of Lake Albano. Today the front as a whole has moved farther than any other since the 3d Div took Cori.

June 5, 1944—EZ Dog Diaries.

Rome is ours. We have it surrounded and occupied. The natives are delirious with joy. What with flag waving and flower throwing and shouting and ringing it is a great show. Our battery moved from Velletri to the fairgrounds SW of Rome. As soon as we closed in the new area we took a flight over Rome. The main streets were thronged with people. The entrance to Vatican City was so crowded with people that we couldn't see the ground. [Margin note: This was the Pope's address welcoming the Allies. A lucky flight for us because flying over the Vatican is strictly forbidden. However this was a special occasion and passed uncensored.] Rome is not badly bombed. Only the railroad yards show any amount of bombing. Our troops are moving well out with little opposition. All troops are advancing straight up the axis on rather narrow division fronts. The Air Corps is still raising Cain in the rear areas. Gerry seems very confused and disorganized.

Allied troops rolled into Rome on June 4, 1944. The German Army had vacated the vicinity mere hours ahead of the Allies. The citizens of Rome welcomed the liberating forces with exuberance. Eddie Muldoon and his two brothers received the news happily. EZ Dog still did not have any real role to play in the mop-up operations so the three relaxed at the villa. The next morning Eddie rousted the two others out of bed bright and early with a cheerful yell, "Come on you yahoos. Let's take a ride." Ace was still a few days from returning to flight status so Eddie still had free use of the L5. The brothers piled into the L5 once again and Eddie took them smoothly into the air. He was really getting the hang of this flying business.

Heading toward the northwest Eddie yelled back over his shoulder, "The city center has been designated as off limits to aircraft, but we can cruise up and fly the perimeter just to see what's happening. Approaching the outskirts of Rome the boys were able to see groups of military vehicles clogging the roads. Eddie waggled the wings as he flew low over groups of doughboys sitting atop tanks surrounded by throngs of civilians. The faces of the G.I.'s were upturned and they threw their arms up in the air cheering the lone two-seater airplane. The dome of St. Peter's loomed in the near distance. "What the heck," Eddie thought. "Let's go give it a look-see." Cruising at an altitude of about 500 feet the little plywood plane sputtered steadily through the hazy Italian morning. As they approached the entrance to Vatican City the crowds on the streets below became thicker. The square was packed wall to wall with Italian civilians with smaller clusters of British and American soldiers. As the plane rounded the corner the brothers looked out at the veranda overlooking the square. They saw the figure of a man in white vestments standing on the balcony with his right arm outstretched. As the man made the sign of the cross in the air Eddie waggled the wings of the plane one more time. Gerry and Seamus whooped in the back seat. "Hurray Eddie! The Pope just blessed us! With the way you fly that's going to come in handy!"

Eddie joined in the laughter. He put the plane into a steep bank and headed for the coast and out over the sea. As they flew low over the Tyrrhenian Sea the late morning sun peeked out from behind a single white cloud. Banking back around toward the east Eddie aimed right at the line of reflected sunlight on the water and plotted a course straight into the future.

--THE END--

EPILOGUE

With the liberation of Rome EZ Dog and the counterbattery unit stood down for rest and refit. They moved to a seaside location on the coast west of Rome. Word came that Allied troops had come upon two large German cannons on a railroad siding at the port of Civitavecchia further up the coast. The two large Krupp K5 280 mm guns were dubbed "Robert" and "Leopold". These were the two guns known collectively on the beachhead as Anzio Annie. After the collapse of the German defenses the two guns had been relocated to Civitavecchia in the hope of being salvaged in a seaborne evacuation but the sheer speed of the Allied advance had forced the Germans to abandon the two behemoths. Anzio Annie's war was officially over.

Gerry was processed out of the army due to his leg wound, the extended period of time as a POW and the time behind enemy lines. Seamus was also released from his attached duty. The two brothers were slated to return to the United States. They would travel by ship to Naples and then a series of air hops along North Africa and then an ocean liner across the Atlantic. From the east coast they would take the route that was now familiar to Seamus. A train would take them to Denver, a bus ride would get them to Greeley and from there they would hitch a ride that would get them to the end of their parents' driveway. Gerry had a duffel bag over his shoulder and Seamus carried a suitcase and his hamster container. Gerry hesitated at the mailbox. "Hey Seamus! One more thing before we see Mom and Dad." He reached in his duffel bag and pulled out the Randall knife.

He had not been able to tell Eddie or Seamus about taking the life of the German soldier with his own bare hands. He had not been able to tell them of the look he saw on the face of Giannina Marie as the man attacked her. He would hold those secrets inside himself for the rest of his life. The Randall knife burned in his hand as he handed it back to Seamus. "This knife saved my life, Seamus. It holds dark things within. Use it in good health, but respect it."

Arm in arm the two boys started up the driveway. Mom was hanging laundry out on the line to dry. Off in the back 40 acres of the farm Dad sat high upon the combine in a sea of thigh-high wheat. The harvest had begun. The seeds planted last winter had taken strong root and the field of golden grain waved softly in the afternoon breeze. The Old Man shielded his eyes from the glare of the sun and looked at the two figures on the driveway. He pulled the combine to a halt. Hopping down with a sprightliness that belied his aging bones he broke into a shuffling trot across the field. Mom joined him at the gate to the fenced yard and their hearts soared as the two young men came home. Mom Muldoon threw her arms around her boys and cried tears of joy. "Thank you Almighty God for bringing my boys back home."

For EZ Dog, the war would continue. His unit rejoined the battleground in the south of France later in 1944 and he served honorably for the duration of the war.

Gerry, Eddie and Seamus Muldoon all went on to lead long and productive lives as solid family men. Early in 1945 Gerry received a small post card in the mail announcing the marriage of Giannina Marie to the young man Giacomo. He would owe a lifetime debt of gratitude to them both for helping to save his life. He never visited Italy again. Seamus put the Randall knife in the very back of a bottom drawer of his dresser and never took it out again. None of the three spoke much about their wartime experiences to their children or grandchildren. They considered themselves ordinary Americans, not heroes.

The three Muldoon boys had played only a very small role in the much greater effort of the Allied Forces in World War II but they had played their role well. Hundreds of thousands of young Americans had come together and functioned as a formidable machine of retribution. They willingly set aside their personal lives in the service of others. They did not seek empire. They sought freedom. They fought not for subjugation but for liberation. Many paid the ultimate price in the service of something greater than themselves. The young men and women of the Allied Forces selflessly and wholeheartedly gave of themselves in order to do that which needed to be done for the simple reason that if they didn't, who would?

War is an ugly and brutal thing. In one of the odd quirks of war the buildings and citizens of Rome had been largely untouched by the immediate horrors of war. Even in the midst of it all EZ Dog had been able to find little glimpses of beauty in the Italian people, buildings and countryside. A peony bush grew outside the latrine.

The liberation of the concentration camps in Nazi Germany was another matter altogether. The joy of liberation was tempered by the atrocities that had been committed and the millions of Jews and others killed at the hands of the Nazis. Subsequent generations should never forget the gift that was given to us all by the men and women of The Greatest Generation. This was the generation that (in the words of Mom Muldoon) "saved us all from ruin."

ADDITIONAL READING

- *The EZ Dog Journals 1943*-1945 by Earl D. Schroeder, transcribed by Randy Schroeder

- *Fatal Decision: Anzio and the Battle for Rome* by Carlo d'Este

- *World War II—The Battle of Anzio by Kennedy Hickman*
http://militaryhistory.about.com/od/worldwarii/p/battle-of-anzio.htm

- *The Ordnance Department on Beachhead and Battlefront by Lida Mayo (Center of Military History United States Army 1991) [Chapter XI—Anzio and Artillery]*
http://www.history.army.mil/books/wwii/Beachhd_Btlefrnt/ChapterXI.html

- *Anzio Beachhead: 22 January-25 May 1944 (Center of Military History United States Army 1990)*
http://www.history.army.mil/books/wwii/anziobeach/anzio-fm.htm#cont

- *Ike's Order of the Day (D-Day 1944)*
http://www.kansasheritage.org/abilene/graphics/ikesmessage.jpg

- *Krupp K5 (Anzio Annie) Heavy Railway Gun (1936)* by J.R. Potts
http://www.militaryfactory.com/armor/detail.asp?armor_id=526

- *Anzio Annie: The Gun That Held 50,000 Men Hostage* by Lee Krystek
http://www.unmuseum.org/anzio_annie.htm

- *Anzio Annie: She was No Lady* by R.J. O'Rourke, O'Rourke Services Co. 1995
- *Anzio Annie: The Story of a Gun* by Louis Wildenboer, Military History Journal Vol 13 No 3 - June 2005
- *A Message To Garcia* by Elbert Hubbard 1899 <courses.csail.mit.edu/6.803/pdf/hubbard1899.pdf>
- *The Pigeon-Guided Missiles and Bat Bombs of World War II* <http://gizmodo.com/the-pigeon-guided-missiles-and-bat-bombs-of-world-war-i-1477007090>